THE HUNTRESS

SEA

SARAH DRIVER

EGMONT

To Mum, Dad and Nick,

for sailing through the storms with me

EGMONT

We bring stories to life

First published in Great Britain 2017
by Egmont UK Limited
The Yellow Building, 1 Nicholas Road, London W11 4AN

Text copyright © Sarah Driver, 2017
Illustrations copyright © Joe McLaren, 2017
Additional interior illustrations by Janene Spencer

ISBN 978 1 4052 8467 7

www.egmont.co.uk

A CIP catalogue record for this title is available from the British Library

Typeset by Avon DataSet Ltd, Bidford on Avon, Warwickshire
Printed and bound in Great Britain by the CPI Group

65148/4

CONTENTS

PART 1: *We Rove*

PART 2: *Winter's Prowl*

PART 3: *Flight*

1 mizzen-mast
2 the hoodwink
3 castle-deck
4 crow's nest
5 aft-castle
6 stern
7 medsin-lab
8 armoury
9 carpenter's cabin

20 hatch
21 aft-deck
22 captain's cabin

26 main-sail
27 main-mast

THE HUNTRESS

10 moonsprites
11 storm-deck
12 hatch
13 archery targets
14 fore-deck

15 oarsmen's benches
16 main-deck
17 stairs
18 crew's quarters
19 orlop-deck

23 eating-benches
24 sleeping-hammocks
25 the hold

28 *fore-mast*

29 *castle-deck*

30 *prow*

31 *fore-castle*

32 *prentice's quarters*

33 *bow*

34 *navigator's cabin*

35 *Pip's kitchens*

36 *bread ovens*

37 *basking shark*

38 *cellars*

39 *cauldrons*

PART 1

We Rove

Terrodyls

The beasts are coming.

I'm below decks in the gloomy kitchens, helping Pipistrelle salt raw reindeer steak, when the first call hacks through the air. As the sound fades, my fingers stop dead and cold chunks of salt dig into my skin. My bones turn to water but I won't let my knees buckle. Pip stops his tuneless whistling and scowls. My heart barely thuds before the clanging of the alarm bell shatters the silence.

Grandma always tells me I'm not to go out on deck when the great winged terrodyls come near. Two summers gone, they killed Grandpa. But this time I've got to keep our ship safe.

I stick my knife in my belt and let out my fiercest battle-howl.

'Mouse!' Pip grabs for me but his hands are slimy with reindeer blood and I wriggle free.

I run from the kitchens, tear through the murky

passageways and into the armoury, with its stink of rot and rust. Spears, daggers, axes and harpoons gleam as I pass. I fling open an elm chest, grab my longbow and a quiver full of arrows dipped in poison-frog venom. Then I burst up the stairs onto the storm-deck.

The deck's a-flurry with running boots and sweeping cloaks. We've been caught unprepared cos the terrodyls should be making for their nests now that winter's prowling closer.

The battle-horn moans. 'To arms! Bows and bills!' Grandma shouts, from the fore-castle above. 'Come *on*, you belching babble of layabouts!'

'Aye, Captain!' boom the crew.

Shadows thicken as the sun drops towards the horizon. Grandma's black-cloaks stand along the port and starboard sides. There's a *whish* as they draw arrows from their quivers. The oarsmen have left their benches so the *Huntress* sways in the sea, buffeted by the waves. I've not been on deck longer than a few heartbeats when a freezing shock of seawater smashes over the rail and drenches me.

The sound comes again, a hideous whip-crack caw. It makes me stagger and throw myself flat with my hands over my ears. My bow clatters to the deck. A shadow falls across me, cast by a pair of vast, hairy wings. They beat, drowning out my heart.

'Mouse!' a shaky voice cries. Slowly I turn my face towards the stern. The hatch is open a sliver and Sparrow's teary brown eyes peer out.

'Sing! Sing to the whales!' I call to my brother, my voice fear-scratched. Sparrow's gifted with the whale-song. Grandma says it's an offering to the whales – the gods of the seas – to keep us safe. Terrodyls hate the gentle whale-song, so might be it's the only thing that can save us, out here with no other trading ships close by.

As I watch, Sparrow opens his mouth and pours his song into the night. The wind gusts and carries his voice over the sea, pulling more strands of song from his mouth – the notes shiver and glow bright blue.

Another scream strikes deep into my brain. A three-strong hunting pack of ten-foot-long terrodyls circles overhead. Their beast-chatter is tangled into one hateful cry of *killdeathdiepaindrownstrikedeathscuttlekill!*

One of them dives towards me but I roll, quick, and its claws tear gouges in the deck. It screeches and comes at me again. I try to stand but bash into its wing, and it sends me crashing into a barrel of salted herring.

There's a thud as the hatch bangs closed. Sparrow must've let it fall shut and now his voice is muffled. Will the whales hear him?

Two of the terrodyls dip lower and use their spear-

5

point heads to strike the hull. They're trying to send our ship down! Arrows skitter off the edges of their wings.

Grandma's voice carves the air. 'Stave the monsters off, but see you don't bring them down on us!' Her silvery hair billows around her head as she strides, clad in merwraith-scale armour. 'Summon my prentice; might be she has a drop of whale-song left in her staff!'

Arrows fly. The terrodyls screech and snap their jaws, furiously rounding on the black-cloaks. Then Vole stalks along the deck, wielding a wooden staff topped with a crystal. Blue wisps of whale-song moan from the crystal; a song-wave that pushes the terrodyls back.

Stealing my chance, I scramble to my feet and hurry along the starboard side. Salt spray strikes my face and the wind whips my hair into my eyes. Grandma don't spy me. If I stick to the left of her she won't, neither, cos of her glass eye.

The tumbling sea stretches into the distance. The moon crawls up the sky, lighting the waves as they roll and crash around us. The arrows and Vole's staff have chased the beasts away. But the staff's whale-song is already trailing off, leaving a silence that makes my skin creep. I can feel the *Huntress* holding her breath for the next attack.

2
Alone at Sea

I glance out to sea and my heart lurches, cos a huge grey fin glides along by our side – must be the bigtooth shark that's been circling our ship for days. *Hunt, weave, death-cold*, it mutters from the water. *Quest, crunch, search-bones. Drowns soon, soon, soon.*

Pip reckons it's the same rogue that munched a whole crew when terrodyls sent their ship down, three moons back. The wreck must be lurking on the seabed, riddled with merwraiths – the blind, scaly victims of drowning – and gulpers that can swallow a person whole. But it ent today that we'll be joining that shipwreck, I swear it. I promised Ma I'd keep Sparrow safe for always.

As the thoughts of Ma nip at me, Sparrow's voice rises up again, high and pure. His glittering blue notes skate across the water.

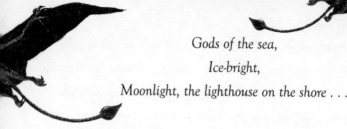

Gods of the sea,

Ice-bright,

Moonlight, the lighthouse on the shore . . .

The next great screech of the terrodyls makes me drop to my knees with my head in my hands. Pain swells behind my eyes. But then the shriek dies and my heart skip-skitters and I can breathe again.

Staggering, I grab my bow and haul myself into the rigging. I shin up the main-mast, the highest of the three. The wind tries to throw me into the sea but I cling tight.

At the top I leap into the crow's nest and peer at the deck far below. The black-cloaks shout and scramble to find the best position to shoot at the beasts, which loop and plunge back down through the air towards us. With shaky hands I string my bow, take an arrow from my quiver and nock it. I rest the arrow on my finger and close one eye, trying to still my breath.

Suddenly I spot a bright wisp of whale-song coiling up from the sea, and a sad song groans through the air – a whale has come! The whale's voice joins Sparrow's and it's the strangest thing, but spooky-beautiful.

Drumbeats,

Snow peaks.

Stare into the fire, see battles of yore . . .

A grey shape lurches clear of the water. If the whale is alone, its song might not be enough to save us. My heart sinks as the largest terrodyl jerks its head towards the shape and dives for the surface of the sea.

'No!' I scream.

Grandma looks up. 'Mouse!' I'm too high to see her face, but it must be frightful-fierce. 'Get down from there or I'll shoot ye down, little fool!'

I can hardly watch as the terrodyl rakes its claws across the flesh of the whale, leaving a bloody tear. 'It can't die for us!' I bellow into the wind.

As the terrodyl hovers in the air above the sea, I take aim, draw and loose. My arrow slams into its wing. The beast gives a sickening scream. Far below, black-cloaks fall to their knees and moan. What if the sound stops our hearts, like the legends say it can?

'Mouse! This ent the day to try my patience!' roars Grandma.

My gut leaps but I grab another arrow and nock it to my bow. The creature draws close on huge wings that stir the air enough to twist the sails into knots. I can see my first arrow, lodged deep in the muscle. Blood beats in my ears.

Suddenly, chief oarsman Bear heaves himself into the basket, towering over me. 'Get out of here, quick!' he shouts. Fear is etched across his kind face.

9

'I won't!' I sink to one knee and angle my bow straight up to the sky. The terrodyl shrieks again and Bear stumbles, but I focus on my breath, sighing in and out like the tides.

A razor-sharp wing slashes at me but I duck low, draw, loose. My arrow *twangs* into the terrodyl's sinewy neck and pierces a thick blood vessel. Black blood hails down on us, hissing as it strikes the wood. A droplet fizzles on my arm and makes an angry red pit in my flesh.

Bear grabs my waist and throws me from the crow's nest into the rigging. Rope burns my palms as I hurtle downwards. The *Huntress* shudders as the terrodyl crashes onto the crow's nest with a great crunch of splintering wood. I jump the rest of the way and roll when I hit the deck. Bear lands beside me. Most of the nest falls away, showering splinters down around us, until all that remains is part of the mast and the bleeding body of the terrodyl. It twitches and finally stills.

The two living terrodyls scream in fury as I lie curled on the deck. All the wind is knocked from my lungs. Inky blood rains down from the broken mast and devours the wood with a smoky crackle.

'Mouse, get below decks, now!' Grandma booms. 'And someone send for Pipistrelle – we need his cauldrons to catch that filthy slime, so it don't eat the *Huntress* whole!'

Bear helps me up and starts to lead me away. 'Oarsmen, to your positions,' he calls down to the rowing benches. 'Someone take up the drum until my return!' I pummel Bear with my fists but he tugs me until my boots slide across the soaked wood.

The captain's hatch has fallen closed again. When Bear opens it, Sparrow's voice reaches us through the gloom. A clump of song knocks against my cheek, whale-skin cold. With it comes a low, sad groan from far across the water.

I twist to look over my shoulder and in the distance, lit by the yellow moon, the dark shapes of whales swim towards us in great numbers. They're a mass of giant tails and fins, blowholing jets of water into the air. A veil of blue whale-song throbs over them, and Sparrow's song rushes to join it. Together, they push against the terrodyls.

Bear stops dragging me and watches the horizon. Terrodyl screeches rip at the air as they reel away from our ship, recoiling from the whale-song. Tears of heart-gladness stream down my cheeks, but I swipe them away with the back of my hand – it's nearly my thirteenth Hunter's Moon and I ent some child.

The drum, the *Huntress*'s life-pulse, begins to beat

steadily as we pull away, heading west. As the black-cloaks gather up their arrows, an icy blanket of mist settles. Frog swings from the ropes, coaxing the lanterns to life. When he reaches the main-mast, he wiggles and weaves around the skewered terrodyl. I glance down; my breeches are torn at the knees and the wound on my arm is crusted with terrodyl blood. When I wipe my nose, my hand comes away bloody.

Grandma stalks towards me and Bear as the terrodyls throb out of sight. She's wearing her danger-face. Without a word she grabs my sodden cloak and bundles me along the deck, past the hidden Hoodwink where the sea-hawks live, and down the steps to our cabin.

Sparrow's stopped singing; now he's just sobbing amongst the bed-furs. My brother's sickly as a merwraith and full of heart-sadness, especially when he sings with the whales. Even more now that Da's been away trading since the last full moon.

Thunderbolt, Sparrow's pet moonsprite, sits on a pillow and chatters softly. Grandma plucks her from the pillow and drops her into a glass bottle, making a silvery moon-lamp that she hangs from a hook. It spills pale light across Grandma's oak table, where the big crinkled map is nailed down, spotted with puddles of blood-red sealing wax. Furs, silks and velvets are heaped

12

in one corner and chests are stuffed with golden eggs, onyx, jade and boxes of pearls. My diving sealskin hangs from a nail, still dripping wet from my morning dive.

That's one of the things I'm best at – diving for pearls. When I collect more than three in a day Grandma tells us her best stories as we huddle amongst our blankets and furs.

Now I ent expecting stories, though. Just a flaming earful.

3

A Flaming Earful

Grandma catches my jaw in her hand, checking my face for hurts. 'You won't be in need of stitching – I've a mind some of my crew will, though. Ent no place for a child on deck when terrodyls come near, girl. Half a hundred times I must have told you!'

'But I ent no child. I just shot one of the terrodyls!' I wave her hands away and fling myself down on the bunk I share with Sparrow. 'And I'm the only one with the beast-chatter, so only I can understand—'

She scoffs. 'You think we need beast-chatter to hear the hate in them terro-wails? You brought the creature down to crush us! Count yourself heart-glad we're striking distance from land, with the damage you've done to that mast. By dawn we should be docked. But we'll have to battle to make it through the night.' Her voice is weary and her brow is furrowed with crags.

'What am I to do with my arrows 'n my poison then?

Save them for the merwraiths, when we're good and scuttled?'

Grandma sits at her table and mixes sea-mud, kelp and herbs to make an ointment for my arm. 'That's enough o' your flaming lip. If your da returned to find you dead and buried at the bottom of the sea, what would I tell him?'

'That I died like any good captain; saving her crew.' I scowl and pick a nib of hardened skin from around my fingernail. Bright blood wells and I suck it clean.

'Twelve moons old and captain already, is she? I think not. I'm hopeful the gods will gift me a few more moons yet, my girl. And any captain knows better than to put the lives of all on board in danger, for the sake of showing off.' Grandma seizes my arm and rubs ointment into my scorched skin. Her silver rings scrape me and I try to push her away but her hand's clamped tight as a limpet.

My cheeks begin to burn. 'I didn't do it for showing off – I done it to avenge Grandpa, and to keep us safe! And it's barely sundown. I'll be thirteen tomorrow night! Sparrow's eight and he ent even asleep yet!' I splutter and almost choke on my words.

A small smile tugs at Grandma's mouth. 'Never mind what your brother's doing, though he should be snoring by now. We might have need of his voice again

15

afore the sun wakes. Off to the privy, now, Sparrow.'

'Yep, off you go,' I say, smirking at my brother. 'Just be watchful that bigtooth shark don't leap up and bite your behind while you're peeing.'

Sparrow yelps and burrows deeper among the blankets. Grandma fixes me with her glass eye. Story goes, her eye went blind when she half turned to merwraith, when the ship of her childhood sank at the hands of wreckers and she nearly drowned. I stare back into its sea-green depths, hard and unblinking.

All of a sudden the fierceness drops out of her face and she starts to chuckle. 'Gods have mercy,' she gasps after a moment, clutching her sides. 'Sparrow, off t' the privy 'n I'll hear no more about it. Mouse, get yourself into your nightclothes. You're to get to bed, and stay put whilst I tend to my injured.'

She turns and clomps up the stairs, herding Sparrow before her. 'My hide's much too ancient for all this child-rearing caper,' she exclaims. 'Not enough that I'm captain and medsin-maker and—' her grumblings fade as she disappears through the hatch.

I strip to my smallclothes, dry myself with a scrap of linen and wriggle into my nightshirt. One of my fingers is grazed raw from my bowstring, so I lick it clean and dab it with Grandma's ointment. When I scoot onto our bunk and prop open the porthole the night rings with the *siiigh* and *shhhhh* of whales breathing.

In the sky, the great green fire spirits dance and ripple, stretching far away into the distance. Grandma says their pictures are gifts, to show us what will come and what has been. She says they showed our Tribe that I'd be a captain, before I was even born. At Sparrow's birth the spirits said he'd be a whale-singer – and sure enough, he was singing before he could talk. I search for some sign of Da among the fire spirits as they flicker with life. But there's naught of him there and my heart aches with it. 'Da?' I whisper.

Sparrow clatters back down the steps into the cabin. 'You ent gonna see Da up there. He's waiting with the land-lurkers.' He jabs me in the ribs with his elbow to make me budge up on the bunk. I'm about to elbow him back when I see the way his hair sticks up in a nest cos I ent got round to brushing it today.

'You better fetch that brush from—'

'Shhh!' hisses Sparrow. He bounces up on tiptoe and grabs the edge of the porthole to peer out.

A knot of women pass along the storm-deck, right below us. 'Carpenters,' I whisper, cos I can hear the little silver hammers on their belts chiming as they lug wood to patch some of the damage to the *Huntress*.

'Bleeding nippers running about, bringing troubles on us,' says one. 'They should be kept below when the beasts come near! Captain's granddaughter or no, it can't go on!'

'Aye, she could've scuppered us! We've a long night ahead.'

Me and Sparrow stare at each other. 'I was just trying to keep our Tribe safe, and this is the heart-thanks I get?'

'I'm cold.' Sparrow pulls the porthole closed with a bang. 'Who cares about the stupid carpenters? Can I have a story?' he begs. He plops himself down amongst the bed-furs and wriggles his hand under the pillow to search out a crispy old starfish.

I sigh. 'Crafty little bargainer, ent you?' I shut one eye and squint at him. 'All right. Just one.'

He pulls off a starfish arm and shoves it into his mouth. 'No sky-monsters! And no stogs – Thunderbolt hates all giants cos they gobble up sprites and spit out their wings.' The moonsprite hops about inside her glass bottle, making a tiny thudding sound like a moth beating against a lantern.

'Gods,' I mutter, rooting around under the bunk to grab the long, smooth walrus tusk with the pictures of Sparrow's favourite story etched into it. 'Next you'll be telling me you still believe in the ghost of Captain Rattlebones or—'

'Don't!' Sparrow shrieks, face gone pale. 'You're

only allowed to tell the story of the Storm-Opal Crown!' He nestles in next to me, peering at the pictures in the tusk. His yellow hair smells like nutmeg and his feet are cold as stones.

'Get them freezing planks off me!' I move the tusk to catch Thunderbolt's moonlight. 'One hundred moons and suns ago, long after the first oarsman beat his drum, but while you was still just a puny sea-spark on the wind—'

'I weren't never!'

'—the last King of Trianukka had a golden crown that got gobbled up by a great whale. Three powerful Storm-Opals were to be set in the ancient crown, to heal the trouble between all the Tribes of Sea, Sky and Land and let them live in peace together. The first Opal held a foam of sea, the second a fragment of sky, and the third a fracture of land. But after the crown was swallowed—'

'Did it hurt?' murmurs Sparrow sleepily, tracing the etched outline of the whale with a fingertip.

'Did what hurt?' I kick his cold feet away again.

'Swallowing a crown?' He belches and I waft away the starfish-stink.

'Ugh! What do you think, clumber-brain? Anyway, the Opals had to be kept safe somehow, didn't they? So the crinkled old mystiks of the Bony Isle guarded them,

19

deep within the walls of Castle Whalesbane, where the last King dwelt.'

I'm getting pulled into the thrill of the story, but Sparrow's breath is soft with sleep, so I skip to the last bit and make it quick. 'And he blamed the Sea-Tribe captain, Rattlebones, for hiding the crown in the whale's belly, and that brought a hundred years of war, and gifted all the power to the land.' My voice trails away. I run my finger across the etching of the first oarsman's drum, then lean down and put the tusk back under our bunk.

Soon Sparrow's garbling in his sleep. The *Huntress* creaks and the wind wails loud enough to almost burst my brain. The whales keep up their moaning; I try to block out their song with my pillow but it's too loud. Shouts drift from Grandma's medsin-lab – must be she's stitching a wound, and I know she's run out of stingray venom for the numbing. 'What are you, True-Tribe or land-lurker?' comes her distant roar.

When I hear her boots creaking down the steps to the cabin I turn towards the wall. I listen to her get ready for bed; taking out her glass eye, peeling off her armour. She flings off her boots but keeps her tunic and breeches on, in case she's needed on deck.

She clambers into bed and I think about calling out that I'm sorry about the terrodyl, but I don't know how to start. I dig my toes into the mattress. She might tell me off if I wake up Sparrow, so I keep quiet, but then another thought makes me bite my tongue – nighttime's always when I think of questions about Ma. Ma was Grandma's own daughter, but we never talk about her. Oftentimes I've lain in my bunk and wanted to call across the cabin: do you miss her? Cos I do. That's the only gap between me and Grandma. The missing Ma and not saying a thing about it.

I open my mouth, turn over, but then Grandma's walrus-snore starts rumbling so I shut my mouth and sigh.

When I'm captain I'll have my own cabin, with no noisy kin to disturb me. I can't wait to fill a captain's boots. My eyelids grow heavy. Da's coming home tomorrow, once we reach port. I grin sleepily into the pillow, imagining the treasures he might bring me for my thirteenth Hunter's Moon. But having Da home will be the best gift of all. He'll make everything right again.

4

The Western Wharves

I gasp awake from nightmares of ship wreckers as first light strikes through the porthole. I'm frighted enough to reach out for Sparrow, but his chest still rises and falls when I put my hand on him and slowly my nightmares fade into the bed-warmth. It's been two full moons since he had one of his shaking fits, and I'm always tensed for the next one.

Sudden as lightning, bubbles of excitement pop and flutter in my belly. Da comes home today! Finally, he can teach me more about stars and tribe-tongues, and I can ask him again about what Ma liked to eat and how sweet she smelled.

I hop onto my knees and swing open the porthole. Only one or two other masts jut into the sky. The squawks of razorbills and black-backed gulls fill my ears.

I shake Sparrow's shoulder. 'We're in port! We're at

the Western Wharves!' He snuffles and rolls over, pulling the furs over his head. I leap from the bunk and fling on the first thing I can find that ent spattered with terrodyl blood. After pulling on my walrus-skin boots I fasten my fur cloak with a bone pin and fix Ma's copper dragonfly brooch to my tunic. It's the only thing I've got of hers, so I always wear it, to keep her spirit close to my heart.

As soon as I step above decks my eyes are dazzle-hurt and my nose fills with the stinks of smoke, fish, sweat, grease and tar.

Kids play amongst jumbled lengths of rigging and a group of Tribesmen struggle under the weight of the terrodyl corpse as they carry it towards the lowered plank, yelling whenever a drop of blood scalds them.

No one greets me. A cold feeling settles in my gut. So they all think me a fool for shooting the beast?

While I'm lost in thought, a heavy hand clamps down over my eyes. 'Guess it, Mouse-Bones. A mouse should have the sharpest senses of all.' A cool pod of something sweet is pressed beneath my nose. Bear must've been trading spices. At least *he's* not being fierce with me.

I breathe in deeply. 'Vanilla?'

Bear's hand lifts from my eyes and he spins me round, a big grin lighting him up. 'Dead right. And look what else I found for you – one of your favourites, I think?' He pulls a small jar of amber goo from his pocket.

'Honey!' I stretch up to take the jar, twist off the lid and scoop out a sweet glob, sucking it off my finger. 'Heart-thanks, Bear!'

He beams, then shivers and wraps his arms around himself. 'You know, 'tis early in the year for such a frost,' he muses. 'Where I was born, we fled from winter. Now, in the company of you northerners, I run further into her jaws.'

'Aye.' I pull my polar fox fur tighter about me. 'You been up to Haggle's Town? Did you pass by the Star Inn?' I ask.

'I've not yet left the dockside. Wanted to come back for you first, little lay-abed, even though I'm heart-keen to see my best friend.' His dark eyes crinkle and dance when I crane my neck to look up at his face. 'Shall we find your da?'

'Yes! Let's go!'

Bear laughs and offers me his elbow. I loop my arm through his and we're heading for the plank when Vole bustles towards us. 'That's your mess, young Mouse.' She nods at the smashed crow's nest and the splintered wood strewn across the deck.

I feel the blood rush into my cheeks. 'Ent my fault a pack of terrodyls chose to—'

She holds up a finger. 'Salvage what timber you can,

help take in the sail for patching and sand down the boards – you'll find fresh sharkskin in the carpenters' cabin.'

'Now, Vole,' starts Bear, reaching out to tuck a curl behind her ear. 'What's the harm in letting young Mouse come ashore to—'

'Don't you *Vole* me,' she snaps, batting his hand away. 'I've a tough enough job keeping the little ones in line as it is, without you leading them astray.'

I gaze across the port towards Haggle's Town, where Da's been lodging while he trades. My heart sinks like it's been scuttled by a fire-arrow. 'But I'm meant to be meeting Da at the Star Inn!'

Vole's blue eyes narrow. 'After your foolishness last night, if I were you I'd do as I was told.' She swishes away, all skirts and ink-black hair. 'Ermine! Squirrel! Little Marten! Stop playing tag and help with the work!'

I chew my lip to keep from hurling insults after her, cos I'm already in enough trouble.

Bear sweeps a bow at her turned back, merriment in his eyes. Then he gifts me a wink. 'You'd better play along with the rules, Mouse-Bones.'

'But—'

'Ah, just for the time being. Some full-growns have forgotten how to loosen up! And, in heart-truth, trouble simmers in many a port, though the war was said to end

25

when Captain Wren were small. You're safest here.'

He plods across the plank and onto the craggy scrubland. I watch him pass into the shadow of towering evergreens and disappear between the lopsided wooden houses of Haggle's Town.

'Mouse!' calls Vole.

With a snarl I stamp over to the mess and start separating the pieces of wood that're good enough to be used for repairs. Once I've finished my hands are full of splinters. For a heartbeat the pain helps take my mind off waiting for Da. What I wouldn't give for a breakfast of fat cinnamon rolls down at the Star while he tells me stories of his travels.

I sneak a glance across the deck and make for the plank at a sprint, squeezing past Tribesmen carrying thin timbers onto the deck.

'Them splinters wouldn't hold up my drawers, let alone a flaming mast!' Grandma yells from the prow. She spies me. 'Mouse! What you about, girl?'

I freeze. Vole catches up to me and grabs my arm. 'Oh, no you don't. Here.' She shoves a broom into my hands.

I curse. 'You can stop spying on me now, I'll do it! Though if you like I could wrench a few of them bad teeth out for you. They're turning proper rotten.' I push past her on my way back to the deck.

'Don't you give my prentice grief, child!' booms

Grandma. 'If you don't want to help on deck you can get yourself to the kitchens and scrub the terrodyl blood out of Pip's cauldrons.'

'All right, all right! Everyone, becalm your sails, I'm doing it!'

As I work, I notice the eerie silence of the harbour. Why ent folk heading for market? Our ship alone must've brought enough goods to trade 'til next week. The only creatures lurking round the dockside are a few scrawny brown mongrels hunting for scraps. Their beast-chatter is knotted and worrisome. *Hungryyip! Frightedcoldgrumblebelly.*

I breathe and force my heart to slow, but nerves have turned my palms damp. I just want to fetch Da home and raise anchor. I can't focus on work, so after Grandma goes ashore with a band of black-cloaks and Vole takes her nagging self below decks, I leap onto a barrel and give a short, sharp howl.

Sparrow stumbles blearily onto the deck, swigging water from a skin bottle. Then Frog and his sister, Squirrel, pop out from behind the mizzen-mast. Ermine, Hammerhead and Little Marten jump down from the rigging.

'Who wants a game of Rattlebones?' I ask, wiggling my eyebrows.

One by one, their faces light up with grins.

5

The Stranger

Sparrow fires off his question again, the one he's already asked me two thousand times this morning. 'Why ent Da home yet?'

'Dunno, shut up,' I say without looking at him.

'But—'

'Quiet!' I'm trying to keep my mind fixed on our game of Rattlebones, named for the ancient captain of the fireside tales, but my nerves are fizz-popping.

Sparrow growls and plops down on the deck, chin in his hands. Rune tokens and reindeer bones lie scattered across the deck. Hammer draws back his arm to roll a pearl, but Frog jabs his spindly fingers into Hammer's ribs. 'Argh, you bleeding half-brain!' The pearl flies from Hammer's grip, hits the mast and bounces off into the middle of a group of women carving bone fishing hooks.

'Take your blinking games below decks!' one of them shouts. 'And Frog, fifteen is too old to be wasting your time with the nippers! Make yourself useful.'

'Sorry!' calls Frog. Then he grins at Hammer. 'Hear that? I'm far too old and important to be hanging about with the likes of you.' Hammer pummels Frog on the arm. 'Ow!'

I hide my grin in my hands. 'My turn!' I angle my wrist and aim. My pearl skitters along the deck and hits the furthest rune token. I snatch the token up and add it to my collection. Hammer clambers around the deck, counting up everyone's runes and bones. 'Mouse has the most runes,' he announces with a small sigh. 'She wins!'

'Again,' adds Ermine.

'Squirrel loses – she has the most bones,' says Hammer.

I whoop. 'Captain Rattlebones will come for Squirrel tonight, looking for his bones!'

Squirrel's face drains of colour. 'Oh, I *never* win! Not never!' She snatches up her breath in little sobs. 'And don't you even think about dumping those bones in my bed again! It's so unfair!'

'Stop your grizzle-gruzzling, it's just a game,' I snap.

Squirrel gets to her feet amongst the clutter of animal bones and runs off, red hair wild.

'One day the tides will turn!' Frog calls after her. 'Mouse is gonna lose and then Captain Rattlebones will come for her, urggghhhhh!' He waggles his arms at me and I shove him away.

My teeth ache from grinding my jaw. 'Makes no matter; this ship'll be mine one day and everyone's gonna have to do what *I* say. Squirrel might as well get used to it.' I gather my pearls and stuff them in my belt pouch.

'Really?' says Hammer. 'That what you reckon a captain's job is, bossing everyone around?' His eyebrows twitch. 'Can't wait to be part of your crew,' he mutters.

'Shut it,' I murmur, peering at the rune tokens I collected. One of them is carved with an *Yr*, meaning bow, which makes me smile cos of my longbow. Others, showing the runes *Fe* and *Ar*, promise wealth and plenty – never a bad thing for a trader. But the last one has a long *I* chiselled into it, meaning ice, and I turn the rough piece of wood over in my hands. Everyone knows the runes hold secret meanings. What could this foretell?

'We all miss your da, but it ent Squirrel's fault he's not home,' says Ermine, glowering at me through his shock of white hair. 'But it *is* someone's fault we're tethered to this ghost-harbour, waiting for the Hagglers to come for us, and that we've traded half our finest wares for timber what's not even strong enough to repair that smashed mast.'

'Say that again with your fists up and your teeth bared,' I growl.

Hammer gets between me and Erm. 'Settle your bones, both of you. Captain's got extra crew on watch, so no one will dare board the *Huntress*.'

'She went ashore without her glass eye in, just to make herself look more frightful-fierce,' I tell them. Ermine breaks into a toothy smile and I grin back, heart-keen to drop the fight.

I grip the ice-rune tightly in my fingers. 'Ent it odd that it's already so icy and all the other ships have sailed?'

Hammer opens his mouth but then a great cry goes up and my head spins to look at the gangplank on the port side.

Grandma and her black-cloaks stride up the plank onto the storm-deck. 'She's back!' I scramble to my feet, slipping on a stray pearl.

I'm running towards her to ask after Da when the black-cloaks move aside to let a tall stranger in a scarlet cloak climb aboard. I skid to a stop and stare. The man plants his gold-buckled boots wide and rests his fists on his hips.

The stranger's face is long and pinched, with a crooked hawk's nose, downturned lips and great black brows. But it's his eyes I keep looking at, as he lets them crawl all over the *Huntress*. They're grey and wide like rock pools stuffed with eels, ready to swallow me up. Suddenly they fall on me, dead and heavy, but I keep my face icicle-fierce. The man smiles, baring a row of sharp teeth.

'What's going on? Who's that man?' asks Sparrow, tugging on my cloak.

'The king of the bleeding sea-cows. How would *I* know?' I wrap an arm round Sparrow's shoulders and rest my chin on top of his tangled hair. Sick longing for Da twists inside my belly.

Grandma's hair swirls in the salt spray. There's a green glint when she moves her head – she must be wearing her glass eye again. She stands arrow-straight and crosses a fist over her heart. Her sea-hawk, Battle-Shrieker, hulks on her shoulder, talons clutching a scrap of cloth. Quiet falls, leaving just the shrilling of sea-birds and the sloshing of waves against the hull. 'Tribesfolk, this is Stag, a long-lost member of our Tribe. Some of you know him—' Someone cheers, and Grandma grins broadly. 'Some of you don't. But all of you will make your captain heart-glad if you join me in welcoming him home.'

Welcoming him *home*?

'Blessings and thanks to you, Captain Wren,' he replies. 'As a hearth-gift I have brought the carcass of the bigtooth brute that's been plaguing these waters, slain by my hand.'

As he speaks, Bear and a group of fishermen struggle up the plank, lugging the colossal shark. Its blood makes dark puddles on the wood. The world melts into deafening cheers, but I don't care about the shark, cos the man called Stag slides his eyes over my face again. Then they dart away, across the deck. My guts wriggle, heavy and damp as a bucket crammed with slimy hagfish. Who is this Stag? What does he want with the *Huntress*?

And other questions stab behind my eyes, in my chest, into the back of my throat, again and again and again. Where is Da? How could Grandma have returned with this strange man instead?

'Stag!' calls an oarsman. 'Too many heartbeats have passed, good brother. Where have you roved?' As Stag strides into the greeting, I notice something folded over his arm. It's a sealskin. My heart jangles and Sparrow's body tenses, cos he's seen it too.

A sealskin cloak just like Da's, stained with dark splotches of blood.

6

A Paw Print in the Ice

Sparrow presses his sticky little hand into mine.

'This cloak was found by washerwomen on the riverbank,' says Stag, passing the sealskin to Grandma. 'As one of your own, I recognised the symbol of the *Huntress* sewn into the skin.'

My belly drops away. Grandma flashes a look at me and Sparrow before she glances at the underside of the cloak. She nods and her face grows flushed and slack. I grip Sparrow's hand tight enough to make him whimper.

'Bear!' calls Grandma.

'I believe it belonged to your navigator. His name was Fox?' asks Stag.

A startled murmur *swooshes* around the deck. Grandma meets my eyes. Stag's words fly between us. *Was?*

Bear appears, breathless, breeches smeared with tar and shark blood. He pushes past black-cloaks and carpenters and comes to stand behind Sparrow and me. His warm hands rest on our shoulders. 'After all these years, he returns,' he murmurs.

'What happened at Haggle's Town? Where's Da?' I ask. Bear shakes his head gently.

Before I can brace myself, the stranger speaks again. 'I gift you a thousand heart-sadnesses for the death of your navigator.'

Bear's fingers tighten and he pulls us closer to him. 'Fret ye not,' he whispers in our ears.

Am I going to have to cut out Stag's stupid land-lurking tongue, just to shut him up? 'Don't you listen to this thundercloud in breeches!' I shout. 'We've got to search for Da!'

Stag's eyebrows almost vanish into his hair when I shout, but it's Grandma who speaks, in her no-messing voice. 'Bear, get my grandchildren below decks. The rest of you, on with your duties. The Wharves are dangerous and empty of trade. The Hagglers blame us for bringing terrodyls close to their shores – land-lurking fools. So finish patching the sail quick-sharp – we raise anchor before sundown. We rove!'

'We rove to trade, to meet, for the restlessness in our bones; we rove at one with the sea!' cry the Tribe in answer. But I stay silent, cos even if we ent safe here, I don't wanna leave without Da, and I don't want my Hunter's Moon celebrations without him.

I tip back my head to see Bear. His eyes are fretful, but kindness fills them when he looks at me. 'Come, gentle-hearts. Word is Pip's got a cauldron bubbling with his best squid tentacle stew.' He steers my brother and me away but I duck under his arm and race to Grandma.

I clutch her tight. 'A blood-soaked sealskin don't mean nothing!' I hiss, flicking my glare between her and the land-lurker. 'We ent leaving here without Da!'

'Enough, child.' She tries to prise off my fingers but I dig my nails in. 'Mouse!' she snaps. 'You heard what I said and I will not have you quibbling so. We sail and that is an end of it.'

I lower my voice. 'Come with me, *please*, I need you in private.'

Grandma smiles sadly. 'Go, dearheart. Fill your boots. A future captain must keep up her strength.' She leans down and presses her forehead to mine in a Tribe-kiss. 'Meet me in my medsin-lab after you've slurped your stew.' Then she turns back to Stag. 'Will you break hearth-bread with me?'

Below decks, I ladle some stew from a steaming cauldron

into a bowl and sit next to Bear at one of the long wooden benches. My stomach's clenched like knotted rope. Bear's oar-scabbed fingers slip beneath my chin to make me look into his coppery eyes. 'Happens your da's a tough 'un, same as you. My silver's on him being the one to find *us*, next time we dock.'

I drop my spoon with a splash and prop my head in my hands. 'But he's gonna miss my thirteenth Hunter's Moon and he swore he'd be back in time. Da keeps his promises, so why ent he home? Ent no way he's dead, I don't care what that Stag says.' My voice wobbles so I kick the table leg and swallow back my tears.

Bear wraps a huge arm around my shoulders and squeezes me tight. 'So as you gathered, I didn't find your da. But I did find this.' With his other hand he brings a small, dark piece of wood from his pocket. It's whittled into the shape of a ship. I'd know it anywhere – it's a carving I made for Da, a tiny model of the *Huntress*. He takes it everywhere with him. A wave of sickness spreads through me.

I steel my heart and bite my lip, hard enough to tear the skin. 'Where did you get it?' I ask, running my thumb across the wood. I try to blink away my tears, but one escapes and drips onto the runes that Da and me etched to spell our names. *Mouse and Da.*

'Now, don't take your sails down just yet, Mouse. I

found it at the Star, and I've half a thought it's like a paw print in the ice – a trail your da's left behind, to let you know all's well.'

His words kindle a spark in my belly. Da knew we were meant to meet him at the Star Inn, so what if he *did* leave it there as a trace of himself? That better be the truth of it. What with Ma gone, I can't lose Da as well.

'So who's the sour-jowls, then? Why's he here?'

Bear rubs his chin. 'I don't know why he's come back. I was just a lad when he left, about your age, and the thing is, his jowls were no less sour then.' He leans closer. 'Some folks just don't know how to have fun.' Bear picks up his bowl, winks at me over the top of it and gulps down the rest of his stew. 'Shall we remember the leaner times and gift our heart-thanks to the sea-gods for this food?'

'Aye,' I mumble, ducking my head close to my bowl. 'Blessings and heart-thanks, you gods of the sea.'

Bear stands and cracks his knuckles against the ceiling. 'Back to work,' he says through a yawn.

I watch the table opposite through a veil of steam. Stag sits on a wooden chair draped with polar fox fur, sharing a flagon of ale with Grandma. A great black crow hunches on Stag's shoulder.

Grandma's voice is low. I strain my ears above the clatter of the crew to listen. 'Not so long ago, the

Hagglers showed respect to a captain when she went ashore to trade, and we could barely satisfy their demand for herring. Now the bakers won't even buy a dusting of nutmeg and there are whispers of slavers and wreckers on every breath of wind.' Scorn bubbles in her throat. 'Trouble's brewing, ports are fast closing. Friends are few. And gods only know what terrodyls are doing so far north this late in the season.' She turns to a scroll and quill on the table, dips the nib into a pot of squid ink and scratches at the parchment.

'Indeed, Captain Wren. Their habits have been odd of late, according to reports from the fishing villages and Hill-Tribe chieftains – though nothing has been heard from Castle Whalesbane for many suns and moons.'

Just then, Sparrow plunks a wooden bowl carved with a jagged 'S' onto the bench and plops down next to me, grubby hands fumbling for a spoon. A gold brooch in the shape of an arrowhead gleams on his tunic.

His face hasn't seen a good scrub for gods know how long and dark circles ring his eyes. *Look after him, Mouse,* whispers Ma in my memory. But some days the looking after feels too hard. I send out a silent prayer to the sea-gods, begging them to keep away his shaking fits.

'Din't Grandma wash your face?' I ask.

'No.' He shakes his head. 'And I don't care. Don't like washing.'

'I can smell that much, slackwit. I'll have to do it then, won't I?' A stray moonsprite runs across my knuckles, covering them in silvery moon-dust.

'You lemme be.' He sighs over his food and rubs his eye with the heel of his hand. 'Can I swap my arrowhead brooch for Ma's dragonfly? Just for one day?'

I shake my head. 'Not on your life. Remember last time, when you let Ermine borrow it and he tried to feed it to a sea-hawk?' At my words, a thrill flickers along my nerves, cos tonight I'll get my own sea-hawk during my Hunter's Moon celebrations. But the thrill feels like a betrayal of Da.

Across the room, Stag's crow *thwawks* and stretches out its wings, hopping from foot to foot. Stag turns his head slightly and the crow grows still as oak.

Sparrow sighs, takes a spoonful of stew, then spits it out again and starts pushing his wobbly tooth back and forth with a finger. 'When's he coming back—'

'I told you, I don't know!' I'm so sick of him asking questions when I'm just trying to get my head clear. Sometimes I wanna live underwater, even if it means being a merwraith, so all I can hear is my own heartbeat and the dolphins and whales calling.

'Well *I'll* tell *you* then. He won't never be coming back,' Sparrow whines, like somehow it's my fault. He pulls off his boots and draws his knees up to his chin.

The stink of his feet climbs into my nose. 'That was his cloak, all right. And it were covered with—'

I thump the table with a clenched fist. 'I saw it too, little fool!' I hiss. 'A man as strong as our da can live without a sealskin.'

Sparrow snuffles loudly and swirls his spoon through the stew. I think of the cloak draped over Stag's arm and bite the inside of my cheek as I push my bowl away.

'Where you going?' pipes Sparrow.

'Anywhere that ent here,' I mutter, weaving past folk carrying bowls and flagons. I head above decks, cos I can feel my longbow calling, like she always does when I need to think.

7
A Skilful Captain

Sundown's an hour away when we raise sail for the Wildersea; the great greyness we have to cross to reach the Bay of Thunder, for the Tribe-Meet. The Western Wharves fade behind us in the mist, and the foghorn booms.

I'm out on the storm-deck, practising my right-handed shooting. Grandma's black-cloaks keep arrows nocked to their bows as we sail past the closed ports of the Hill-Tribe chieftains, who watch, shields up, from their jagged fortresses.

Leaving without Da feels every kind of wrong. But I ent gonna doubt him. If he says he'll come home, then he'll be here, sooner or later. I keep a tight hold of the carving in my pocket and treasure what Bear said – that it might be a paw print Da left for me.

My last arrow thrums into the animal-skin target. As I lick the salt from my lips and stoop to gather my fallen arrows, I remember with a jolt that Grandma said to meet her in the lab. My pulse flickers as I race below.

Grandma's medsin-lab is marked with a sign saying 'Leave Me Be!' but I push open the heavy door and step inside. The stinks of boiled sea-slugs and algae greet me. I'm dwarfed by tall shelves crammed full of brown bottles, with labels written in squid ink. There are vials of wolf-fish blood, for keeping divers' blood warm, and the dragonfish luminescence Grandma worked on for moons and moons, to make into night-vision eye drops for the night-watchmen. On the wall is a note: 'A new-birthed oyster ent no bigger than a peppercorn,' to keep her impatience in check.

Grandma stands at her table, tipping a blue powder onto measuring scales. Beside her, glass tubes of jewel-bright liquid seethe and bubble. The table's strewn with chisels, mallets and saws, and stained with dark patches of blood from her amputations and tooth-pullings.

'Young Mouse,' she says, without turning. 'Come and help me brew this potion for Sparrow's shaking fits. Fetch me three sea-slugs, if you please.' I'd a mind I was being silent. How'd she know I was there?

I dump my bow and quiver on the floor and turn to the shelf behind me. When I find the right jar I grab a rusty pair of forceps and pick out the scaly green slugs, dropping them onto a square of cloth.

'So why's this Stag here, then?' I ask, idly digging the

forceps into the flesh of a slug.

'He's a navigator.' Grandma looks at me like she's about to say more but her jaw closes again with a *pop*.

'Aye, but we don't need a new navigator; we've got you til Da comes back.' I spot the mortar and pestle, add violet root and start to grind it up for the potion.

She laughs croakily and turns back to her work, dropping the sea-slugs into a small cauldron, where they burst and sputter. 'Happens I've got too much shrimp on my platter and I could do with the help. Think of that?' She sets the cauldron over a flame and adds a gooey ball of rotten kelp to the slug-sludge. 'Fetch the porpoise bladder, dearest.'

I scuff over to some barrels filled with the odds and ends that Pip can't find a use for in his kitchens, and haul a big white bladder out of one.

'But why *him*? Could've had any of the crew be a navigator if you ordered 'em to. Da was training up a few good 'uns, anyway.' I dump the bladder onto the table. It makes a soft *ooooohh* sound as the air's knocked out of it.

Grandma ladles the cauldron gunge into the neck of the bladder. 'Ha! Being a captain ent about giving orders.' She threads a needle and starts to stitch the bladder shut. I add my violet root to a glass tube with a ladleful of elder wine and set it boiling over a flame. 'A crew's like the sea herself: full of wild moods. A skilful captain learns to weather stormy seas, but *only* once she's learned to weather her crew.'

I squint up at her.

'Ack, such solemn grey eyes, always finding me out since the day you were born!' She laughs. 'Stag was a young member of this crew, moons ago. Any Tribesperson may return after a wandering if the captain judges them to be heart-sore for their true home. Stag is True-Tribe and his skills are much needed here – he is a truly exceptional navigator.'

'He's a sombre old loon, is what *he* is. Besmirching our deck with his sneering jowls.' I use tongs to lift my glass tube from the flame and fix it in a vice to cool.

Grandma's mouth twists like she's trying not to laugh. 'You ent frighted of him, now, are you, Bones?'

'No, I flaming well ent!' My face floods with shame. I slam my fist down onto the table as Grandma hoots with laughter. 'But he can't be trusted.'

Grandma stretches across the table for a rag. 'Time will tell, dearest heart. Shall we gift him a chance to prove himself?' She wipes her hands on the rag. 'Truth be told, my girl, the sea is the only one you can trust, though she's no fool and she claims anyone who don't show her rightful respect.' Her good eye flickers between both of mine, and deep inside her glass eye, little flecks of gold begin to swirl. Ent noticed that before – less it's just my imagination.

'I wonder if turning thirteen's lent you the strength for what I'm about to say.' Her mouth draws into a grave line.

'What?' I gape up at her, my heartstrings pulling and thudding.

She pushes loose strands of hair away from her face. 'Stag's moving into your da's cabin.'

The words hit me hard in the chest, like Grandma's thrown the whole stinking porpoise bladder at me. 'You ent serious.' I back away, a storm in my veins turning my cheeks hot.

'Mouse, calm your bones, you know I don't want to heart-bruise you.'

'So why are you, then? You still sore with me cos of that terrodyl? I never meant to bring it down on us!'

'No, course I ent.' Grandma's eye burns into me. 'But if you ever try a repeat performance I'll do far worse.'

I nod, quick. 'I thought you wanted Da back as much as me 'n Sparrow do!'

'Course I do, Little-Bones.' She folds herself onto a wooden stool, looking more crumpled and tired than ever. 'There never was a finer man. I've loved him like my own son, ever since your ma first fell for him at a Tribe-Meet. And gods know we could do with him aboard. But you saw that sealskin, clear as stars.'

'So what? Anyone can lose a cloak. I'd bet it weren't even his blood!' I bite my lip, hard.

'Aye, that's a point. I don't know exactly what it all means.' Grandma sighs, her craggy face pained. 'But if he *is* alive, your da's more than capable of crewing another vessel until he can return – then the cabin will be his again. Meantime, we've to forge on, and Stag needs a place to sleep. Tonight we celebrate your Hunter's Moon. I'm heart-certain your da will be with you in spirit.'

'I couldn't give a twisted fishing hook for any birth-moon without Da!' I turn my face away as tears prickle the backs of my eyes. 'I ent ten, so don't talk to me like I am. I want Da here, body *and* spirit. Don't let Stag have his cabin. *Please.*'

Grandma smiles gently and reaches for me. 'Listen. The cabin was yours for a heartbeat, when you shared it with your da. But you're half-grown now, learning the ways of a captain. Looking after your brother. Does a captain pine after past lives? We can't own a thing in this world, and a cabin's wooden walls, that's all.'

'Ha!' I shout bitterly, swiping at my face with my sleeve cos the tears are dripping down even though I'm fighting hard. 'You always say there's so much of our blood in *Huntress* she's like our living, breathing kin! Now the truth comes, that you think –' I snatch for breath '– *you* think she's naught but wooden walls!'

Grandma looks at me. Her mouth's turned down at the corners and her good eye shines bright. 'Aye, girl. There's Stag's blood in the *Huntress*, too. Like it or not.' She bundles me into her arms and I breathe her warm, herby scent.

Someone taps at the door. 'Mouse! Are you in there? It's time for your gift-giving!' calls Vole.

My pulse quickens. I wipe my nose on my sleeve and pull away from Grandma, looking up into her face.

She brushes the hair off my forehead and nods briskly. 'Come and greet your first sea-hawk.'

Hunter's Moon

Near the prow Frog, Vole and Big Marten play pipes and drums. Moon-lamps hang from hooks along the deck, bright against the dusk. My heart lifts when I see my moon rising, a full yellow orb that bathes the sea in milky light. Wherever Da is, maybe he's looking at the moon too, and thinking of me.

Pip lays out a feast beneath the stars: oranges and cinnamon buns, lobster claws, whole spiced tentacles, roasted snowshoe hare, toasted anemones and sweet curd tartlets.

Folk stuff themselves with grub and leap in the firelight, clad in animal masks and hoods. I take an orange and run my thumbs over its cool, bumpy skin, but I can't eat. The fire spirits twine overhead, flickering white, green and purple, but they still don't gift me any sign of Da. Bear rumbles his loudest growl and the littlest ones shriek with laughter.

High above us on the top of the fore-castle, a group

of women gather moonlight. I crane my neck to watch as they spin orbs of light between their hands and drip pools of it into glass bottles to make moon-lamps.

A Tribeswoman lets out a cry as she drops a silver splash of moonlight onto the boards. It quickly forms a moonsprite that runs off, streaking silver footprints across the deck. Squirrel chases it, giggling, red hair braided over her shoulder.

I send imaginary arrows and my fiercest battle-howl into the night sky, as the pipes and drums and horns and fiddles play faster and faster. The whirs and clicks of the orcas' song fill the air. 'The whales are dancing with us!' Sparrow shouts, cheeks nipped with cold.

Bear hears him. 'Aye, the sea-gods have blessed your thirteenth moon, Mouse-Bones!' He grabs our hands and spins us in a circle. Sparrow squeals with laughter.

All the faces around me are familiar ones, and I'm heart-glad, but how can Grandma say the stranger is True-Tribe when he ent even bothered showing up for my celebration? I wrinkle my nose. He must have too much work to do, given he's such an *exceptional* navigator.

Squirrel clambers down from her best spot in the rigging to gift me with a tiny arrowhead chiselled from jet, hung on a hook. I thread it through my ear and grin at her. 'Took me three sunrises to make it!' she chirps through a mouthful of sugared almonds.

Sparrow's gift is a wooden whale that he carved himself, with chips of jet for eyes. It looks like a great shapeless lump of wood, but I keep my mouth shut about it.

From Bear I have an amulet of dark amber, wrapped in silver and hung from a string of dried sinew. 'It'll bring you luck and protection,' he tells me, grinning as he lifts it over my head. My gift to him is a proper toothy smile.

'Can I have something, too?' begs Sparrow, eyeing my gifts sullenly.

'Your birth-moon, is it?' I ask.

He sticks out his tongue. I make a grab for him but he wallops me on the arm and darts out of the way. Then he gasps. 'Look!'

I turn as Grandma appears, cradling my sea-hawk fledgling, and before I can think I'm jumping in the air and shouting for joy. I startle the bird so much that she poos a white river all down Grandma's arm.

'Mouse, you witless sculpin!' Grandma scolds, but laughter sparkles in her eye. 'Don't unsettle her so!'

I rush to her and grip her arm, peering at the hawk's spiky feathers and up-to-no-good face. She's got yellow eyes and a white crest like spilt sea-foam. She stares at me but no words come yet. I can sense the beast-chatter in her, though, and it stirs the wild-crackle in my blood.

'Can I take her?' I gasp, opening my palms.

'Gently,' Grandma says.

The fledgling settles her feathers against my skin and cosies her face up to my neck. It tickles and makes me laugh. Her heart drums wild against my frozen palms.

'My granddaughter has claimed her thirteenth moon, and will take her place by my side at the next great Tribe-Meet!' announces Grandma. 'Let it be known the fire spirits named her hawk Thaw-Wielder.'

Folk begin to cheer, howl and clap. Sparrow wanders up to me and scuffs his boot against the boards. 'She ent even half as good as Thunderbolt.' His moonsprite flits around his head, shedding moondust into his hair. Her light shows up the jealousy in his wrinkled nose and stubborn chin.

I open my mouth to tell him what I think of that stupid moonsprite when Thaw-Wielder poos down my cloak. Sparrow laughs so hard he bashes into the mast.

How much of that stuff have you got in there? I ask the bird.

She stares at me and makes a soft peep that nearly sounds like *lotslotslots*.

Grandma smiles. 'It's good to hear the wildness of the beast-chatter in your throat, my girl. This hawk is lucky to have you.'

Heart-pride blazes in my chest. But I wish, fierce as

anything, that Da could be here to greet Thaw-Wielder with me.

Tonight Grandma's let me sleep out on deck with my sea-hawk, in the hammock Da uses when he takes the watch. Thaw-Wielder tucks her beak into her feathers and her sides rise and fall with tiny beast-breath. The only other life out here is the night-watchmen and the creatures lurking below the starlight-silvered sea.

In the light of the Hunter's Moon I cradle the carving of our ship in my hands. Grandma's words echo around my brain. *There's Stag's blood in the* Huntress, *too.*

Worms, croons Thaw sleepily. I fetch a pink wriggle-treat out of my pocket and she slurps it up. *Wormswormsworms.*

The tiny model of the ship has all three masts and jutting sticks for oars, though some of them must've snapped off. *This ship belongs to me and my kin*, I whisper to the snoozing hawk. *Not that Stag.* The wind rises and gusts suddenly, filling the sails, and the *Huntress* speeds along like she agrees with me.

I'm about to put the carving back in my belt pouch when my finger brushes a knotted lump in the wood at the base of the tiny fore-mast. I pluck at it. *Thaw, lend me your beak and you can have lots more worms.* Her eyes flick open and she looks where I'm pointing.

She nibbles and drags at the knot with her sharp beak, and it extends into a thin cord.

Wormswormsworms? Worms? she asks, fanning out her wings and tail feathers.

Shh, wait! Frowning, I grasp the cord and pull.

My breath lodges in my throat like a fishbone. Beautiful, silken white blooms unfurl, attached to the miniature masts. They're little white sails. My eyes fill with tears. We were meant to add the sails together, Da and I, but he must've finished the job without me.

I turn the carving over to look at the other side and suddenly I sit bolt upright, heart hammering. Thaw bursts into the rigging with a shrill hoot.

Etched in spidery squid ink around the edges of the sails are runes, delicate enough to look like decoration to eyes less sharp than mine. My eyes follow the symbols:

KEEP THIS HIDDEN, LITTLE-BONES.

I CANNOT RETURN, THERE IS GRAVE DANGER.

SEEK THE SCATTERED STORM-OPALS OF SEA, SKY AND LAND, BEFORE AN ENEMY FINDS THEM AND USES THEM TO WIELD DARK POWER.

TAKE THEM TO THE GOLDEN CROWN BEFORE ALL TRIANUKKA TURNS TO ICE, TRAPPING THE

WHALES BENEATH A FROZEN SEA.

REMEMBER THE OLD SONG? THE SONG
WILL MAKE A MAP.

KEEP YOUR BROTHER CLOSE BY YOUR
SIDE, AND KNOW YOU'RE NEVER ALONE.

I WILL FIND YOU WHEN I CAN.

DA.

My heart flutters like a wild thing. A message from
Da – I *knew* he was alive! Then his message starts to
settle about me like a heavy cloak. *The Storm-Opals
are real? I thought they were just part of a story!* My mind
tries to catch hold of this new knowing, but it's too
big. *There's so much power in them Opals, Thaw! The story
says they can bring all the Tribes together in peace, if they're
returned to the crown. How'd they end up scattered? And how
am I meant to find them?*

My eyes gobble the runes over and over. Wasn't I
just pondering the meaning of winning that ice-rune
this morning and now here's this message, talking
about ice again!

Thaw-Wielder zooms down to land on my knee
and stares up at me. *Da used to sing me the old song,* I
tell her. *But that was many Hunter's Moons ago, when I
was little.* I search my mind, but I can't remember the
words.

She pecks my ear with her cold beak. *Lift throat-warble to sky!*

Reckon she's telling me to sing, but I frown and shake my head. *I don't know the words, Thaw.* And anyway, singing ent my strong point, mostly cos the beast-chatter clogs my ears all the time.

I pull the cord from the other side and the tiny sails collapse and disappear back inside the carving. I've got to keep Da's message secret. *Bear's right; Da did leave the carving as a trail!*

Trail! Old song. Worms? she peeps.

I stow the ship in my belt pouch and pull the furs up to my chin as I sway gently in the hammock, feeding worms to the sea-hawk.

For hours I lie awake and stare at the full moon, etching Da's message onto my memory. I don't mind keeping it hidden – for once I can have a secret, just for me. But how can a song be a map? And what kind of danger has kept Da from coming home?

When my eyelids grow heavy I'm restless. I know I should settle my bones good and proper, cos otherwise my spirit's gonna pull free and fly through the night in a dream-dance. That's what happens if my mind can't stay still.

As I slip into the dreaming world, my spirit tugs against my body. Fright pangs beneath my skin; I fight, but it's too late. I climb *out of my sleeping self, cold night air brushing my spirit. I flit away from the hammock and fly below decks. Something drags me like the tide, towards Da's cabin. But when I reach the door the din almost shocks me back to my body.*

A man shouts and cries out like a frighted bab. I drift inside and the stranger's there, asleep in Da's bunk. A candle burns by his bedside – is he afraid of the dark? He thrashes and yells. 'Lost. Dark. No! Gone. Almost had them. But I'll find them again, can't have been for nothing–' Then he startles awake and stares about him for a long moment. 'Who's there?' he barks. But he can't see me, cos only my spirit is there, dream-dancing.

9

The Frozen Wastes

Darkness falls earlier every night, now this fearsome winter's stirring. I watch through the porthole as the *Huntress* prowls past a stretch of ice-flats. These skinny sea-paths through the ice are perilous, cos the land-lurking Fangtooth Tribe rule this place with terror.

Grandma's orders float along the deck. 'Lamps doused! Shields up! Oarsmen below! Black-cloaks, be watchful for Fangtooths. The *Huntress* is entering the Frozen Wastes – Sparrow's whale-song is the only sound I want to hear, from this beat on. May strong winds fill our sails.'

The drum fades and Sparrow's high voice rises, like a bell, to chime along with the whales. Blue puffs of song blow past my face. His voice will keep the whales close and they'll guide us forwards in the dark, so we don't crash into the ice.

Thaw-Wielder clings to my shoulder. *How does Grandma think I'm gonna be captain if she don't let me join*

58

the watch when danger lurks? I mutter.

Danger? Thaw trills.

I need to be out on deck, where I can watch for polar dogs and keep an eye on that Stag. Suddenly I snatch a yawn, and Thaw catches it in her beak. *Last night in my dream-dance I saw Stag thrashing in his sleep, and babbling about something being lost.* My mind flits to the missing Storm-Opals in Da's note.

Feather-fear, chirrups my fledgling, hiding her head under my chin.

You stay here then. I nest the hawk in a swirl of bedding. *But I ent frighted of the Fangtooths, just cos they wear bones round their necks and file their teeth into daggers. What if they're out there, hunting us?* I can't stay put a heartbeat longer.

I pile on another walrus skin and some slippers, then grab my bow and quiver from under the bunk.

Outside, cold blackness steals my breath. The *Huntress* glides through a forest of icebergs, some tall enough to hide their heads in the clouds. There's a sadness to them, like they hold too many secrets.

Sparrow plays with the whales, mixing up the words of his song to make the bowheads chuckle, whilst a pod of orcas *hunthunthuntPUSHhunthunthunt*, driving fish up through the thin ice on the surface. Sea-hawks swoop silently over the waves to seize herrings from the sea and plunk them onto the deck. My eyes drink it in as I turn in circles. Grandma was going to let me miss all this?

I feel my way along the frosty deck. Grandma's in the mended crow's nest, blowing softly into a bone pipe, in time with Sparrow's song. A dark shape ripples next to her head – when I squint I can just make out the ancient sea-hawk, Battle-Shrieker, perched on her shoulder.

Sparrow sings at the prow, his hair and furs glowing white under the moon's light. He spots me and grins. By his side, Vole captures drifts of whale-song in the crystal atop her prentice-staff, making it glow midnight blue.

We break free of the ice forest and drift down a narrow path through the middle of the frozen land. The whales fall silent as they're forced to dive beneath the ship.

An eerie moan carves the night, spilled from the throat of an animal.

My heart becomes a wild bird, thrashing against my ribs. Grandma hoots into her cupped hands and black-cloaks step out of the shadows, all along the storm-deck and higher up on the fore-castle. Icicles hang from the men's beards. Stag's with them, eyes glittering.

I scan the ice but it's too dark to see. Then Sparrow's song strikes deep into my bones.

Do you remember
When the sea
Lay, still, in wait for me.
Don't you remember?
Watch and see, they tread the paths, swim the seas.
They fly wild through the skies,
Fathoms deep and mountains high.
They are three,
Sea, land and sky.
On the sea
One travels wide.

It's the old song, the one in Da's message! I pull Da's carving from my pocket and open the sails. The runes glow. I blink, hard, but the glow burns brighter. The whales sing with Sparrow, stirring the runes to life.

Might he claim this sea,
Claim it for his own?
Witches call to me, atop the Wildersea,
The hearth-stones treasure their memory.

The moan becomes a bones-deep baying for our blood. The runes whizz around the sails, then settle into a pattern of arrows. Da must've enchanted the message!

You must remember
What waits there,
You'll find it at the point high in the air—

The *Huntress* brushes an iceberg. Sparrow stumbles, the song knocked from his mouth. 'Hold steady!' shouts Grandma. 'Keep your wits about you!' I stuff the carving into my pocket and tear along the deck towards the prow, opening my throat to make room for my battle-howl.

Grandma's voice calls, cracked with worry. 'Sparrow, get away from the side.' She's scuttled down from the crow's nest and stands with her black-cloaks on the fore-castle.

There's a feathery bump as Thaw-Wielder lands on my shoulder – I must've left the porthole open. *What's Grandma seen?* I whisper. *What's out there?*

The hawk nips my ear painfully. *Danger, danger, danger!* she shrills.

Before my brother can move, something big and white blurs through the darkness, crashing onto the rail on the port side.

'Black-cloaks, string your bows!' Grandma booms. 'Nock, draw—'

'Do not draw!' Stag's voice cuts through the night like a whip.

Great plumes of whale-breath rise from the sea, encircling the *Huntress*. The whales are trying to keep us safe with a protective circle of seawater, to stop Fangtooths or their beasts from boarding, but they're too late.

A huge shaggy creature crouches on the rail, bristling and snapping. It swipes a paw and knocks Vole's staff from her hands. The crystal smashes, letting the whale-song escape, its midnight-blue glow weaving up into the sails. Vole tries to shield Sparrow, but the creature lashes out again and Vole screams as she falls to the deck.

I've seen etchings like that beast – it's a polar dog, one of the savage hounds that pull the Fangtooths' sleds and guard their homes.

Sparrow's fright-frozen; the only part of him that moves is the white cloud of his breath.

'Black-cloaks, loose! Sparrow, move!' Grandma's voice has a dangerous edge now. I wait for the arrows to fly.

'Black-cloaks, ready, but loose on my say!' Stag barks. What's he think he's doing, trying to give commands right under Grandma's nose?

A murmur of confusion runs along the deck. A few of the black-cloaks lower their bows.

'What are you doing?' hisses one. 'Bows in hand, nock your arrows!'

63

Another shakes her head. 'Sparrow is too close to the beast, what if we strike him?'

Grandma's words are chipped by fury. 'Stag, what are you—'

He thumps the rail. 'The moon is behind cloud. If we—'

'Are *you* captain? Close your blowhole, now, or—'

Filthy sea-slug child, kill, kill, kill! the polar dog growls, full of hate and hunger, gums foaming, bared fangs gleaming. Thaw's feathers brush my ear as she flits away into the rigging.

If the full-growns won't loose their arrows I'll have to do it myself, even after all the trouble that terrodyl brought me. I unhook my bow and slide an arrow from the quiver at my belt. My mouth feels dry.

Crack small one's bones, gobble-slurp marrow! keens the polar dog.

I nock the arrow to my bow. The moon appears from behind the clouds, casting me in a pool of light.

'Mouse, get back! I told you not to leave the cabin!' Grandma hurls her voice like a spear. 'Sparrow, run!'

'It's saying it's gonna slurp my brother's marrow, Grandma!' I shout.

'Well for the gods' sake don't let it slurp yours as well! Black-cloaks, you good-for-nothing lot of eel-brained—'

I close my ears and creep closer to the rail. 'Sparrow,'

I call, but he won't move. The polar dog snaps its amber eyes onto my face. Its growls change as it watches me, distracted from Sparrow. *Bigger. Juicy. Kill, kill, kill. Hungrrry.*

When it growls *kill* my bones shudder and I want to run, but I won't leave Sparrow. I move forward, legs jellyfish-weak.

Frighted girl-child! it rasps gleefully.

As I pass Sparrow I shove him out of harm's way but I keep my eyes on the creature. I put my heart-strength behind my longbow and draw my bowstring taut. *I ent frighted, stupid beast. Stop your chatterings and get ready to die.*

It laughs. I clamp my fear behind my teeth and scowl.

Behind me comes a scuffling. Probably Sparrow and Vole making for cover. Distant shouts reach my ears. 'Black-cloaks, listen to me. As your captain: take aim, draw—'

Too late, Grandma.

When the polar dog's muscles tense I let my arrow sail, a battle-howl ripping from my throat. Another heartbeat and the creature leaps.

My arrow punctures its chest. Four deadweight-heavy paws land on me. I fall backwards onto the wooden boards, the breath punched from my lungs.

10
Mouse Arrow-Swift

Warm breath rattles in my ear but there's no beast-chatter. I lie still as the grave. *This is it*, my bones scream. Got by a wretched polar hound.

Muffled shouts hail down around me. Grandma's voice comes closest. 'Hold your arrows else you'll strike the child! Draw daggers, now!'

Suddenly the hound's body falls limp. A beat later the dead weight's lifted and Grandma hauls me to my feet. I'm in her arms as sheets of tears wash down my cheeks. Stupid warm salty tears.

'What you bawling for, kid?' She looks straight into me as usual, so there's naught I can hide. 'You saved your brother's life.' The little crinkles round her eyes dance as she hugs me again. 'Mouse Arrow-Swift, they'll be calling you afore break of day.'

Battle-Shrieker peers down at me with bright gold

eyes from her perch on Grandma's shoulder. *Arrow-Swift*, she chirrups, beak stuffed with fishtails.

Grandma points. The polar dog lies sprawled on the deck, its dirty white fur already nipped with icicles. But the shock and the shaking still won't let me smile.

Grandma's smiling enough for the both of us, though. 'That'll make you a fine cloak, dearheart.' She presses her forehead and nose to mine in a Tribe-kiss.

I pull away from Grandma, to look into her eyes. 'So I'm not in trouble this time?'

'Trouble?' Grandma's good eye glints. 'Not half so much as my rotten crew are. But you, Little-Bones? You took action when all the full-growns were dithering like guppies. You kept the promise you made to your ma, to keep your brother safe.'

A deep voice severs Grandma's warmth. 'That's as may be, Wren. But what will keep the rest of us safe from the Fangtooths, now that she's shot one of their prized polar dogs?' Stag asks. I turn to face him and his unblinking eyes pin me to the spot. 'We still have half the Wildersea to cross.'

'You can call me Captain.' Grandma glares at Stag, full of fury. 'My grandson still draws breath, no heart-thanks to you. If you're fearful of a few land-lurkers, then perhaps I've been too quick to judge you True-Tribe. Get yourself below decks. Mouse is more than ready to take your place.'

Stag's face darkens. He turns and stalks into the gloom, then a door crashes in the distance.

Grandma gifts me a wink with the eye that works. 'I ent nearly finished with him,' she growls. 'Now rest your bones – you'll be skinning that beast the best part of the morrow. I won't keep you from my side at times of danger again – you've proven your thirteen moons this night.'

Heart-pride fills me as she strides away, giving orders. 'Secure the nets! Send for Bear and his oarsmen!' Her voice dwindles as she moves further away from me. 'There may be others – so help me, if the Fangtooth scum sent that creature—'

Sparrow slams through the shadows and almost knocks me off my feet, burying his face in my cloak. I press my forehead to his. Thunderbolt zips from his pocket and streaks up my neck, across my cheek and onto Sparrow's shoulder, leaving a sparkle-cold feeling on my skin and covering us in a trail of silver footprints.

Thunderbolt thanks her for saving sweet Tangle-Hair's life! she chitters.

He's my brother, stupid. I swallow the lump in my throat. *Course I flaming saved him.*

Thunderbolt blows a moon-dusted raspberry. So much for her thanks.

'What's she saying?' Sparrow asks, stroking the moonsprite gently.

'Just the usual bilge-warblings.' Then a thought drifts into my head. 'That song you were singing. Did Da tell you what the words mean?'

Sparrow shrugs and wipes his nose on his wrist. 'Dunno,' he says through a yawn. 'Lessgo inside now – I'm freezing!'

Vole limps along the deck towards us. Gods. Not even a swipe from a polar dog can get her off my back. 'I know you two are tired,' she says, running a hand through her hair. 'But we need Sparrow to sing for the whales more than ever now. And Mouse, could you fetch me a poultice and some goldenseal from the medsin-lab? I've a few cuts need tending. Sparrow, come with me.' She takes my brother's hand and leads him off.

I pull my most gruesome faces after her. Thaw-Wielder thuds onto my shoulder. *Just cos Vole's chief prentice, don't mean she's the boss of me*, I tell her, stooping to grab the polar dog carcass. It drags heavily along the icy deck, a trail of blood slugging from the arrow-wound. Above me, crew scuttle like spiders in the rigging, unfurling a huge net to keep enemies from boarding.

My hawk rubs her feathers under my chin. *Leave chores, play! Fly!*

I chuckle and stroke her black wing tips. *But if I don't do Vole's bleeding bidding she'll spill, and I like being in Grandma's good books too much to mess up now.*

Thaw-Wielder jostles her wings in disappointment. *Sorry, Thaw-beast.* I put her to nest in the Hoodwink, before scuffing off to fetch the medsins.

Before I get below decks Sparrow's voice rings out. The whales answer him, and Vole starts singing with them, to wind the protection tighter around us.

I wish I'd thought to ask Da what the old song means. I've got to work it out – cos the ice, the terrodyls, Stag, the polar dog attack – they've all got me feeling like things ent right, like there's a stain spreading over Trianukka. And maybe, if I can find them Opals, they'll lead me to Da.

11

Whale-song

I've spent all day skinning the polar dog and my nails are clogged with blood. Pip took the carcass to his kitchens to use for meat, broth and glue. The bones will be made into other things we can use or trade: cloak-pins, fish hooks, toothpicks, chisels.

Now I'm cross-legged on the storm-deck, watching the sky – it sprawls above our ship like a grey wolf, with fat black clouds smudged across it. A flock of sea-swallows streak past on their journey south for winter.

Bits of old song roll round and round my brain, making my head throb. *You must remember what waits there, you'll find it at the point high in the air.* What does that mean?

Stray whale-song from last night is snagged in the sails, noisy and glowing. Thaw-Wielder swoops at it, chortling when it gets caught in her feathers. *Reckon a squall's coming, Thaw,* I call to her. *That why you've gone all loony?*

Storm comes, she hoots in agreement. *Feather-fun!*

Stag strides from the hatch, face full of thunder. Frog follows him, carrying a logbook, lead and line for measuring the sea's depth. 'The Frozen Wastes are far behind us,' Stag barks. 'But the Fangtooths may yet catch up, and rainstorms are ahead.'

He moves to the rail and stares across the water. 'Look, where the sunlight touches the sea,' he tells Frog, pointing at the path of glitter that shows when the sun peeks through the clouds. 'The widest patch of light equals the roughest sea. I need the sails song-swept and my crew in position.'

His crew? Wait 'til I break all the bones in his stupid old head, I murmur.

Thaw hops onto my shoulder, smooths her wing across my cheek and peers into my face with keen yellow eyes. Then she spreads her wings and leaps from my shoulder. As Stag straightens up, she swoops for him.

'Control your hawk!' he shouts. 'You've made enough trouble already.'

'Saving my brother ent trouble-making!' I yell.

Thaw-Wielder circles gleefully around Stag. *Fast, zip, quick, fast, swoop, soar, shiny-bright, hungry, worm, shrimp? Poo! Poopoopoopoopoo!*

Stag jumps out of the way, just before a white splatter hits the deck, splashing the bottom of his breeches.

I shout a laugh before I can swallow it and Thaw zooms onto my shoulder, resettling her feathers.

'Sea-hawks are not pets!' Stag hurls out the words like throwing knives. But when he strides away, it hits me as a punch to the gut. Stag *knew* to move – he heard what Thaw-Wielder said. He understands beast-chatter! My feet itch to tear after Stag, cos I ent never met someone else with beast-chatter before, but just then Bear strolls along the deck and stoops to admire the work I've done on the pelt.

He nods his approval. 'What was all that about?'

I tell him about Stag chucking his weight around like he owns the place, and how he heard my hawk.

Thaw sits in the crook of his arm and Bear strokes her head. 'Aye, years ago he used to boast about his beast-talk. But what I'd like to know is what he's been doing all that time he's lurked on land. Word of last night has swept through the oarsmen's benches. I don't like Stag crossing our captain, not one bit.' He leans closer. 'Watch him, Mouse-Bones. That's what mice are best at. They're small enough to hide, quick enough to run and silent enough to listen.' He straightens and heads back to his post at the rowing benches. Thaw-Wielder zips towards me.

I call after Bear, but he salutes me and keeps going. 'Got to get back to work. But look.' He holds up a long white bone. 'I'm carving a story-telling of you and the polar dog into this!'

'Heart-thanks, Bear!' I call, grinning.

Thaw-Wielder crash-lands into my lap and peeks up at me. *Stag heard you, Thaw,* I breathe. My brain whirls. *Grandma says that in the old days, hundreds of years past, lots of Sea-Tribesfolk had the beast-chatter. But now it's just me – least, I thought it was.*

Bad one. Get his blubber off sea-prowler!

Aye, Thaw. But how?

A movement catches my eye and I scramble to my feet – a mighty plume of water erupts into the air on the horizon, sunlight lending it a golden sparkle.

The breath of the sea-god at Whale-Jaw Rock! Look. I stretch out my arm to point. *The stories say that there's an ancient whale trapped beneath that mountain – Whale-Jaw Rock. It still blows water through its blowhole; that's what we just glimpsed in the distance! It means we're making good time for the Tribe-Meet at the Bay of Thunder! And Da might be* there, whispers my heart.

As we watch, the jet of water falls back down. Ten beats later, it erupts again, *high in the air . . .* the old song pulls at my mind.

Tell Grey-Hair! my hawk chatters.

Yes! Let's find Grandma. We can talk to her about that old loon Stag, too. Maybe she'll say we can dump him when

we dock next. My hawk hoots happily at that idea. As the dusk deepens I'm starting to shiver, and in the distance rain smears the sky.

I tear down to our cabin, the polar dog pelt over my arm and Thaw huddled in my hair.

Shadows drift as the ship creaks and rocks. 'Grandma?' I call, dumping my pelt on the floor. 'I finished the skinning! And we saw—'

'Settle your bones, Mouse Arrow-Swift,' she lilts. 'The whale-singer is sleeping.'

Sparrow moans from our bunk. 'S'all right, chook,' croons Grandma, and he settles.

I clam up and move through the shadows, towards the soft light of the moon-lamp on the map table. Grandma sits in her rocking chair, hands working a piece of cloth over a green lump. It's her glass eye; she's taken it out to polish and let the socket rest – now it's crumpled like the neck of a drawstring pouch. These days she seems to rest the socket more than ever – but if *I* had a glass eye I'd take it out just to fright people. Her good eye studies me, clear and bright. 'Look at this girl!' she whispers, but her eye smiles. 'Stinking like a polar dog, covered in blood and scrapes, eh?'

She beckons me close. I move to her side and before I can bolt the comb appears in her hand. 'Some of this black wilderness needs hacking off!' she declares.

'There.' She releases me from her bony grasp.

'What about you?' I point to the stray silver hairs wisping free of her braid. 'Can't recall the last time I saw you brush that tangle.'

She guffaws, but then Thaw-Wielder flaps onto the map table, lifts her tail feathers and poos a white splodge onto the crackly old map. 'Tsk, away with you, feather-fool!' scolds Grandma quietly.

Thaw giggles, then burps up a tangled loop of whale-song. She must've gulped it off one of the sails. It moans, glistening with hawk-spit.

Grandma tuts. 'Catch that song before it wakes your brother! It's as drawn to him as the whales themselves are.'

I catch it and cup it between my hands. It thuds about, feeling like ice-silk. 'Grandma, we saw Whale-Jaw Rock blowholing on the horizon, so we're making proper good time for the Tribe-Meet! But that Stag's throwing his weight around something rotten. He looked at me like he hates me for shooting the polar dog.' I chew my lip. 'And he just called the crew *his* crew.' My blood boils with remembering.

A thoughtful look crosses Grandma's features, swift as a storm-cloud. She fits the glass eye back into its socket with a small sucking sound.

'Grandma, I really don't trust him. I was thinking,'

my words rush. 'What about if we just get rid of him at the Bay of Thunder? You could say—'

But she's stopped listening. 'Ah, a whale shark never changes its spots,' she says. 'That one always wanted to be captain, but the fire spirits didn't write it in his destiny.' Her face fills with keenness. 'What he should stick to is navigation – he's brought some very interesting instruments with him. You know, he studied books of all sorts at Nightfall, the great City of Smog.'

The whale-song tries to squeeze through my fingers, so I clamp my other hand over them. '*Da's* a better navigator. He don't need instruments, neither.'

'No, Bones. You're right, that was foolish of me. I'm sorry.' For a heartbeat the depths of her glass eye seem to swirl.

'What was it like, turning half to merwraith?' I blurt. Rain beats at the porthole and waves *slosh* against the hull.

She blinks, startled. 'You do ask me some stinkers, Mouse-Bones.' She stares into space and I'm wondering if I should nudge her, but she comes back to me. 'Painful. Dragging, like how you talk about your dream-dancing. The process—'

I jump as a fist suddenly thumps against the cabin door. 'Captain?' calls Stag's voice. 'We have a carpenter who has fallen from the rigging and two oarsmen with teeth that need pulling. I thought I'd send for you at once.'

My heart flies into my mouth but Grandma winks at me. 'Good of him, eh? Fetch some grub for your brother and me while I talk with the whale shark. I want Sparrow to eat well when he wakes up – but you ent to disturb him until then, let him *rest.*' She stoops to pull on a pair of iron-capped boots. 'I'll gift Stag a pair of pliers and see how he likes pulling the ruddy teeth himself,' she mutters.

She almost trips over my polar dog skin on her way out. 'Mouse! For the gods' sake get that pelt pegged out to let the fat stiffen. Don't you leave it to stink out my cabin!'

It's only after she's clomped up the stairs that I realise I forgot to tell her about Stag's beast-chatter, and my dream-dance. *Gods! I can't never get more than ten heartbeats with either Grandma or Bear these days!*

I open my hand, but before the whale-song can flee I grasp it between my thumb and forefinger, where it wriggles like a worm. Thaw-Wielder tries to slurp it up again but I push her beak away, laughing. *It's not food, Thaw!* I listen hard, frowning. *It's – singing.* The strand of whale-song still has words from the old song throbbing inside it.

Eel-quick, I grab the carving and open the sails.

Aches and Pains

When I dangle the whale-song over the enchanted runes in Da's message, they start to burn and quiver. The song tries to coil around my finger, but Thaw-Wielder plucks at it and it falls onto the message, blending into the sailcloth. *Heart-thanks, Thaw!* She puffs out her crest.

They fly wild through the skies, fathoms deep and mountains high, moans the fragment of whale-song.

When it touches the note, runes skim across the sails like skipping stones. They stir little hand-drawn waves to life, and through the waves rise hazy sketches of icebergs. When they settle, an outline of a towering mountain burns faintly to the right of the message.

Bleeding shipworm, Thaw, this is just like one of Da's sketches! Looks as if he drew a map, but . . . my head aches as I mull my idea over . . . *he somehow made it invisible?*

Three coloured orbs, smaller than pearls, are scattered around the cloth – one green, one blue and one amber. But as I stare at the message, barely breathing, Da's sketch begins to fade again.

Thaw! You got any more belches? I ask desperately.

My hawk starts bulging her eyes and spitting as she tries to burp more whale-song. I press my hands over my mouth to keep my belly-laughs in. Finally, with a *squawk-hiss-pop*, a wet, tangled loop glides from her throat.

Watch and see, it wails. *They tread the paths, swim the seas.*

It squiggles towards the ceiling but I leap to catch it, then throw it onto the message. More runes whizz to life. They streak a path of arrows that point to the green orb.

The orb begins to rove up and down, left and right across the sailcloth. *Why's that green one moving all over the place? D'you reckon it's a Storm-Opal?*

Thaw shuffles her feathers. *Map. Open peepers, look there.*

I go to the map table and chip off Thaw-Wielder's dried poo with my fingernail. As it crumbles away, the Whale-Jaw Rock sea-god appears on the map, shown as a plume of steaming spray that reaches into the sky, touching the mountain's peak. *Thaw, the last bit of the song said 'you'll find it at the point high in the air' – what if the sea-god's breath points to where one of the Opals is!*

More wiggle-worms? she asks, eyes bright. *Beg too-soon for song-worms!*

I snap my fingers and spin to face the bunk. *Yes!*

Sparrow snuffles in his sleep. I dash over and poke him. Thunderbolt sparks and growls at me from the pillow. 'Sparrow! Can you sing that song from last night? I need more of the words!'

'No. People always want more song, but I'm sleepy and I've got aches *everywhere.*' He sticks a foot out of the blankets and waggles it at me. 'Ent you gonna fetch me and Grandma some grub afore she comes back?' he murmurs.

I make to slap his foot but then Grandma's boots thud down the stairs so I scud past her and head towards Pip's kitchens.

Thaw sits on my shoulder and rubs her feathers under my chin. As I think about Da's message, my pulse flickers hard. *Thaw-Wielder, our next port after the Bay of Thunder is near Whale-Jaw Rock. Maybe we can search for one of the Storm-Opals there!*

Suddenly voices float along the passageway. We dart into an empty cabin, leaving the door cracked open.

Stag and Frog walk together, talking in low voices. What's Frog doing with him? Maybe he does think he's too old to hang about with nippers, now he's fifteen. They pause under a moon-lamp.

Stag lights his pipe and sucks in a big breath of smoke. 'How long have children been permitted to run riot? Where will it end – with a war waged against us by the Fangtooths?'

'Aye, sir, you have the right of it.' Frog shrugs. 'Though it's the way it's always been round here.'

Stag smirks. 'When I was a child there was discipline, there were *rules*.' He breaks off into a coughing fit, then quickly draws another lungful of pipe-smoke. His cough settles. 'Women were not captains and little girls were not *renegades*, answering to no one.'

Rules are for jelly-brains. I chew my tongue to keep the words locked inside my head.

'Aye, you speak the truth of it,' quavers Frog.

'You know she thinks she's the future captain?' Cold mirth twists Stag's voice. 'Just because the old woman interpreted some lights in the sky as the girl's destiny. She's just a trouble-making little girl, too small for her age. She'll never be captain.'

Fire whips through my blood. Frog begins to stutter a reply but Stag rants on. 'And why should we risk everything to reach the Tribe-Meet? Most of the other Sea-Tribes drowned long ago and the remnants are nothing but hopeless fisher folk.'

'Cap'n reckons Fox might return to the *Huntress* there,' says Frog.

My heart slams into my mouth. Grandma thinks Da's alive, too!

'She's merely holding out hope for the sake of her grandchildren – everyone knows the navigator is dead. And this is a new era.' He puffs himself up. 'I have studied the art of navigation. Instruments and calculations will keep this ship afloat and on course, not singing songs and following whales.'

My muscles tremble with rage. He scorns the whales – our sea-gods? And *my* da?

Frog laughs with him, but his voice holds a spear-edge of fear. 'Aye, sir, but you might want to keep ideas like that quiet. There's folks here what mightn't take well to that kind of thinking.'

Suddenly Stag grabs Frog around his neck and pins him against the wall. I gasp and clap my hand to my mouth. Frog's eyes bulge. 'And yourself, young man?' Stag drawls. 'Do you take well to my thinking?'

Frog scrabbles at Stag's hands, trying to prise them off his neck. 'Y–'

'I'm sorry, I can't hear you?' Stag smiles, sharp-toothed.

'Y– yes,' Frog squeezes, purple in the face.

Finally Stag lets him go, with a nod. 'Good.'

Frog hurries off, rubbing his neck, but Stag lingers in the passageway. I watch him, legs cramped, hardly daring to breathe. Suddenly a huge black bird flaps through the shadows and lands on his shoulder. Thaw bristles.

The crow stares around with bright golden eyes. I duck deeper into the murk, willing Thaw-Wielder to stay silent.

'She never should have shot that wretched polar dog,' mutters Stag. The crow *thwawks* and resettles its inky feathers. There ent no trace of beast-chatter. What's it hiding? Then Stag stalks away, boots ringing through the gloom.

Baaaaaddddd, exclaims Thaw, letting out all her fishy breath.

Aye, don't I know it. I step out of the cabin and glance up and down the passageway. It's empty. Then, above and all around, thunder *booms*. No wonder Sparrow felt unwell – foul weather gives him the aches and pains. A pang of guilt ripples through me for forgetting about him. *I'll be the one in trouble if I don't get Sparrow to eat something,* I tell my hawk. *We'd better get going.*

Thaw-Wielder glides ahead of me as I move through the moonlit passageways. In the kitchens, Pip's spattered with grease and his face is smudged with soot and flour. He barely looks up at me so I snatch a crusty loaf and a clay flagon of broth to dunk it in.

As I climb the stairs I almost get flung flat on my face cos the ship's rolling so much. When I reach the main-deck I stare through the portholes at the storm that's seized the sky. Each time the ship crests a wave, she plunges down again, and the world's a wall of iron-grey water.

Nest nest nest, chirrups Thaw, fanning out her wings. I open a porthole for her and she zips out, to settle herself in the Hoodwink.

I battle to keep the flagon upright as I head towards our cabin. Lightning flares. A few heartbeats later, thunder cracks through the *Huntress*'s timbers. When I reach the door I stop and stare. A sudden dread clangs around inside me. Grandma told me to get food for Sparrow and I dawdled too long; he's been alone for beats and beats. I press my forehead against the rough wood. Please let him be safe, whispers a voice in my head.

When I open the heavy door, the darkness inside the cabin rushes up to swallow me. A sharp stench of spew and pee hangs in the air.

I stumble towards the grainy shape of the map table and put down the bread and flagon. 'Sparrow?' I call, peering across the room.

My eyes focus – there's a pale shape, falling, *flowing*, down the side of the bunk. I gulp a breath. It's a *skeleton*. My pulse gallops.

Captain Rattlebones has come for me!

The ship pitches and the skeleton starts moving. It jerks and writhes, slipping suddenly, heavily, all the way off the bed to puddle on the floor.

I back away, urging the shakes from my voice. 'Stay away, Captain Rattlebones! We'll repay the debt; we'll return your bones!' Then a bolt of lightning pierces the porthole, spilling eerie light over the cabin. I see a tangled mess of yellow hair and before the darkness resettles I know what a flaming fool I am.

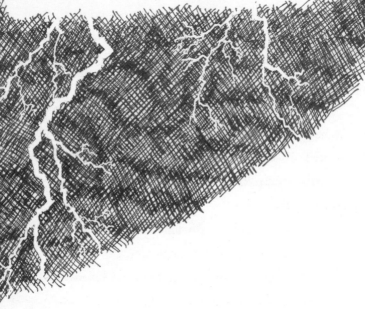

13

Storm

'Sparrow! Oh gods, not again!' His arms and legs jerk, striking stiffly against the floor, over and over. When the lightning crashes, the room glows white. My brother's lips are frothy with spit and tinged blue around the edges. His eye sockets are purple-black, startling out of his ghost-white face. A low clicking sound comes from his throat. He's having another shaking fit.

I knew it would come again, so I dig my toes into my boots, cos I've spent half my life running away from Sparrow's shakes but this time I know I can't.

'Grandma!' I scream, but the thunder's moved closer now and the rain lashes through the open porthole.

No one hears me. No one comes.

The sound of Sparrow's head smacking the boards snaps me to my senses. 'Don't move him, just cushion his head,' I mutter to myself, Grandma's voice flooding my memory. I bound across to the bunk and grab a pillow, damp from sea-spray.

Sparrow's eyes are rolled back and pearls of sweat stand out on his brow. I sink to the floor beside him, trying to breathe and steady my trembling hands. Quickly I slip the pillow under his head.

I wait. Something's fearsome wrong. The clicking sound grows louder.

'Stop it now, stop!' Hot tears snake down my cheeks and into my mouth. 'Grandma, help!' Thunder grumbles like a giant's belly. Who will hear me?

Suddenly something slams into the ship and I'm flying across the room. The impact of the wall against my back knocks the wind from my lungs. The *Huntress* leans sharply to the right and gives a low groan. Grandma's bed drags along the floor towards me and stops when the ship rights herself. Then the *Huntress* tips the other way and the bed crashes onto its side, dumping the furs in a heap on the floor.

I blink, dazed and stupid, even as the lightning slaps again. Thunder cracks overhead, carrying its burned smell.

Sparrow's body still jerks. His face looks bloodless and his brown eyes are wide but frozen, unseeing. His arms rise, slowly, like he's a doll on strings.

And skinny tentacles of – my breath falters – purple

lightning crackle from his fingertips.

I pinch myself, but I'm awake. For a heartbeat I'm hollow, then horror scratches my insides. My hand flies to cover my mouth and my heart zooms into my throat and I try to swallow it down, but I've got no spit. Sparrow's shaking fits ent never been like this before. Is it cos of the storm?

Grandma bursts into the cabin, water dripping off her nose. Stag follows. I'm so glad of help coming that I'm halfway happy to see *him*.

'What bewitchery is this?' Stag utters, cold grey eyes fixed on my brother.

I stumble to my feet. 'Just help him!'

'Mouse, don't you move!' Grandma orders, setting a moon-lamp on the table.

'What's happening to Sparrow?' I wail.

'Your brother's out of control,' Stag mutters darkly.

Grandma gives him a hard look. 'Get yourself back out on deck if you're not going to help my grandson.' She sits by Sparrow, crooning softly to him. I ignore her command to stay still and crawl to her side. 'Well done, young Mouse. You remembered to protect his head.'

Pride fills me but it don't quell the threat of tears. 'Someone tell me what's going on.' I try not to let my voice waver.

'We've got to stop this shaking fit.' When Grandma takes Sparrow's hands in hers, there's a purple flash and she yells, her hands flying to her mouth. The stink of singed flesh fills my nose.

I try to pull Sparrow's arms down to his sides but they're fixed firm as iron. Grandma tries the same. 'His strength is that of a man grown,' she breathes.

I draw my knees up to my chest and wrap my arms around them. 'Is he going to die?' I whisper.

Stag stares down at me. 'If we don't stop him, we will all perish. Sparrow is stirring the sea into an inferno. He's drawing the whales to us, to smash us into pieces.' As he speaks his voice trails off and he stares away into the distance. Then another giant crash hits. Stag's knocked off his feet and thrown across the floor.

He slides to a stop, smacking his head against the leg of Grandma's map table. The moon-lamp smashes and its moonsprite slips between the floorboards, deepening the darkness.

When the lightning flashes again Stag scrambles to his feet, cursing, blood dripping down his face. I shrink from the sight of him. He strides for Sparrow, knocking Grandma over.

Stag grabs Sparrow's shoulders and starts to shake him, shouting anger-twisted words that flash in and out of hearing.

I'm on my feet, screaming. 'What you *doing*? Get away from my kin!'

Grandma hoists herself up and kicks Stag's feet out from under him in one sweeping movement. The sea crashes and the thunder echoes and drums.

The thin snakes of purple coming from Sparrow's fingertips thicken into blazing, tangled vines that burst up to touch the ceiling.

Suddenly, I'm flying across the room and the mantelpiece rushes towards me.

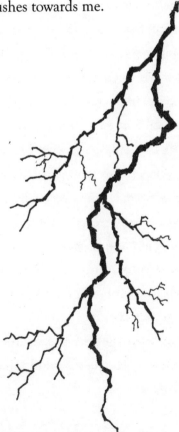

14

Turning Tides

Pain fills my head and my spirit tugs against me. Ent no chance to fight it this time – my spirit drags free from my body in a dream-dance.

There's a creeping blood-stink and the air is crackle-hot. The new bab is ready to be birthed, but the women are frighted. They say it comes too soon.

Grandma bends down to peer into my face. 'I remember your own birth very well, Mouse-Bones. Born in the caul, you was, I had to grab my hook to cut you free!' She straightens up and musses my hair. 'It means you'll likely never drown, so you'll never turn half to merwraith, like me.' Her glass eye shines in the light of the moon-lamps. She winks. 'And now the whole Tribe knows how at home my little granddaughter is in her sea-mother's arms.'

I want Ma but she's away into some other world, eyes lolled back, skin slip-sliding with sweat. 'What's she doing?' I pipe; five moons old again but still knowing I'm dream-dancing back through the stew of time. 'Where's my new bab, is it here yet?' Grandma's prentice shushes me.

Ma clasps her head and lets out a long moan. Is she dream-dancing, too? Smoke fogs into my eyes and nose. I can't get to her.

Women fuss round my ma. They carry lamps, make chanting speeches.

A tiny pink bab is bundled quick-smart into my arms. It crumples up its face like an old man. It's got purply eye skin and a cross red mouth and it looks like it wants to stay asleep in that nether world where it's sprung from.

Ma reaches for me and the bab. 'His name is Sparrow. Take care of him, always.' Tears snag her breath.

'Why? Why, Ma?'

Ma's telling me what I've got to do but I don't—

I look down at the little too-soon and he's getting smaller in the blankets, growing tiny sleek feathers to take us far away.

That crackle-hot feeling in the air has settled on his skin; it turns to a soft bristle of lightning.

'I promise, Ma.'

But she's gone from me and there's pain and shaking and fear and blood and she's gone.

Sparrow. His pebble-smooth skin feels cold. I wrap him tighter and sing him a song, even though Vole says I ent got a good song-voice. The bab don't seem to mind, though. All the full-growns are rushing around and we're forgotten.

I rock Sparrow further into the world, willing him to stay with me and leave the shadows behind.

When I wake, smoke fills my nose and the copper taste of blood coats my tongue. I gag and splutter, then reach up to touch my hair and my hand comes away sticky. The dream-dance that took me back to Ma still has its claws lodged in my brain. That's the first time I've been carried backwards. This storm has brought some proper strangeness.

I lie on the floor, missing Ma. The cabin's full of strange purple light. Where's it coming from? Then my heart floods with remembering. Sparrow! I promised Ma on the day she left us that I'd always take care of him.

As I crawl towards Sparrow the smoke makes my lungs tighten and my eyes stream. My brother's body still shakes and spit foams at his mouth. How long has he been lost in this shaking fit? Is it too late to bring him back?

Grandma's propped against the doorframe, breathing quick and soft, as though she only fell asleep. 'Grandma!' I drag myself across the cabin. 'Wake up!' But even when I reach her and press my forehead against hers in a Tribe-kiss, she don't stir.

Stag's slumped on the floor with a trail of blood trickling from his ear to his chin.

With the next flash of lightning, an idea strikes me

– the potion I left in the medsin-lab. Could I use it to help Sparrow? I crawl over to him. 'I bet you can hear me,' I say. 'Don't you fret – I know what to do. You're not to leave this world. Ma said.'

A woeful chattering comes from the bunk. I find Thunderbolt whimpering under the pillow, grab her and drop her into a jar on the map table. Her fearfulness makes her light weak but it's better than naught. Then I dig out some old terrodyl-hide bootlaces and tie Stag's wrists together, in case the wretch wakes up while I'm gone.

I climb over Grandma and leg it down the passageway, though I'm so dizzy I could fall. I've got to get to the medsin-lab but the wind's so fierce the hatch won't lift. Then, when the wind's fury changes direction, the hatch rips open, almost tearing my arms with it, and I'm out in a world of stabbing rain and crashing waves.

Crew run and shout, eyes wild. A wall of seawater smacks over the deck and hits me, leaving me gasping for breath. I stagger across a deck cluttered with fish and seaweed and fling myself up the steps of the fore-castle. I'm jumping through the hatch just as the thunder booms again. It sounds like the sky-gods are hurling rocks and spears down on us.

The heavy door to the medsin-lab has swung open and glass bottles and tubes are strewn across the floor.

'Please be here, please don't be smashed—' As I plunge into the lab, a splinter of glass slices my sealskin slipper, jabbing into my foot. A scream rips from my throat.

My tube of potion is still clamped in the vice, so I unscrew it and pour it into a bottle. Then I cork it and stow it in my belt pouch, along with some needles and a glass syringe.

Before I go, I grab the last bottles of wolf-fish blood and dragonfish luminescence, cos if this ship goes down we're gonna need them. As the next crack of thunder dies away I hobble back out on deck and limp as fast as I can between the folds of the storm.

I slip below decks and feel my way along the passageway, sending up a prayer to all the gods of the sea. 'Let it work, gods, let it work. Don't let it kill him, *please*.'

When I reach our cabin, Grandma's still dumped in the doorway like a bundle of linen. But Stag kneels by my shaking brother, hands pressed down on his chest. My terrodyl bootlaces are strewn uselessly across the boards.

'Get off him!' I rush at Stag but he just shoves me away with one hand.

'Can't you see we're scuppered? We'll all drown if I don't get the cripple to stop.' His voice quavers, which shocks me worse than the things that thud against the ship's hull.

96

Ignoring Stag, I take the brown bottle and pull its stopper out with my teeth, using a needle and the syringe to draw out the purple liquid like Grandma showed me.

My eyes strain in the flickering light. Have I drawn up the right measure? Too little won't do the job. Too much could kill him.

But when the lightning spills again I know there's no time to fret about it. Stag takes a pillow from the floor and brings it to Sparrow's face.

'No!' I scream. I drop to my knees by Sparrow and drive my needle deep into his thigh. Then I press down the plunger.

The force of the explosion knocks me backwards and makes lightning shoot from Sparrow's blackened fingertips into the ceiling, where it burns a ragged hole in the wood. The shaking stops and Sparrow's arms fall lifelessly to the floor.

15

The Unseeing Eye

'Is he breathing?' My voice sounds moons and stars away, and I wish Da was here more than ever.

'We're saved,' whispers Stag. I want to boot him in the shin, but then Grandma sits up and rubs her head. She's stunned only for a heartbeat. Then her good eye fixes on Sparrow and she shoots from her nest of rubble like she's been burned again.

'What did you do?' she snaps at Stag, as she kneels by my brother.

'This was not my doing.' He looks at me like he's tasted bile.

But Grandma ignores him. She props Sparrow's mouth open and listens for his breath. I've seen her do it to folk too many times to count, but now I feel about as useful as kelp.

Grandma blows into Sparrow's mouth, twice. Then she starts to press on his chest, regular as his own heart, if it were pumping. I bury my face in my knees. As Grandma

98

works, I'm dimly aware that the worst of the storm has settled, sudden as it flared, though rain still taps against the porthole.

I drag myself across to Grandma and push Sparrow's head back, gently, to keep his pipes open like she showed me before. When she's counted to fifteen heartbeats, she nods to me gravely and I blow air into Sparrow's lungs, watching as his chest rises and falls.

Nothing.

Come on, come on . . . it's not your time, little too-soon. Not today.

It feels like a thousand heartbeats pass. Beneath my fingers Sparrow's skin feels too cold, like old candle wax. Why was that lightning coming from him?

Stag's voice floats down but I shut my ears and breathe for my brother. Grandma pumps his heart, sweating, silver eyebrows knitted together in concentration.

Then—

I dart back as Sparrow splutters and chokes. 'Grandma!' he cries, hoarsely, the tears rolling down his cheeks.

She bends over him, smoothing the hair off his forehead. 'You're safe now, my chook, my dearest heart, I'm here.'

He loops his arms around her neck. 'It hurts too much,' he gasps. Then he starts spewing his guts. When he opens his eyes, one of them's not brown no more. It's lifeless and white, like Grandma's before she got her glass eye. Foggy like a merwraith's eye. My lower lip trembles, so I suck it in and bite down, hard.

'I hope you're satisfied,' rumbles Stag. 'You almost killed your brother.'

I glare coldly up at Stag. 'You *know* I saved him.'

'Saved him?' Stag hacks out one of his grim coughs. 'I saw what that witch's potion did to the boy, not to mention the ship.'

I get to my feet, rage boiling my blood. 'I saw what *you* were about to do to him! Now you can get out of our cabin, you great ghoul!'

'Little monster,' he growls. 'You ought to be filled with shame.'

'Is that so?' Grandma cradles Sparrow's head in the lap of her breeches. She lifts her chin and the look on her face could curdle the sea. 'My granddaughter is right. You're dismissed from the captain's cabin, navigator. See that you survey the damage, aid the carpenters and take the first night watch. I'll summon you after my midnight rounds.'

Stag's cheeks flush purple and his grey eyes blaze. He opens his mouth and closes it again, like a fish. Finally, he turns to go, stepping over bedclothes and candle stubs. But in the doorway he pauses. 'Count that the last time I'll involve myself in family matters. This is a working trade ship. Not a nursery.'

Grandma rolls Sparrow gently onto his side and then rises slowly. I sink to my knees in her place and scoop an arm around my brother. 'What happened to me?' he whispers, but my throat's too thick with tears to answer.

Grandma dusts off her breeches, never taking her eyes from Stag. 'So be it.' She stalks towards him. '*Black-cloaks!*' she bellows, straight into his face. 'I am heart-sore with you, Stag. What did we say about him, Mouse? A whale shark—'

'Never changes its spots!' I call.

'Quite so.'

Within a few beats of the drum, a half-score of Grandma's black-cloaks appear. They look as battle-worn as I feel, but when they see their captain, they stand arrow-straight, ready to listen to her.

Grandma points a knotted finger at Stag. 'This man has repeatedly obstructed my orders. Now he has attempted to harm my grandson. Seize him.' As she utters the words, she steps back and the black-cloaks surround Stag. 'Clap him in irons and imprison him in the hold. See to it he is fed only seawater and fish guts!' she roars. 'He will receive his judgement at the stone circle, when we reach the Bay of Thunder.'

As the black-cloaks haul Stag out of the cabin, joy rises in my chest and breaks into my throat. Finally, everyone's gonna know Stag for what he really is. '*No one* messes with my brother!' I spit as Stag's led away.

But then Stag turns to smirk at me. 'We shall see,' he whispers. His voice cuts marrow-deep and his hatred claws through my belly and my bones.

PART 2

Winter's Prowl

16
Dragonfly

It's Dread's Eve – the festival of the dead. The *Huntress* skulks towards the docks at the Bay of Thunder. With every beat of the drum, we draw closer to what I reckon might be one of the clues in the song – the breath of the Whale-Jaw Rock sea-god; the next place we'll drop anchor after this one. The egg-stinky hot springs nearby will gift us a welcome chance to bathe, too.

'This dawn's colder than any newly birthed winter has a right to be,' grumbles Grandma, breath fogging in the air. The boom of drums and the bellow of horns burst around us as we stand on the fore-deck, longbows slung across our backs. 'Still, we made it to the Tribe-Meet in one piece. Just about.'

My glance flits to her fingernails, still blood-clogged from the amputation work the storm gifted her. 'Aye.' I've piled on extra furs but the ice still bites my bones. I think of Da's warning, about the sea turning to ice. How would we rove, then? How would the whales guide us, or breach the surface to breathe? I've got to do as he says: find the Opals and take them to the crown. I've got to find out as much as I can at this Tribe-Meet.

Thaw-Wielder soars over the rail and thuds onto my shoulder, dripping seawater down my neck. *Oh, Thaw!* She swallows a fish head, then chortles at me and fluffs her feathers into a ball against the chill.

'Didn't get much rest last night, eh Bones?' says Grandma.

I shake my head. 'My eyes feel full of grit cos Sparrow kept me awake with his nightmares again.'

Trouble flickers across Grandma's brow. 'Don't help that the poor mite has to listen to that turncloak bellowing for his life half the night through.' Mischief curls her mouth. 'I've told the black-cloaks half a hundred times, the best way to seal a prisoner's gob is to spin tales of the old-time drownings. My blubber's itching to chuck that traitor overboard and be done with him.'

Stag. Even thinking the name pits a cold hollow in my stomach. 'He's got a bigger blabbermouth than a monkfish when he's frighted of the dark.'

Grandma chuckles throatily. 'I should've listened to you from the beginning, dearheart. You sensed the bad blood in him the moment he stepped aboard.'

Suddenly a Fangtooth longboat glides between the hulls of the *Huntress* and some battle-worn warship named *Devil's Hag*.

'Hard right rudder!' Grandma roars towards the stern. 'We didn't fix this ship to her finest only to see her scuttled by bone-clatterers!'

'Aye aye, ma'am!' comes a distant shout. The helmswoman grips the whipstaff and steers the *Huntress* left, saving her from a splintered hull. The Fangtooth chieftain sends crude noises up at us as the longboat passes. I glare down at him something fierce. He bares his pointed teeth at me and rattles his necklace of bones. In a heartbeat I've strung my bow and I'm aiming my arrow down at his chest. 'You never should've left your pox-ridden Wastes, cos land-lurkers can't sail straight!'

'Dread's Eve is for honouring the dead and respecting the living,' Grandma tells me, gently touching my elbow. I lower my weapon, to a mocking jeer from the Fangtooth vessel. Grandma and me hurl curses at them, while Thaw-Wielder screeches and spits half-chewed worms over the side.

Grandma sighs. 'I shouldn't have done that, but they had it coming. Did I mention my keenness for peace-talks, little Bones?'

'Why would you talk to *them?*'

'Because to begin with, if I'm talking to 'em I'll be able to keep an eye on 'em.' She winks. 'Wear your armour close to your heart—'

'And your enemies closer,' I finish dutifully.

The Fangtooths speed away. 'Who else is gonna be at this meet?' I ask, staring towards the hazy outline of land.

'Oh, let me see,' ponders Grandma. 'Our friends from the Icy Marshes. All kinds of Land-Tribes, of course, tree-dwellers and the horsemen of the east and wolf-riders. I'm hoping to meet with a hearth-healer or two from the foothills of Whale-Jaw Rock. Their knowledge of healing is the greatest in Trianukka!'

Hearth-healers. I stare down at the water and think about the old song. *The hearth-stones treasure their memory* . . . Maybe if I can find one of these hearth-healers, they'll help me with the clues.

The oars of another longboat churn through the sea, scattering my thoughts. Smells of smoke and salt fill the air and in the distance the cliffs are touched by winking green light.

'The dread-fires of thunder,' says Grandma, following my gaze. 'Fire-pits in the circle's heart, lit for the Gods of Sea, Sky and Land to mark the coming of winter – though this time, winter's already bared her teeth.'

She frowns, but I grin up at her, excitement bubbling. 'When we drop anchor, I'm heading for the stone circle to trade with Bear. I've gathered my best ever stash of pearls and merwraith scales and I'll make a purse full o' silver for you.' And maybe I'll trade some of my pearls for learning about the Opals. Or even – my heart stutters and makes my breath catch – find Da.

'That's my Mouse,' she says, gold flecks glimmering in her glass eye. 'Now you've got your sea-hawk you'll be by my side at the Meet, too. How would you like to represent your Tribe and offer the whale-song to the dread-fires?'

I leap in the air and let out a whoop, making Thaw squawk angrily at me. *Catch no fishes for wingless one.* She dives into the air and glides along the deck, heading for her nest in the Hoodwink.

Sorry, Thaw-beast!

'That a yes?' Grandma looks down at me, laughing; then a frown flits across her crinkled face. 'Where's your dragonfly?'

My hand flies to my cloak, meeting coarse wool, fur trim, bone pin . . . but no smooth copper. I drop my bow with a loud *thunk*. 'I must've left it in my trinket chest.' But I never take the brooch off – I've worn it every day since Ma gifted it to me. My heart thrashes against my ribcage and suddenly I'm running towards the fore-deck hatch.

'Mouse! Take some breakfast for your brother and get him out o' that bed!' Grandma yells after me. 'Tell him I want to check on that eye of his. The fire spirits have always shown a shrouding over his future, and I'm heart-sick it means he'll lose his sight.'

Gods. 'Aye!' I shout over my shoulder, though bringing Sparrow breakfast is the last flaming thing I want to be doing.

Before I reach the hatch, Grandma curses. 'What are *they* doing here?' she says, loathing on her lips. 'Banished from Nightfall and still thinking they've leave to creep all over Trianukka?'

'Who?' I ask, curiosity stalling me for a beat.

'Hmm?' asks Grandma, turning to me. 'Oh, them red-cloaked tricksters lined up along the cliffs there, Mouse. See 'em?'

I look. As the ship crawls closer to shore, I can just make out threads of purple fire weaving into the sky.

'Banished mystiks, from the Bony Isle.'

'Mystiks! Like from the stories?'

She nods grimly. 'Wish they was just a story, Bones. They're disgraced scholars, not a good bone amongst them, and they won't be sharing hearth-bread with us. Go, find your dragonfly. And when we dock, you ent to let Sparrow out of your sight. I don't want him getting tangled up with any of them mystiks.'

'Why not? Is it something to do with all that light shooting out of his hands? Was it the same stuff?'

'Truth is, I really don't know.' She sounds vexed, then her voice drifts into thoughtfulness. 'I've been wondering if the key could lie with his birth, and what

110

happened to . . .' Suddenly she catches herself and clams up, so I know she won't talk about Ma.

I race across the deck towards the hatch, fling the door open and clatter down the stairs, into the ship's depths.

Pip sweats over his bread ovens. A fat black rat skitters across his feet and he stamps and curses, clouds of flour puffing white in the moon-lamp light.

'Morning, Pip. Grandma says I'm t' beg bread for Sparrow and me?' I'm minding my mouth and my manners, though all I want is to find Ma's dragonfly.

'Ye'll get your bread 'n broth with the rest o' the crew, when it's good 'n ready,' he barks. His knife-stump is smeared with blood from the basking shark carcass that hangs from a hook in the meat cellar behind him. He wipes the blade with a rag. 'Ye can lend a hand – I've cauldrons want scrubbing and fires want stoking and bones want drilling for marrow.'

My gut twists coldly – I have to get to our cabin. 'Can't, Pip. Happens there's something urgent.'

He raises his sandy eyebrows. 'Aye, ent there always with you scallies?" He steps towards me but I twist away, grabbing two piping-hot spiced buns from the sideboard. He roars and grabs the back of my cloak but I give his shin a good hard kick and I'm off, flying down the passageway.

When I slip into the gloom of our cabin, Sparrow's still a little lump in the bedclothes. 'Why ent you up yet, lazybones?' Since the storm, there've been mutterings that Sparrow's fits ent just a threat to *his* life – now they're a danger to the whole ship. 'If you've heard Erm or Little Marten gabbing about you again I'll sort them out, don't you worry.'

'It's just tummy ache. You lemme be,' murmurs the lump. Thunderbolt snoozes on his pillow, puffing out tiny clouds of moonlight.

'Gods, when *ent* you got tummy ache? You're to get some food down you and haul your hide above decks, Grandma wants to see you.' I drop the fresh buns onto the bunk and fall to my knees next to it, digging my trinket chest out from under a pile of tunics and breeches. Taking a deep breath, I open the lid and rake my floury fingers through the treasure. My brooch ent here. I breathe deep, trying to still my hare-skip heart.

I rock back on my heels and stretch to grab Thunderbolt from the pillow. Then I cast the moonsprite's glow over my collection, ignoring her growls. The piece of red coral Da gave me, a bone pin in the shape of a mouse-head, the jet arrowhead carved by Squirrel, the first pearl I dived for. No dragonfly. I let go of Thunderbolt and she zooms away to a cobweb on the ceiling.

I search Grandma's bedside table, just in case.

There's her silver ring in the shape of a merwraith, with its hidden nook for poison-frog venom, her scroll of different Tribe-speak for trading, the worn leather pouch for her glass eye. My gut clenches. I search the bunk, the furs and my clothes chest.

It's not here. My heart clangs. Dread's Eve is the *worst ever time* to lose a thing of Ma's, cos it's the day for honouring dead kin. My mind whirls, then I remember the day we sailed from the Western Wharves, when Sparrow wanted to borrow my dragonfly . . .

'I'll *kill* you, little wretch! What you done with it!'

'What you on about?' comes my brother's sleepy murmur.

'Where is it?' My voice is danger-quiet.

He moans and turns over. 'I never touched nothing of stinking yours.' One of the spiced buns rolls onto the floor with a soft *smack*.

I make to grab for his foot but the *Huntress* lurches, chucking me hard against the mantelpiece. '*Gods!*' I rub my arm and dart at my brother again, tearing the blankets off him.

'Leave me alone,' grumbles Sparrow. He sits up and glares at me with red-puffed eyes. The blind one's got no shine, no movement. There's a thick white film creeping across it, shutting out more light every day since the storm.

My head's starting to ache. 'You give my dragonfly back, or else. You always gripe on about borrowing it!'

'So? That don't mean I took it,' he huffs. Thunderbolt drifts from her cobweb to sit in his hair, shrilling at me angrily. *Leave poor Yellow-Hair in peace!*

I grind my teeth, hard, worsening my headache. If he's not got my brooch then he must have lost it somewhere. 'It don't belong to you, it was Ma's and she gave it to *me*, afore you came sneaking into the world. It's *mine*.' I want to bawl like a stupid bab. I'll never forgive him for this.

'Why'd you always think things're *my* fault?' he pipes.

'Cos they always *are*!'

'That ent true!'

''Tis!'

''Tis *not*!' He throws his legs up and down, faster and faster, in a rage.

I shove him out of the bunk and pin him to the floor. My knee sinks into the soft bun, squashing it flat. Sparrow struggles and lunges at my face, my arms, biting with teeth sharp as little blades.

'*Yaaaarghh!*' Pain shoots up my arm as he twists out from under me and bolts for the door. There's a smudge of blood on my wrist and two teeth marks.

I fall back onto the floor, breathing hard. 'I *hate* you for this!' I scream. Sparrow's face grows still, frozen.

114

'And I hate you for Ma, 'n all!' As soon as I let the words fly, I wish I could call them back. But they hover in the air, snarling and hissing.

Sparrow's good eye shines with tears. 'I never took it,' his voice quakes. Then he flees.

17

Dread's Eve

The sky's so full of unshed snow that it veils the sun. Me and Bear wait for the crew to lower the frosty plank to the earth. I bounce up and down on the spot, cos I'm clamouring to get off the ship and away from my thieving brother. I'll look for Da and see if I can find out anything about the Opals from the other tribes. Then maybe I'll run off and find my own way to Whale-Jaw Rock, since Sparrow and Grandma ent never on my side.

I feel Bear watching me as he pushes our barrowful of goods, but he don't say a thing, cos he always gifts me the time I need with my thoughts. We walk down the plank, arms outstretched so as not to slip, then our boots snap the silvery skin of frost that's crept across the harbour. Thaw-Wielder rides on my shoulder, gasping at all the new sounds and smells.

Dockside women squat at fires, steaming razor clams and singing coarsely.

'I offered the sand some salt for her troubles, and she spat her clams at my feet!

Won't ye buy some clams and some cockles, they don't 'arf make for a treat!'

I keep my spine arrow-straight. I've pulled merwraith-scale armour over my tunic and my polar-dog cloak over that, the muzzle of the beast still bloodstained. Bear's amber necklace hangs round my neck. A few little 'uns hop about, gobbling clams and sweaty onions, but when they spy me their jaws fall slack and their mothers call them close. I'd be heart-proud if it weren't for missing my dragonfly brooch; my last closeness to Ma.

'Captain said yourself and young Sparrow been scrapping?' asks Bear.

I scowl, kicking a clump of weeds. 'The little thief stole Ma's brooch, and now Grandma ent gonna let me bring the whale-song to the Tribe-Meet!'

When Bear stays quiet I strain my neck back to look at him. He winks.

I bite my lip. 'Why ent you taking this serious? Sparrow's the one what did the stealing, but Grandma took his side, like usual!'

'Use the head the gods gifted you,' he tells me kindly. 'She has no need to take your side – you stand tall on your own. Sparrow's the one who needs others to fight his battles.'

117

Bear's right. I *should* be fighting for Sparrow, not against him. And I'd swallow my words about Ma if I could. I sigh heavily.

'The brooch will turn up, and 'til it does you must shelve your spears,' says Bear. 'This is the one day in the year when all the Tribes of Sea and Land show unity – it's forbidden to shed blood at the stone circle, as well you know.' He don't mention the Sky-Tribes, cos no one's seen feather nor tail of them for ages and ages – not since Grandma was a nipper, when the war ended. Bear waggles his eyebrows at me. 'Unity starts at home, wouldn't you agree?'

I shrug gloomily. 'I weren't gonna *shed blood*, don't fret. But what about the old war over the Storm-Opal Crown? The stories are true, ent they?'

Bear guffaws, clapping me on the back. 'Look in a person's eyes, whether they're born of Sea or Sky or Land, and you'll learn there's not so much difference between you.' He pounds a brown fist against his cloak, over the place where his heart beats.

Hammerhead catches up, pushing a creaky wooden barrow stacked with shark fins, quivery lumps of seal blubber and other odds and ends. Everything our sea-mother gifts us gets used or traded, and we only take enough from her to survive, unlike some.

As we move further from the ship, the smoke from

the dread-fires grows thick and stings my nose and throat. My belly clenches and my brow feels sweaty – it never takes long for my land-sickness to start. Spicy smells drift between gaps in the smoke. Scores of other traders flood in from port, talking in quick, gruff tongues.

Bear's eyes twinkle as he gives me a nudge. 'C'mon, Little-Bones. We want to get ourselves a good trading pitch afore these other scoundrels reach market.' He pats his belly. 'And we should find some pancakes and fried dough-balls before they're all gobbled up, cos Dread's Eve is the day for food with enough grease—'

'To tempt the dead!' I finish with him, despite myself. He musses my hair and we pick up our pace.

Hammer trundles ahead, yelling out his wares. 'Fins 'n skins! Furs 'n blubber! Candlefish – the best for fat – kelp, lobsters 'n coral!' The barrow wheels spatter mud over his moss-green breeches.

Ent no way I want him shouting louder than me. 'Polished amber! Fine pink seawater pearls! Moon-lamps and merwraith scales and poison-frog fangs!'

All the while I'm yelling my wares, I watch folks' faces and clothes, trying to work out what Tribes they're from. Soon the Sea-Tribe Gateway Stones loom above us, carved into the shape of two merwraiths. Then we're on the windy Sea Path to the circle of stones that stands upon the cliff top.

Before us, a group of Marsh-Folk from the Icy Marshes draggle along in mourning garb, singing sadly for their dead. Their warship, *Frog Witch*, sank ten moons ago.

Most of the other Tribes meeting here are travelling the Land Path, entering between Gateway Stones in the shape of horses' heads. But the Sky Path lies overgrown with weeds, and thorns strangle Sky Gateway stones in the shape of eagles.

Suddenly a flash of bright gold snags at the corner of my eye. I twist to look – in the distance a blood-red tent of dyed animal skins sits between two stones. I'd swear by all the sea-gods that I saw a tall, golden-haired man disappear inside.

My heart flies into my mouth. 'Da?' I quicken my step.

Bear catches me with a gentle hand. 'Mouse, settle your bones. If your da's here, he'll find you. You ent to go chasing after strangers.'

I tilt my chin to look up at Bear, my cheeks burning. 'I can't wait another heartbeat! If he's here, I'm finding him *now*.' I shake off Bear's hand and race towards the tent.

'Mouse!' he shouts after me. The squeal of Hammer's barrow stops and he shouts my name along with Bear, but soon I'm lost in a thick press of traders.

Eastern Tribesmen, with ropes of purple hair falling to their saddles and skin almost as deep a copper as Bear's, ride the Land-Tribe path on horseback. I shudder at the sight of the horses; only land-lurkers could trust a bunch of skittish land-ships that can't be rowed. Iron chains are wrapped round the Tribesmen's fists, tethered to the floating thunderclouds they're bringing to trade.

I cut into the Land-Tribe path, cos it'll take me to the tent quicker. Three Tribeswomen prowl towards the marketplace on the backs of giant white wolves. Thaw-Wielder soars over the wolves' heads, brushing their ears with her wing tips and chortling when they snap for her.

A wolf lifts its muzzle to howl in the direction of the dread-fires and my startled hawk swoops back to me. I howl along with the wolf as I run. 'Your howl is wild and true, little sea-sister!' calls one of the Tribeswomen.

I call out my heart-thanks but press forward, cos Da might be here and I can't waste a beat.

18

The Stone Circle

I run, feet slipping on the icy ground. Raised voices come from the tent. If anyone's starting a quarrel with Da it's *my* fist they'll answer to.

As I step through the flap of the tent me and Thaw are sucked into darkness. I stand, blinking, and scan the wooden crates, animal pelts and stray black feathers scattered across the floor. On the far side there's a silk curtain, and murmurs drift from behind it. I pause in the gloom to listen.

'Crow, what d'you think you're doing here? I told you, I don't want to see hide nor hair of you again until—'

'I ain't going back there, Weasel, not now. D'you want me to beg? If I'd known—'

'Stag ain't paying you to whine,' snaps the first voice. My skin prickles at the mention of Stag. 'He'll take it, whether you're man enough to finish the job or not. It's waiting in the water like unguarded gold.'

Thaw-Wielder bristles. *Warbling about bad-blubber!* she squawks.

I know, I chatter softly. *But why? He's locked in the dungeon.* My heart's sunk like a ship, cos neither voice belongs to Da, though I was so heart-sure – I'd have sworn my brother's life on him being in here.

Behind the curtain, the voices die. I freeze. A grubby hand appears, pushing back the cloth, followed by a pair of colourless eyes.

The man has a mop of dirty yellow hair and a hate-blistered stare. Pustules burst on his cheeks and chin. His mouth is a bloodless sneer and his eyes flit about restlessly. 'What's this?' he grates. 'A spy?'

I take a step back. 'I ent no spy! I'm looking for my da, you seen him?' I gabble. 'Tall, golden-headed, kind-faced?'

'There's been no one like him round here.' The man's clothes are salt-gnawed and his jaw's tight from stooping against fierce winds. He's a filthy Haggler if ever I saw one, or a ship wrecker – and that sort's forbidden from the stone circle on Dread's Eve.

But whoever he is, I vowed to seek knowledge of the Opals and might be he's a useful full-grown to ask, especially cos he was gabbing about Stag. 'All right then, so who you talking to?' I peer into the gloom behind him but he blocks me with his greasy bulk. 'What's waiting in the water?'

He turns away. 'You should get out of here, little gnat, if you know what's good for you.'

'Wait!' I grab his arm. 'I'll trade some pearls for whatever you can tell me.'

The man sneers and grabs a fistful of my cloak. Thaw puffs herself up and hisses. 'How about this,' rasps the man, putting his face close to mine. 'You give me them pearls and I still don't tell you anything, but I let you leave this tent in one piece.' His breath reeks.

A wave of fury rises in my chest. Thaw plucks at my ear with her beak. *Waiting in the water,* she chatters.

I turn my face to meet her bright eyes. A tingle spreads through my blood. *Thaw, you flaming wondrous hawk, you!* Maybe I've already heard what I need to know.

When I try to wrench away, the man holds onto the back of my cloak, so I swing my boot into his shin and he unleashes a piteous wail. 'Vicious little swine!'

I run, my hawk gliding next to me. *Never mind trading pearls for words,* I pant. *Might be it's an Opal what's waiting in the water – and I'm gonna dive for it!* Thaw-Wielder makes a gurgle of heart-gladness.

Outside, the stone circle buzzes with folk preparing for the Tribe-Meet. My belly's all knotted up cos I ent found Da yet, but if Grandma don't want me with her at the Meet, cos of my fight with Sparrow, at least I'll be free to search for him. And maybe I'll have the first Opal for him by then.

Suddenly I bash into a gangly boy in a tattered black cloak, with fury-filled golden eyes. 'Watch it!' we yell at the same time, then stare at each other, startled. I ent sure whether to wallop him or break into a grin. As he shakes a lock of rust-brown hair out of his eyes his look softens, but I've already started shoving past. He yells curses at my back.

As I tear along I get the feeling someone's following me. I glance around, but no one's paying me no heed. Then the shadow of a bird falls on the grass. When I search the sky nothing's there, though I can't shake the feeling.

I weave between horses pulling carts until I find my ship, then run up her plank and head towards the port side. Everyone's busy trading or supping their stew below decks. I'm heart-glad there's no black-cloaks keeping watch, cos diving's forbidden here – the sea's stuffed with shipwrecks. That means *gulpers*, and enough merwraiths to deck out an army with their scales. But I ent frighted – if anyone can find that Opal, I can.

I think about fetching my diving sealskin, but then I search my pockets and find the wolf-fish blood that I took from the medsin-lab the day of the storm. This way I'll stay warm without wasting a heartbeat. I throw off my cloak and armour, then kick my boots off and peel away my sealskin stockings. I fish Da's carving out of my pocket and poke it into the toe of a boot, then stash all my garb on the deck, in the shadows under the rail, where no one will see it.

When I climb onto the rail, I swallow a drop of wolf-fish blood. It slimes down my throat and I shudder, but it quickly lights a fire in my belly. As I stow the bottle in my breeches pocket, a black shape blunders into the rigging. I crane my neck to look. It's Stag's crow, shuffling its feathers, watching me.

Thaw-Wielder gives a furious scream and soars towards the crow. It takes off with a disgruntled *thwawk* and Thaw chases it out of sight. I forgot about that wretched bird. Did it follow me here; is that what the shadow was?

Then another thought strikes me – I still didn't hear its beast-chatter. Shivers ripple along my spine, strangling my breath.

19
The Merwraith

Wild grey waves smack against the hull. I rake a giant breath, then fling myself through the air, sailing, bending, arcing, before I plummet straight down like an arrow. The cold stuns me for a heartbeat. Salt stings my open eyes.

I kick hard, plunging deeper, my swiftness startling an octopus so it twists away from me, blushing blood-red. Darkness gathers as I sink. All around, sea-beasts slither. A shadow passes over me and I flip, quick, to watch a giant ray sail along grandly like a blank-eyed king.

A wrecked ship emerges from the gloom, tattered sails moving as though the water was air. A silver shoal of pollack drift sorrowfully around the wreck and a bloated eel slithers through a hole in the hull. A wreck is a grave, so I think a quick prayer for the crew. *May the sea-gods swim close to you.*

I take a good look around before I have to fill my lungs again. What does a Storm-Opal look like? I watch for anything that shines or glitters. Three big pink oysters sit near the rotting wood of the wreck, surrounded by clusters of coral, rising like hands from the seabed. Scattered here and there are the bright grey scales shed by merwraiths. I twist my mouth in excitement, cos pearls and scales will fetch a pouch full of gold for my Tribe – I'll gather some of them, then I'll swim further away from the harbour to look for the Opal.

I kick off the sand, feeling my chest tighten as the air runs out. The blurred shape of the *Huntress* looms above me.

On the surface the sea-birds' caws punch into my ears, too loud after being wrapped in my sea-mother's arms. I gulp a breath quick-sharp, in case someone spies me, then tuck into a dive again.

When I reach the seabed I collect a dozen of the sharp scales and drop them into my pocket. Then I grab my knife from my belt, swim over to the largest oyster and begin to pry it apart.

My fingers close around a rosy pearl but I sense something moving, other than water and weeds. I turn and some of the coral that looks like hands has lengthened, like arms pushing out of the rock.

I spring from the sand, but after a few kicks it's like

I've swum into an invisible net. Panic shoots through me.

Something's pulling me backwards, without even touching me.

No. Oh gods, no . . . it can't be . . . I glance back over my shoulder and there it is, half hidden by rust-red weeds – a gulper! If a crew find a dead one and cut it open on their deck, it'll puddle into white slime and not a single trace can be found of what – or who – it's eaten.

Devour bones. Hungryyy for human morsels. Crunch, snap, guzzle.

I kick and kick, stretching my fingers for the surface, but the *Huntress* might as well be moons and stars from me. I risk a look round and glimpse the gulper huddled near the wreck; a white, shivering lump of jelly. Its eyes are black, dead and draining. The blood-red slash of its mouth opens wide, dragging me closer.

My strength seeps away as I kick uselessly. The ship glimmers in the distance and I yearn for her timbers and sails.

Black dots swarm before my eyes and there's a crushing pain in my chest. I will my heart to slow but panic makes it race faster. When I look back the gulper is nearly all one huge mouth.

What's the bleeding use of the fire spirits saying I won't drown, cos of being born in the caul, if I ent safe from gulpers?

Thoughts of Sparrow flash inside my brain. I wish I never said I hated him. I should've told him I'm sorry. How will I protect him now? I've failed Ma. And Da. Everyone. I think of the carving – and Da's message – and urge every muscle and nerve towards the surface, but blackness starts to close in.

Suddenly a pale face glides from the murk. Rust-coloured hair swirls like scraps of ancient sailcloth. The coral-hands grasp for the creature as she passes them. Her eyes are two white marbles, unseeing. Her fingers are webbed with pearly fish roe and dark scales sweep downwards from her belly to form a powerful tail.

I start to thrash in the water as the blood pounds in my ears.

The blind eyes of the merwraith suddenly look straight into me, like they ent blind at all. Reminds me of being in Grandma's bad books, when even her glass eye seems to uncloak all my trouble-makings.

The merwraith presses a song into my head. *Do you remember when the sea lay, still, in wait for me?*

It's the old song. My heart clangs and stutters. She swarms up to me in one hideous slithering movement.

Her voice invades my head. *Mouse!* she calls.

I forget all the rules – my mouth opens and I let out the last of my breath in a short scream of bubbles.

The merwraith's hand closes around my wrist with a

grip of iron and her voice floods my head again, words sparking like stars. *Find the Storm-Opal of the sea, before he does! It is not here, in my realm; it is closer to your home than you think.*

20

Cut Adrift

Shivers wrack my body. I struggle against the weight of furs. Colours and faces swim in and out of focus. My spirit pushes against my skin, *drags free, calling for Da – and I'm flying across the sea to a time moons past, when Da skimmed flat stones across the water, making them skip like little running creatures trying to stay afloat.*

'Six skips!' screams Sparrow, laughing.

Da laughs too, eyes dancing. He sweeps us into a hug.

'Mouse, can you skim this one?' he asks, holding out a cool grey stone that fits inside the palm of my hand.

I try and try, using up all Da's stones. But each one sinks quicker than the last. Da takes my hand and shows me how to angle my wrist, but still the stones sink.

'I'm cold,' says Sparrow, lifting his arms to Da.

Da catches Sparrow's hands and blows into them to make warmth. 'There are ancient songs in the air, waiting to be hooked, like fish,' Da tells him. 'Shall we sing?'

Da starts singing a song that turns round and round in a

circle like the wheel of the seasons. Sparrow joins his voice to Da's. The spell weaves across the water, bringing a seethe of fins and tentacles to the surface.

I can't sing with them, cos I can't even hear myself think above the din of the beast-chatter. But I can hunt for food. I fill our boat with fish and an octopus and a shark the length of my arm.

Da leads us in the respect-words; the words we always say in thanks to the creatures that give us their lives so we can survive.

In my heart I vow that one day I'll be able to skim stones across the water, like magyk, just like Da.

I wake again, pouring sweat, coughing and thrashing, but someone holds down my arms and however hard I fight I still sink into blackness.

Finally I'm awake good and proper. A faint trace of dream-dance plucks at my mind but I'm too fogged to remember it. I'm in our cabin. The sea's got to be wild cos the ship sways like a mad thing. A lantern squeals as it swings back and forth on a hook, making the shadows dance. My mouth's clogged and dry and sickness crawls up my throat.

A quiet tapping comes from across the cabin. I lift my head but the memory of a pale, marble-eyed face flickers behind my eyes. I touch my wrist – there's a bruise raw enough to make me wince. But the tapping comes again so I shake myself and heave onto an elbow to look.

A shadow hunches over Grandma's table, swamped in a red cloak with the hood drawn up. My heart lurches when I see the hand – it's holding a pipe, tapping it on the wax-spattered map. It can't be; he's locked in the dungeon-hold . . .

'How'd *you* get here?' I rasp.

Stag looks round in surprise. His face is gaunt. 'Lie still,' he booms. He stands and comes to sit on the edge of my bunk, close enough that I can see the wiry hairs poking out of his nose.

I shrink away from him. 'Where's Grandma?' Something flutters in the corner of my eye. When I twist my head it's Thunderbolt, trapped in a bottle.

'She has watched over you for the past three sun-and-moonrises,' he says. His grey eyes are fathomless pits. 'The old woman has to rest.'

I've slept *that* long? Then I gasp. 'The Tribe-Meet! I was gonna—' Quickly I bite my tongue to keep from gabbing about the Opal.

Stag smiles smugly. 'The festivities of Dread's Eve are long finished.'

'*Flaming cockle-dung!*' Tears burn my throat. I didn't find the Opal and I missed my chance to find out more from the other Tribes. I hide my face in my knees as a sob rises in me, but I swallow it down. Then hope creeps into my belly. 'But—' I'm hardly daring to wonder. 'My da, did he come home?'

Stag raises an eyebrow and shakes his head as though I've made a joke. 'Of course not.' He stands and clunks up to the top of the stairs. '*Frog!*' he bellows.

My breath rushes out like Stag's punched me in the gut. I dig my nails into my palms. How'd that stupid old lugworm get free? Has Grandma shown him mercy? Confusion drags through my head. What if he's done what that man in the tent said? *He'll take it, it's waiting in the water like unguarded gold . . .* Could he have found one of the Opals?

I shut my eyes against the dizziness, breathing better without Stag looming, but in a few heartbeats his weight presses down on the bunk again. I grab fistfuls of furs, drawing them up to my chin. 'I want to see Grandma.'

Stag looks as though he's tasted something sour. 'It is not, in fact, always about what you want. *Frog!*' he bellows again. I almost jump out of my furs.

Frog springs down the steps into the cabin, carrying a steaming pot of broth and a covered dish. Before the door bangs shut I hear waves crashing onto the deck. 'All better then, Mouse-Bones?' he asks, squelching about in his sodden boots. 'You must've swallowed half the sea from what I saw pumped out of you.'

'I do not recall inviting you to speak.' Stag glares at him. 'What delayed you?'

'Sorry, sir, Stag, sir. Pip dropped the first pot.'

'What you calling him *sir* for?' I snort.

Frog don't reply but his face flushes livid as he ladles the broth into a bowl and hands it to Stag. I frown. 'You seen my brother out there?' I ask. 'Can you get him to fetch Grandma down here?'

Frog darts a look at Stag, who shakes his head and gestures for Frog to go.

I'm starting to get the fear. I sit bolt upright against the wooden headboard. When Frog barges out the door, the clamour of the crew rises and fades again as the door slams shut. I wish I could join them, but I can't get out of the bunk cos I'm just wearing my smallclothes and Bear's amber amulet.

Stag passes the bowl of broth, cluttered with little fish roe. My stomach dips and heaves as I remember the merwraith, how she got inside my head.

'Eat,' Stag commands. He takes the cover from the other dish and plucks a small octopus out by the head – it's still alive and clings tight to the bowl, but Stag pulls harder and the tentacles wrap around his wrist.

The sight brings another hazed flash of memory.

'I saw a gulper. I should be dead, but – a merwraith saved me.' Reckon she tried to tell me something, too – my mind whirls, but her words keep falling through my memory and I can't catch them.

'Nonsense,' he drawls. 'They have no will to do such a thing.' He grasps at the octopus, but it don't budge.

I sip a spoonful of broth to dampen my painful throat. 'She left me marked.' I show him the purple-black bruise coiled around my wrist.

He eyes the bruise dully. Then the octopus leaps out of his hand and onto the wall with a sticky *thud*. Stag gives a long sigh. Then he leans across me and stabs the wall, raises the octopus on the point of his dagger and stuffs it into his mouth whole. He chews and swallows loudly. When his mouth opens a tentacle still clings to his tongue. A shudder rolls through me, from toe to crown.

'You owe your life to *me*, not some wraith.' His face hardens. 'Most likely Sparrow did that.'

I shake my head. I *know* the merwraith left the mark. I can still feel her grip on my skin and the heavy seriousness of her words, whatever they were. 'Why would *Sparrow* have done it? Where is he?' I ask. Fear swishes round in my bones.

Stag sighs. 'He fought hard to stay with you. I've

still got the gouges on my arm where the creature dug his nails in.'

Thunderbolt zooms frantically round her bottle, shrieking, but I can't hear her words through the glass.

'*Good.*' I smile at my brother's heart-strength. 'But he can stay with me if he wants to; don't matter if I'm sick.' I listen but I can't hear him singing.

'You must understand, Mouse,' Stag says, clearing his throat as he lumbers across the cabin to lean over the map. 'A large trading ship is no place for a child like Sparrow, who was orphaned too young—'

'He ent orphaned!' I shout. Thunderbolt flashes bright and slams the glass with silvery fists.

Stag stares blankly and continues. 'And is too sickly to be of any use. You have useful skills. But Sparrow is skin and bone, his development is stunted. He cannot function without someone to help him. Weakness is like blood in the water – dangerous and intolerable.'

'You're wrong, Stag,' I say, trying to keep the shakes out of my voice. 'He's only eight, he's still learning.'

An odd smile plasters itself across Stag's face. He gives a short, rumbling laugh. 'Child, by eight I could skin a seal, shoot fire-arrows from my father's longbow' – his eyes glitter – 'and swim through underwater caves as deep and dark as the tomb.'

I shrug. 'Sparrow's got the whale-song. We need his

songs to offer up to the gods.'

'Your grandmother has encouraged your imagination too much, and that is a worthless trait. She will stay with the *Hunter* as midwife and be supported in old age as befits a captain's widow. But she will no longer make a captain's decisions aboard this ship.'

The *Hunter*? Bile rises into the back of my throat. The lantern sways, throwing light across the cabin, and the wrongness of it glares out at me. The drapes have been taken down and piled in a corner. Grandma's rocking chair has vanished and in its place sits an open chest full of men's garb. Gleaming brass instruments, rulers and notebooks, and jars full of dark, floating shapes sit atop the map table. There ent a trace of my kin left.

Panic spreads through my blood. What has happened while I slept? What if Stag found the carving, and Da's message? 'The fire spirits picked Grandma for captain, after Grandpa died, and I'm to be next.' My voice cracks but I make it loud all the same.

'The natural phenomenon you refer to is simply an attractive display of light, nothing more. I will not have "fire spirits" spoken of again,' says Stag firmly. 'There is no place for she-captains here. I've been waiting for you to wake up, in order to move you out. The old woman claimed it could kill you to have you moved whilst the fever endured.'

I stare. What's this bilge-squaffle he's spouting? Something icy has taken root in my stomach. 'Where is my brother?' I ask coldly. I remember the storm, when Grandma's black-cloaks marched Stag from this cabin, and how he seemed so calm. *We'll see.* That's what he told me when I said no one messes with my brother.

'Somewhere far healthier for him. The boy needed a more . . . *suitable* environment in which to mature. After we found you floating in the sea we raised sail for the Western Wharves.'

'*Why?* We were on course to pay our respects to the sea-god at Whale-Jaw Rock,' I splutter. Then I think of Da's message and groan. Now I'm moving further *away* from the clue in the song.

'Because now we sail where I say we sail,' Stag replies flatly. 'And traders pay good gold for orphans young enough to learn a variety of trades.'

'They're *slavers*, Stag!' I scream, flinging my bowl of broth at him.

21

The Hunter

Stag dodges the bowl. It crashes into the wall and shatters, spraying the cabin with oily fish roe. His face is slack with shock, and my heart riots to see it.

'You've sold him as a slave and he's just a bab!' Tears prickle my eyes but I shake them away violently.

Stag tries to sit on my bunk but I kick at him. 'Get out!' I scream.

His face is steel again. 'If you're feeling well enough to lash out I suggest you clean up the mess you've made and leave my cabin. I'll send for Vole to take you.'

'Get out of here, Stag. This is our cabin. I need to get dressed and this ent no place for some man.'

Stag laughs again. 'I don't intend to leave you alone in my quarters! But if you're so modest, I shall turn my back for you.' He turns around, still chuckling.

I fling myself out of bed like a tornado, throwing on my salt-stiff clothes, wrist frightful sore. That's when I realise that Grandma's been nowhere near me. If she had, she'd have daubed 'n dressed my wound. And she'd have waited by my side 'til I woke up. I search for my knife. Stag must've heard me rooting through the bedclothes cos he turns round before I tell him to.

'You won't find anything of yours here, child,' he says, watching me with cold eyes.

I make mine hard and dangerous. 'Gimme my things and I'll be off. Where's my trinket chest, my knife, my pearls?'

'Your fripperies have been sold.' He yawns and I want to smash his face. 'Knives, valuable goods and diving are no longer any concern of yours. You will assist the women in stitching cloth and sails, weaving nets and rope. If you are well-behaved and ladylike you may progress to chiselling arrowheads.'

I spit at his boots. 'You ent fit to be captain of a rowboat. You're no better than a slaver and a thief! The fire spirits said—'

'I will not have such arcane beliefs spoken of agai—' begins Stag.

I yell over him. 'The *Huntress* is to be *my* ship after Grandma.' I turn and run up the stairs to the deck. 'And you can clear up that mess yourself!' I yell down.

Above decks, the wind has whipped into a frenzy and slivers of ice slash through the air like tiny daggers. I stumble in the dark, fighting to run away from the cabin door, but the wind throws me against the rail on the port side. The sea rages and I imagine all the hateful creatures that swarm down there, willing our ship to sink. I feel like joining my will to theirs. Maybe we'd be better off as merwraiths.

No. Then I'd have to spend eternity with Stag.

I kick out at the side of the ship. With a pang I remember the carving again. I drop to my knees and search the space beneath the rail where I left my stuff before I went diving, but there's no cloak, no armour, no boots. No carving.

'No, no, *no*, they have to be here!' I whisper. Fright trickles from my scalp to my toenails. What if Stag finds the message? Da said to keep it secret. And – the merwraith said I had to – I strain my thoughts back under the sea, feel my chest tighten again, see the merwraith's long-dead face. *Find . . . before he does . . .* Suddenly footsteps thud behind me and all my muscles tense. I spin round, still crouched on the deck.

'*Mouse?*' Bear's face is too heart-sad for me to take. I jump up into his arms.

'Thank the gods! I thought I'd lost you,' he whispers into my hair. He takes me by the shoulders and holds me away from him, studying my face closely. 'I should never have let you run off at the stone circle! Are you hurt? It's been seven sunrises!'

My heart jolts. 'Stag told me I was asleep for three!'

He flares his nostrils and bunches his hands into fists. 'More lies.'

'Where's Sparrow?' I whimper. 'Is Grandma looking for him?'

'No.' Bear's face is full of sorrow. 'I tried to stop Stag, but he's got a seventy-strong crew of murderous mutineers – mostly Fangtooths – enough to overpower us that stayed faithful to Captain Wren. He's locked her below decks with the other women. They smuggled Sparrow away while we were trading on Dread's Eve. I don't know where they sent him – I'm so sorry.' He gathers me close. 'When I returned Stag had given my chief oarsman's drum to one of his mutineers and then they chained us to our rowing benches.'

My breath catches. 'How'd you escape?'

'Days of sawing at my chains and tonight I finally broke free. I've been hiding in Pip's kitchens, watching for you. We've got to release Captain Wren and reclaim our home!' He pulls away from me, fire burning in his eyes.

'Aye,' I whisper, frightful-fierce. 'No one locks up my Grandma and gets away with it! We'll get her out, Bear, and then we'll find Sparrow!'

Bear watches the stars, his mouth downturned. The stars are the hearth-fires of our ancestors, Grandma always says. My heart hardens. They're just plain old stars. 'If I'd known what Stag meant to do I'd not have left the ship for a moment,' murmurs Bear. 'But when he's clapped in irons again, he'll soon tell us where he sent Sparrow.' It's the first time I've ever seen Bear brimming with hate and it's the worst thing in the world, even worse than that gulper.

My mind reels. 'Stag said he sold Sparrow at the Western Wharves!' I tell him, heart-glad to know something useful.

Bear scans the deck. 'We have to keep quiet and stay out of sight. Poor ship's crawling with Fangtooths and their hounds.' He tugs me into the shadow of the main-mast.

A new fear grips me. 'Stag thinks he knows it all but he don't. Without Sparrow aboard we won't have his songs to gift to the whales!'

Bear nods, thoughtful. 'And that means less protection from the terrodyls. Gods swim close,' he prays. 'Listen, Bones. I'll go back to my post and pretend to be chained, and you hide in the sea-chest I keep my garb in. When we dock, we make a break for it—'

'With Grandma!'

'Aye,' Bear whispers, pressing a finger to his lips.

'So, one of my oar-slaves has abandoned his post.'

Stag's voice cuts into the night like a blade through blubber. I flinch. 'Get back to your bench. You will be punished for your impudence.' A heavy hand clamps down on my shoulder. 'And you, girl, come with me.'

I try to wrench away from him but he won't let go of me and my neck twists painfully. 'Why would I go anywhere with you?' I spit. I put my hand in Bear's.

Stag laughs, low in his throat. 'I tire of this, child. Come. I will not ask again.'

Bear pushes me behind him. 'Let the girl be, Stag.'

'Or what?' Stag barks, harsh as a hungry polar dog. 'I'd be careful if I were you, Bear. Oar-slaves are *replaceable*.'

Bear looms over Stag, fury etched on his face. 'When a truth flicks its tail, it travels faster than a whale,' he says. 'The truth about you will travel, quick, and folk won't choose your side for long.'

For half a heartbeat I can sense the fright that gnaws at Stag and I almost send up a cheer. But that's the thing about heartbeats. Before you know it they're over and it's the next one you've got to worry about.

Stag sends up a piercing whistle and red-cloaked figures emerge from the murk to surround us. They train their bows on me and Bear, and huge shaggy polar dogs pad along by their sides, all snarled gums and teeth. 'And see how quickly *my* truth travels?' Stag drawls.

22
Dungeon

'Stand down!' I roar. 'As your next in line, I say stand down, archers!'

No one moves – except one of the polar dogs. It sniffs round my ankles, hunger splintering its beast-chatter.

Young meat, blood-rich, lick-taste clamp teeth?

Bear pulls me away from the beast and it growls, ribs shifting under its fur. 'He's keeping 'em hungry,' I breathe.

'I'm keeping them obedient,' says Stag, looking at me like I'm less than nothing. 'Get this oar-slave back to his bench!' Next beat, beast-chatter gruffs from his mouth. *Dogs, help your masters!*

It takes five red-cloaks and two polar dogs to drag Bear away. He bellows and fights, trying to throw them off.

Stag pulls me towards the aft-deck hatch. If I had my longbow I'd splatter his blood across the deck before he could draw another breath. 'Where you taking me?' I yell.

'Where you belong, at last.' He stares straight ahead, crushing my arm so hard I cry out.

'When Grandma finds out what you've done to Sparrow she'll have your guts for rigging and your eyeballs in Pip's cauldron!'

'It truly amazes me,' he says, as my heels skate across the ice-slickened deck, 'how you continue to underestimate the gravity of your situation, Mouse. You will no longer have free rein to behave like the insolent brat you have been since you slithered into this world.'

'You dung-gobbler! I knew you was land-lurking scum, from the heartbeat you stepped aboard!' I dig my nails into his arm and kick out at his legs. But it makes no difference.

'Where's my sea-hawk? I've got to go and get her! Get off me!'

He barges through the hatch, pulling me down the steps. I drag my boots as we struggle through the passageways, right into the bowels of the ship. Then I make myself limp as a doll and let my feet slide until Stag yells and – I see what's coming before he hits me. I flinch as he slams the edge of his hand across my temple and my spirit *nudges out of my body and I'm* weightless, zooming away from him, seeking Grandma. The moon-lamps glow brighter as my spirit passes by.

An old woman, with one fierce green eye and a plume of silvery hair, sits in the corner of a cabin, her skin grey and slack. Her other eye is a smooth stone. Grandma! My heart startles. There's a gag in her mouth and her hands are bound.

A woman wearing a necklace of bones questions her over and over. 'Tell us, or you die!' Grandma lifts her chin and shakes her head. Someone grabs her arms and hauls her to her feet. I can't catch my breath. Then Grandma looks straight at me. I'm pulled towards her blind eye. She don't speak, but she gives me a tiny nod. *On the sea*, whispers my memory. *One travels wide.* My spirit zooms back towards my body.

'She's waking up!' swims a voice near my head.

Nibble, tear, fangs sink in, slithers something's beast-chatter.

'She don't look well!' another voice whispers.

'Would you, if someone whacked you across the head?' hisses the first.

Cramp-legs, air bad. Forest gone, sighs some grand beast.

'Why's he brought her down here? I thought she was his special pet,' says a third voice, bitterly. 'He kept her above for long enough, didn't he?'

I wake amid a cluster of grubby faces. The thick air stinks of animals, dampness and soiled bedding. I retch, griping pain wringing my empty belly. The bitter taste of bile fills my mouth. I try to sit up, but my head throbs. 'Too many voices,' I croak.

Squirrel's oval face is squashed into worry. She presses a damp cloth to my forehead. 'Bring her some water, quick!'

Little Marten stumbles through the gloom, clutching a cup. I glug the stagnant water – it's foul, and it'll probably end up coming out again – then I try to rise but the pain in my head beats like a drum.

'Where am I?' I run my tongue around my gums. My mouth feels like it's stuffed with ash.

'Don't you know?' Little Marten asks, fixing me with round brown eyes. 'This is the children's 'n animals' quarters.'

I stare at him like he's speaking Fangtooth. 'Children and animals?' I twist my sore neck to look around. The damp floor's littered with heaps of straw, grimy blankets, rag dolls and a few rune tokens. Puddles of pee shine on the ground.

Crates are filled with snow geese and berg-owls and poison-frogs. Three great polar deer stand in a pen, their black antlers reaching up to scrape the ceiling of the hold. The beast-chatter of them all is deafening. 'Grandma would never keep any living thing like this,' I mutter. 'Except . . . Stag.'

Suddenly everything floods back to me. I clamber onto my hands and knees. 'Sparrow! Grandma! The merwraith!' I gabble. This time my dream-dance didn't fright me so much. It's the first time I've ever flown into a dream-dance half by choice. What if it can be a friend, a thing that gets me where I choose to be? It showed me Grandma . . .

'Settle your bones,' says Hammerhead. 'You're unwell.' He pushes a strand of black hair out of his eyes with a stained sleeve.

'I'll settle my bones when I'm dead,' I hiss. 'What you all doing down here?'

'Stag's stuck us all in this filthy pit to rot,' spits Ermine. 'He reckons we're no better than animals.'

I blink. 'He's right, ent he? Why should we be better than animals, when all creatures are worth respect?' I tug hard on my hair. 'That ghoul's got no right to keep kid nor beast down here!'

'Stag steals the beasts from the land,' whispers Squirrel. 'They're for trading. And so are—' Her voice collapses and she nibbles her bloodied fingernails. But I know what she was gonna say. So are we.

A flickering candle sends a coil of smoke up to the ceiling. I watch the others' pale faces as they stare at the flame, their wide eyes gobbling the light.

They never get to see the light no more. Horror heats

my insides. What if Sparrow's in a place like this? What if – no, I won't think what might be worse. I should've kept him close like Da's message said. I never should've said I hated him.

His name is Sparrow. Look after him, Mouse, says Ma's voice in my head. But I didn't, and now the little too-soon is all alone somewhere.

I curl into a tight ball to keep from quaking. Sorrow crashes over my head in waves that leave me gasping like a fish trapped on land.

23
Endless Night

I use a merwraith-scale from my pocket to carve runes into the *Huntress*'s flesh:

> This is OUR ship. She is OUR kin. WE make the rules!

Then I scrawl the outline of a sea-hawk into the wall. *Thaw-Wielder*, I write. The best hawk that ever flew. I miss her too much. That Stag better not harm her.

Across the hold, Hammer's telling the story of the Storm-Opal Crown to Ermine and Little Marten. 'One hundred moons and suns ago, long after the first oarsman beat his drum—'

'But you haven't got a story-etching,' interrupts Little Marten.

'I know it by heart,' Hammer promises. He clears his throat. 'The King of Trianukka—'

'The *last* King,' says Ermine.

'You two want to hear this story, or not?' asks Hammer irritably.

My skin prickles. Hearing someone tell the tale again is proper strange, cos now it ent just a story. It's as real as the dirt under my nails.

A rat sinks its teeth into my leg and scurries off. *Argh! I'll kill you, just you wait!* I bellow at the putrid scuttler.

Got to catch me first, stupid two-legs, it chatters, sniggering.

'Mouse, you should get weaving or the guards will beat you,' warns Squirrel. Her hands work quickly, twisting tough brown strips of dried walrus hide into rope.

'I ent doing no work for him,' I snap. 'I'll take as many beatings as I have to.' I need to make a plan but the polar deer stamp their hooves, *forest snow-stink gone gone gone*; the poison-frogs mutter, *kill, kill, squirmy-bones, sink-fangs in flesh, kill, kill, kill.* All the beast-chatter muddles my thoughts.

From high above us comes a din of voices and drum beats; some crazed death-dance. Feels like it's been going on for hours and it's making my palms sweat. Then the polar dogs join in with barks, yips and howls. I tense. 'Squirrel, we've got to get out! How long you all been down here?'

Her hands pause on the rope she's weaving, then

quicken again. 'They brought us here when we raised anchor, after they took Sparrow and Stag fished you out of the sea. Must be about eight sunrises by now.'

I scoot back against the wall and drop my head onto my knees. 'What about Stag?' My voice is muffled. 'How'd he escape?'

'None of us knows for sure,' Hammer replies, breaking off his story. 'But when he got out, more than half the crew were already his. The mutiny saw most of the rest desert Captain Wren within minutes. One or two ran, most turned their cloaks. Stag made your grandma's loyal ones into oar-slaves.'

'He had help from our own Tribe.' The words taste like old blood in my mouth.

Hammer nods. 'And Fangtooths.'

'That's got to be why he didn't want me to shoot that polar dog. He was already in league with the Fangtooths.' I curse and leap to my feet; can't stay still a moment longer. 'I've got to get out there and free Grandma.' I've still got the picture my dream-dance showed me stamped behind my eyes, of Grandma with bound wrists and a gag in her mouth. And I can't shake the feeling that she saw me, too. But how? And what did that Fangtooth woman want Grandma to tell her?

'Don't you think we've tried to get out?' asks Ermine. 'It's useless.'

I pace the hold, my boots making deep prints in the muck covering the floor. 'We ent giving up, Erm. Not while I draw breath.' I run to the door and pound on it but the lock don't even rattle.

Suddenly keys jangle outside. I whirl to face the others, digging a merwraith-scale from my pocket in the same movement. 'Who comes down here?'

'Fangtooths,' hisses Squirrel, pressed tight against the wall. 'They bring the slops, when they remember.'

'Get back from there!' whispers Little Marten.

I shake my head. 'I might not get another chance!' I crouch behind the door, the scale jutting between my knuckles like a blade.

Hammer and Ermine glance at each other. Then Hammer nods. 'We'll rush at them when they come in.'

The lock clunks open. I snatch a breath and leap out from behind the door, barrelling into a figure wearing a red cloak. 'Urgghhh!' it moans, sinking to the floor beneath my weight. I hook my arm around the Fangtooth's neck, pressing the scale against his skin.

'Get the weapon!' shouts Ermine.

Hammer grabs a long, curved dagger from a sheath at the Fangtooth's hip, engraved with an 'H' flanked by two jagged antlers. 'H' for *Hunter*.

'It's me, you wretches!' yells a familiar voice.

'Frog?' He pushes me away, wriggling to his feet.

'Still doing Stag's bidding, then?'

Hammer points the dagger at him but Frog holds up his hands. His skin is pale and his freckles glare like warnings. 'I ent one of them – not for real,' his voice scratches. 'Stag's crazed! Poor *Huntress*! He's building great machines in her flanks – he calls them canons – that can spit fire and rocks, and he's making a huge claw out of whale bones for dredging merwraiths off the seabed and–' He falters. The noise above decks grows louder, a frenzy of chanting and drumming.

Suddenly I know what's coming and the knowing smashes me to pieces. I swallow away a stone in my throat. 'He's plotting to kill Grandma.' My vision flashes red.

Weary bodies and voices stir behind me. 'What?' says Hammer. He passes the dagger back to Frog, who sheathes it and nods, fear blooming in his seaweed-green eyes.

'I overheard him talking to Axe-Thrower, his Fangtooth first mate. He said he's gonna drown Captain Wren, cos she won't play by his rules, whatever that means.'

'He can try,' I seethe, 'but I won't let him.'

I take a step but Frog blocks my way, one hand on the hilt of his dagger. 'I don't know what you think you can do about it, Mouse-Bones. Stag'll just throw you back in here, if he don't kill you first.' He rubs his temples. 'He might not stop at you, either. What if he hurts Squirrel to punish me for letting you escape?'

'Never had you pegged as such a quiver-heart.' Fire whips through my blood.

'Squirrel's the only kin I've got.'

Squirrel bolts from her nest of filthy blankets to wrap her arms around Frog's waist. 'When you gonna let me out?' she whines. 'I can be a guard, like you.'

I chew my lip and drop my voice to an urgent whisper. 'You said it yourself – Stag's crazed. He's such an old loon he'll probably kill or sell us all, whatever you do.'

'Shhh!' Frog hisses, looking around at the others. But they all stare back at him, eyes dull, cos they know I'm right as well as he does. He rubs his face and groans in frustration.

I make my eyes hard. 'Why'd you even bother coming down here if you ent gonna let me—'

'All right, all right!' he snaps. But before I can run he grabs a fistful of my tunic, rooting me to the spot. 'When Stag finds you, the story goes you slipped out when I brought the grub – and for my sister's sake, you tell them I never noticed you. Got it?'

I nod. Then I'm out in the empty passageway, silent as a spekter. I run my hand along my ship's walls, heart-glad to be free of that place.

As I move up through the decks the darkness thins and the light half blinds me. The air tastes clean and I breathe to the depths of my lungs. As soon as I've saved Grandma I've gotta let the others out, so they can taste air this pure again.

I follow the drums and voices until I'm at the hatch leading above decks. When I crack it open and peer out, bright daylight stabs into my sore eyes and for a few heartbeats I can't see a thing. Then boots haze into view on the storm-deck and fat silver raindrops splatter to the boards.

The crew chant, their voices strange and drunken. But each and every throat erupts with the same message.

'Drown her! Drown her! Drown her!' they cry, stamping and baying for blood.

24
Bad Blood

Grandma – I've got to reach her, cos she's in danger right now. The crew face away from me, towards the starboard side. A few Fangtooths hunch over the rail, violently spewing their guts upwind of the oar-slaves' benches – the land-lurkers ent used to dwelling at sea so long. Half-starved polar dogs shelter from the rain under hammocks and rails. They snipe at each other, a tangle of jutting ribs and filth-streaked fur.

Quietly I slip out and crouch behind a cluster of barrels.

The plank juts out over the waves with a bundle of rags and ropes hunched at the far end. My stomach flips – as I stare, I see that the bundle is a thinner, grubbier Grandma than the one I know. She's got one hand clenched tightly across her heart, one empty eye socket and a fighting look on her face. Stag walks towards her, pointing a blunt, long stick of metal.

Something sways in the corner of my vision. I turn

my face up to the rain and my scalp prickles in horror – Grandma's sea-hawk, Battle-Shrieker, hangs from a length of rigging, plucked bald and limp as seaweed, her beast-chatter long since flown. Oh, *gods*, please let my fledgling be safe. What if that loon's done the same to all the sea-hawks? A growl throbs in my throat.

Suddenly a shape darts through the rain and Thaw-Wielder pings straight into the folds of my cloak. She nestles on my lap, shivering, feathers soaked. *Thaw!* I chatter softly. *I'm proper heart-glad to see you!*

All-seeing strong-arm leader! she chatters. *Grey-Hair trouble-times?*

Aye. Trouble is the word, Thaw.

All-seeing . . . The words make me think of the merwraith who saved me. Her eyes were blank stones, but the way she looked right into me spoke of a deeper kind of seeing. She saw all my frights, wishes, nightmares, struggles. Thaw-Wielder peers into my face and in a blaze of memory the merwraith's fingers clamp my wrist. *Find the Storm-Opal of the sea, before he does!*

Stag rummages in his pocket, lifts the metal stick and puts something in the end of it. Then he raises it to his shoulder and points it at Grandma. 'Jump, witch. Before I shoot.'

Grandma fixes him with her splinter-eye. 'What of

Hare's memory?' Her sudden mention of Ma startles me. 'Think before you take her daughter's future. Is it not enough that you have taken her mother's home?'

Home . . . Finally, the rest of the merwraith's words flood my memory. *It is closer to your home than you think.* The old song burns bright in my head like sunlight striking ice. *On the sea one travels wide.* That's why the runes in Da's message showed an orb roving all over the place. Because it was on a ship – *our* ship.

My heart thuds in my chest as suddenly I know what Grandma was trying to tell me in my dream-dance – her eye is one of the Storm-Opals! Maybe the Opal was what let her see my spirit. I stuff my fingers in my mouth to keep from yelling.

Hungry wingless gobble claw-worms? asks Thaw-Wielder, blinking. I don't know whether to whoop or bawl, so I just shake my head.

Stag shrugs. 'Hare is long dead, and Mouse will learn to approach life from a more rational perspective, free from your influence.'

'What you've become,' Grandma snarls in disgust. She lifts her chin high. 'May the bad blood stain your soul!' Her fury carves the air like thunder. She lifts her hand from her chest and opens it to the sky – a shine of green sits on her palm. Her glass eye.

My muscles tense, ready to run. *Thaw,* I murmur to

my hawk, as a plan begins to form in my mind. *See that green in Grey-Hair's claws?*

Thaw wriggles out from my cloak and zips onto my shoulder to look. *Seen green. Green!*

Thaw, you get that green. Get it for me and find Sparrow – little sickly-wing?

She trills in answer.

Fly across the sea and find him, I whisper in a rush, careful not to let Stag hear. *Ask the whales, they can help you. Keep the green safe and stay with Sparrow until I find you.*

She puffs up, shaking raindrops from her feathers. *No more feather-fear. Thaw-Wielder do journey to find little lost one.* She rubs her smooth head under my chin and my eyes fill with grateful tears.

'You leave me no choice,' Stag says, dagger-calm. A smile leaches into his words.

'I should have known,' cries Grandma. 'Curse my weakness for the past.'

Just then a massive, mange-ridden polar dog snarls at me around the barrel, but I'm already hurtling across the deck with a sea-roar in my ears and fire in my blood.

At the same heartbeat Thaw *whooshes* over my head, wings clipping my ear. *Getthegreengetthegreengetthegreen of all-seeing strong-arm!* she chatters.

Stag hears it too. I curse under my breath for

forgetting to warn Thaw to stay silent. Stag's long, pinched face whips towards my sea-hawk. 'The green? What – the eye? Why does it want the eye?' he murmurs.

I launch my battle-howl beneath Thaw-Wielder's wings. 'Fly swift, Thaw!' I reach Stag's side and grab his arm, trying to rip it off the strange weapon, but he swats me away and I fall to my knees. The polar dog grabs my ankle in its jaws and shakes me, but Stag hits it with the end of his weapon and it slinks away, yowling, in time for me to look up and watch Thaw.

She reaches Grandma and plucks the glass eye from her outstretched palm. Then my brave hawk flaps away across the sea. Grandma smiles.

'*You!*' Stag shouts at me. 'You really think you have the power to change anything?' He levels the metal stick at my head. The laughter of his crew hacks into the air like throwing knives.

'Stag!' Grandma screams. 'She's just a child – I remember you at her age, before you became this *monster!*' She sounds proper frighted now, and I've never heard her like that before. But Stag don't even seem to hear.

There's a hole in the end of the dull metal stick, like a big blank eye staring at me. 'You've got to let my grandma go,' I spit, lifting my gaze from the stick to his face.

My belly writhes. Ent nothing human in his look. Even his fury has dropped away, leaving a smooth mask, half peaceful.

'No.' He turns back towards Grandma. A sudden sharp burst of fire blasts from the strange stick. The smell of burning fills my nose.

Before I can scream a plume of blood splatters into the air and Grandma topples from the plank. There's a huge crash as her body hits the water. The polar dogs send up frenzied barks and howls.

'*Grandma!*' I sprint down the plank, my bones screaming that she can't leave me; I ent ready, I won't never be.

'Stop her!' bellows Stag. Rough hands catch me and bring me down. I feel the skin on my knees rip open. Someone grabs a fistful of my hair and drags me backwards until I'm on the deck.

I'm pinned down by a Fangtooth woman with a wide grin on her face, revealing her pointed fangs. My whole body shakes. The cries coming from my mouth sound stars away. 'You'll all *rot* for this!' I scream. '*Grandma!*'

She's drowning. She's underneath the ship, getting closer to death with every skip of our hearts. Her blood might be drawing sharks close. Her lungs must be screaming for air. My feet scrabble against the boards but I can't get away. I can't get to Grandma.

'This little one is spirited,' the Fangtooth woman purrs.

I bare my teeth at her and growl.

Stag stands over me, his shadow blotting out the pale sun that's snuck between the clouds. 'Yes, she is.'

He kneels and grips my chin. Mad rage burns in his eyes and a muscle twitches in his cheek. Blood has dried in the corners of his mouth. 'You need to stop fighting me, girl,' he murmurs. 'You will lose every time.'

I spit in his eye. 'Grandma!' I wrack my brains – she can dive for two hundred and twenty heartbeats. There's still time to get to her . . .

'You're wasting your energies, and I tire of it.' He rocks back on his heels, fevered eyes locked on mine. 'You and I are not so different – you abandoned your own brother, after all. And you need me now that you're utterly alone in this world.'

I close my eyes against the wave of sickness that comes when I remember how I screamed at Sparrow, and the confused look he wore when I did it. Fury spills shaky words from my mouth. 'I will find Sparrow.' Stag laughs but I talk over him. 'I *will*. And Da's still out there somewhere. He'll find us and *kill* you. Grandma!' I yell.

'You'll never find your brother. And why you should cling to that sickly wretch when he killed your own

167

mother is beyond me.'

'It weren't his fault!' I shout. 'He was a new bab!'

Stag's eyes flash and his bloodied mouth twists into a strange grin. 'As for your father, it's time you gave up on him as well. He's *dead*.'

'He ent!' The message hidden in the carving told me why Da can't come home. And now I'm heart-certain that Stag must be the enemy it speaks of. Gods, please don't let Stag have found the message!

Stag draws his pipe from his cloak, lights it and watches the leaves crackle and burn. 'Oh, I think you'll find I know what I'm talking about.' He sucks smoke deep into his lungs, looking mighty pleased with himself. 'You do realise I'm the one who killed your father?'

I narrow my eyes and wrinkle my nose. 'You're lying again. Why should I believe a word you say?'

A frown flickers across Stag's brow. Then he springs forwards and seizes a handful of my hair, pulling me up onto my knees.

He blows smoke into my face. I breathe it in and cough and splutter, but that don't stop me screaming and spitting through my tears. 'Grandma!' She might be struggling in her ropes. She might have heartbeats left . . . I try to move but Stag tightens his grip on my hair, forcing my head still.

He draws a knife from a sheath at his hip. 'Keep the arm steady,' he instructs the Fangtooth. She grips my forearm.

'What are you—' My breath stops as he presses the tip of the knife to my skin and gouges a deep 'H' into it. My scream sounds muffled, my skin grows hot and clammy, blood rushes in my ears, and for a heartbeat the pain takes the real hurt away.

When he's finished, the 'H' is flanked by two curved slashes, like antlers. Bright red blood trickles onto the deck. He slaps my cheek, almost gently, to rouse me. Then I realise Grandma's really gone, cos she never could dive as long as me, and a great ragged breath surges up my windpipe, choked with shuddering sobs.

'You're part of my Tribe now.' Stag's cold eyes gleam. 'You belong to me and you *will* obey, or I'll throw you overboard like seal guts.' I thrash against him, kicking and sobbing and cursing. 'The only way to protect yourself in this world is to keep your heart hard, Mouse. Only then can you know real power.'

He stands and dusts off his breeches. 'Come to me when you want to learn the strength of a true warrior.' He swaggers away.

Sorrow bites deep into my bones and makes me gasp. Grandma's face swirls around my brain. The ship rings with her spirit, so how can she be gone? I try to yell my worst name-callings after Stag but my voice is too tight and scratched raw and I can't breathe.

I fall to the deck, retching and screaming my throat inside out. My tears flow faster and fiercer than a raging river. Rain slices through the sky to stab into me.

I'm dragged back through the hatch and into the depths of the ship. As darkness folds itself around me, a thought flashes through my head like a lightning bolt – it's cos of me that Sparrow's gone and Grandma's dead and Stag's got Da's carving. The wrongness of it clangs inside me, dread-dull.

I did this. It's all my fault.

25
Moonrise over the End of the World

'Don't be heart-sad, Little-Bones, for I have returned to my sea-mother's arms. Now your voyage continues without me, but you are ready. I've been training you for this journey all your life. A hawk brought the Opal to me just eight sunrises past, with a note from an unknown hand – protect the Opal and the girl for as long as you can. But now it is your turn to be the protector. Know you have made me heart-proud, every beat.'

As I drift awake, the ghost of someone's voice dies in my ears, and I can't hold onto the words. I curl into a ball, trying to cling to sleep, but other voices whimper in the grey light of the dungeon. When I reach across for Sparrow, to soothe his nightmare, my hand meets freezing air and scratchy floor. The memory of what Stag did pierces my gut again. I jump onto all fours.

Thaw-Wielder zoomed off across the sea with that

Opal cos of me. I pray to all the sea-gods that she keeps it safe and finds my brother. I've got to get out of here and search for them.

'Squirrel?' I call. 'Little Marten?'

'He's gone!' sobs Squirrel.

I follow her voice and find her huddled against a wall with Ermine and Hammer. They're wrapped together in filthy blankets, trying to keep warm. 'What happened?'

'Last night, while you were sleeping, we reached port – I know cos the ship stopped moving. A Fangtooth guard dragged Little Marten away.' She shivers and hugs her knees. I sit close to her and put my arm around her shoulders. She snuffles wetly against my neck.

'Stag must be planning to sell us to slavers all over Trianukka,' spits Hammer.

'We're not goods that he can trade. We're getting out of here!' The wound where Stag etched his Tribe-mark itches sharply. If the cut's healing it means I'll be branded forever. I'd rather have my arm sawn off. I scratch the scabs open again and bite my tongue against the pain.

'How?' asks Ermine, cold eyes flitting between my face and the *Hunter* mark on my arm. 'You ent the captain's granddaughter no more. You're as powerless as the rest of us.'

'Our Tribe is made of survivors,' I tell him fiercely. 'When the Land-Tribes wiped out most of the Sea-Tribes, ours refused to die. None of us is powerless, you should know that!' Then the fierceness falls away from me. 'But you're right, I ent, cos Grandma's dead.' I rub my nose with my sleeve. Suddenly I can't meet anyone's eye.

'What?' asks Hammer, mouth gaping. 'Gods swim close!'

'Oh, Mouse!' says Squirrel in a rush, eyes filling with tears. 'Captain Wren!'

Ermine looks away, tugging his fingers through his white hair, cheeks ablaze.

Suddenly footsteps thud along the passageway and a key rattles in the lock.

'They're coming to get us!' shrieks Squirrel.

Axe-Thrower stomps into the hold and grabs me by my tunic, hauling me to my feet. 'You will see Stag now,' she barks.

'Get your foul mitts off me!' I stare up at her as she marches me through the passageways, and won't look away even when she bares her fangs. *You'll pay for what you did to Grandma*, I think, then wish I hadn't cos the horror gulps me again.

When I'm pushed into the captain's cabin there's a faint smell of Grandma and I can still picture the room how it used to be. Pain rushes up my nose as tears spring into my eyes.

Thunderbolt sees me and chirrups like a mad thing. Stag's got his feet propped up on the map table and the moonsprite trapped in a bottle. He's using a magnifying glass to flash sunlight at her, making her fizzle and shriek in pain. Her face is mournful and her body is blackened. My heart pangs.

Stag dips his other hand into a dish of shark eyes, popping them into his mouth and crunching. 'How is your arm?' he asks, without looking at me.

I watch him coldly. 'Give me my brother's moonsprite.'

'A crew flocks to the strongest captain, you know.' He still don't look up. 'You're going to have to get used to it.'

'You might have the crew, but you'll always be alone, in your heart.' I make a fist and hold it to my chest.

He glances at me, his expression darkening, before boredom resettles in his thick black brows. 'I see you still haven't grown up. But if you prove yourself to me I'll consider sparing some of those little friends of yours. Young Hammerhead should make a fine warrior. But Squirrel? Completely useless until she's of marriageable age.'

I curl my toes and swallow, hard. 'You won't touch her.'

Abruptly he twists in his chair to reach a pile of books and runs his finger down their spines, searching. He slides one from the stack, turns and holds it out to me.

Curiosity presses fists into my back, so I step forward and take the book. I stare down at a yellowed, waxy cover showing a crown studded with three gems of blue, green and amber. The Storm-Opal Crown. I try to keep my face frozen, cos I don't want him guessing I know a thing about it.

'You have to earn your place on the *Hunter* – birthright will not suffice.' He watches me closely. 'Open the book.'

On the first page there's just a nest of scrawled black letters that don't mean nothing to me, cos they don't look like runes. I flip through the musty pages. There's an etching of a whale with a golden crown inside its belly. I peel apart the next page and a picture of wrongness screams out at me.

It's the same whale, but it's been torn to pieces, and a hunter with a long knife rips the crown from its belly.

Stag takes his feet off the table and rises. 'All true warriors in my Tribe have to kill a whale. You want to be the strongest, don't you? You want to be a captain one day.' He twists the magnifying glass between his fingers.

Kill a whale? I gag. 'They're the gods of the sea, sacred to my Tribe.' I throw the book at Stag's chest. It bounces off and slides to the floor.

'They are not,' rumbles Stag. 'They are inferior beasts, to be made use of as my will sees fit. To worship beasts is savagery.' His words make my skin crawl. 'You seem to think we should be against each other, Mouse. But we're both looking for the same thing, aren't we?' He smiles.

My skin prickles and I stare at him agog.

His smile broadens as I squirm. 'Since I first stepped aboard I have glimpsed the potential in you. You could know what it feels like to hold real power. You've seen what happens to the weak – don't let it happen to you. Join me. I'm all you've got.'

Rage takes away the pain for a heartbeat. 'I hate you,' I whisper hoarsely.

'Good,' he replies. 'Hate is power. Use it.'

'Give me my brother's moonsprite. She ent your plaything.'

'No.' He throws the magnifying glass down on the map table and cracks his knuckles loudly.

'You said Grandma—' My throat closes, but I push my voice through the pain. 'You said she encouraged imagination, that it was worthless. But it ent imagination when it suits you, you two-faced—'

176

'I am studying the creature,' he interrupts, nodding at Thunderbolt. 'When I have finished it will be disposed of. Moon-gathering will no longer be practised on this ship. And at moonrise you will join my hunt, if you want to protect your friends. Young slaves fetch a princely sum across the land.'

'I ent hunting whales! We don't—'

'Being a captain is about serving your crew,' he says, like I don't know a flaming thing. 'You may find this hunt distasteful, but if you have to choose between doing your duty and saving your friends, perhaps you ought to question whether you are entitled to the role of captain.'

A flush flares in my cheeks. 'I know what being a captain is about, better than you! And nothing I can do will keep anyone safe from you, cos you're a murderer. I won't ever help you kill more innocent creatures!'

He shakes his head, mirth smeared across his mouth. 'The whales will provide rich materials for food, fuel and trade. One day perhaps you will learn – the greater good matters more than sentimental superstition.' He picks up Thunderbolt's bottle and rattles it.

That's when I see Da's carving, all the little oars snapped off. The bottle was hiding it. Fright squeezes my chest. What if Stag's found the message?

I dart forward and grab the carving, my blood leaping

177

in my veins. But something's frightful wrong. The cord to raise the sails is snapped in half and around the masts hang tattered scraps of white cloth. The message has been ripped away. My gut boils and spots dance before my eyes.

'Put that back at once.'

'No.' My voice comes out small so I clear my throat to make it strong. 'No. This is mine.' I slip the carving into my cloak pocket. 'And I ent gonna listen to any more of the poison that's leaking outta your stupid face!' I shove Thunderbolt's glass bottle out of his hands and it smashes on the floor. She whizzes into my pocket with a shrill of *Helphelphelphelphelp!*

Disgust and rage lick across Stag's face. 'You have nothing, yet still you cannot find the strength of a warrior.' His lip curls as he nods at someone behind me.

Rough hands clamp down onto my shoulders. 'I'll saw the tongue from your head for talking to your captain like this!' rasps Axe-Thrower.

I twist and bite until she lets go with a furious yelp, then I kick at her shins and dodge away. I'm about to hurtle up the steps when my breath falters – there's a glint of copper sticking out from underneath Stag's pillow. I snatch it and a gasp spreads through my chest. My dragonfly!

Stag roars to his feet so I tear from the cabin and crash through the hatch, into a deepening dusk.

Beyond the harbour stretches a wild, foggy marsh, cluttered with animal-skin canoes. Wooden dwellings tower into the air, built atop stilts in the ice-crusted water. Steam seeps between cracks in the ice. To the north looms an ice-capped mountain range. Stories etched in bone tell of this place – the Icy Marshes. We're further south-east than I thought. And Sparrow might be at the other end of the world.

What was that wretched navigator doing with Ma's brooch? Grandma's voice drifts through time. *What of Hare's memory?* I clatter across the deck with my face on fire and palms slick with sweat. Suddenly a soot-smeared man pushes open the fore-hatch, wiping his knife-stump on an old rag.

'Pip!'

'What are you doing out here?' he husks.

'I ent sticking around – this ent my home no more.' I flinch as behind us, a hatch squeals open and someone shouts.

Pip scowls. 'They're coming for you.'

26
Hawk-courage

In a few quick strides Pip catches my arm and hauls me below decks. We crouch beneath the hatch, listening, until boots and paws stomp past overhead.

'Heart-thanks, Pip,' I whisper.

A soft warbling floats from my pocket. When I peek inside, Thunderbolt has fallen asleep.

'You won't escape Stag.' Pip's voice is flat, his eyes empty. There's nothing in him of the cook I remember; the one that used to roar, frightful-fierce, whenever I nabbed a cinnamon bun or let the stew boil over. 'This is how the voyage ends.'

I wrinkle my nose. 'Where's your fire-crackle? We're True-Tribe, not like that Stag and his Fangtooth scum!'

Pip blinks. 'You're the captain's granddaughter, all right.' A faint smile touches his mouth. 'But if you're going you'd best go now. They'll not stop hunting you.'

'I want to find Bear first!'

'No. It's too dangerous, believe me.' He grips my

shoulder. 'You run, now. I know what that soft-hearted oarsman would tell you to do.'

'Bear would never leave me! And he's my da's closest Tribesman. How can I leave him here as a slave?'

Pip looks into my eyes. 'Listen to me. When you make it back here, I'll be waiting with Bear, to help you reclaim the *Huntress*.' Fire-crackle burns in his eyes again.

I nod. 'Blessings and thanks, Pip. I'll bring Sparrow back with me, and we'll both fight for the *Huntress* with you.'

'Aye.' He presses his forehead to mine in a Tribe-kiss. 'May the gods gift you a stronger bite than a ray, and a longer life. Now go!' He turns and hurries off, towards his kitchens.

Above decks night has fallen, thick as fox fur. Sorrowful whale-song flicks through the dark. Moaning blue strands of it snag in my hair. I brush it away and hide behind an archery target to watch as crew scuttle down rope ladders and drop into hunting boats. Harpoons, clubs and axes are lowered into the boats with clanks of iron. The whale hunt. It's really gonna happen.

When there's no one in sight I scan the deck – ahead of me looms the mizzen-mast, set with the round wooden door of the Hoodwink. I race towards it, shin up the mizzen-mast, fling open the door and tumble inside, breathing hard.

A great flapping and squawking starts. I sit up and pull the door closed. *Shhhhh!* I hiss. Rows of yellow eyes glare at me. I'm sitting on a bed of sea-hawk feathers, drizzled with thin lines of white poo and sticky with old fish guts.

I crouch in the gloom and press my eye to a gap in the wood, just as Axe-Thrower and Stag prowl past. 'Where has that obstinate creature concealed herself?' he snarls.

'Let us hunt the girl later,' says Axe-Thrower. 'For now, the whales. Give me first cut,' she pleads with Stag.

My belly flips when a group of red-cloaks march to the rope ladders, forcing Hammer and Ermine before them. But where's Squirrel?

'I think the first cut should be made by one of our newest young warriors,' Stag replies. They hoist themselves over the rail, onto a rope ladder and vanish from sight.

'No!' I whisper.

Hawks fly away now, fly far, leave foul place! husks a voice. I startle and turn, just as the oldest hawk, Storm-Tamer, spreads his wings wide and drifts down from his lofty nest. The haughty-faced bird used to be Grandpa's sea-hawk. *They killed my life-mate, Battle-Shrieker.* He shuffles his feathers and dips his head sadly. *They stole her feathers and her life-breath!*

I nod, heart-sad for Grandma's hawk and my own. Thaw better be safe, wherever she is. I'm bursting with heart-pride that she nabbed Grandma's eye. *When I open the door make certain you fly fast, don't let them shoot you!*

You, he croaks. *Hawk-courage.*

Blessings and heart-thanks, Storm-Tamer, and all you others, I tell them, looking round at the eyes glowing like lamps. I smear fresh droppings across my cheeks for war-paint. *If you find Thaw-Wielder, tell her she's the bravest hawk that ever lived.* A rustling hoot spreads through the Hoodwink and Storm-Tamer inclines his grand head.

I kneel and pin Ma's dragonfly to my cloak with trembling hands. Then I press my eye to the wood again and wait a beat. The deck's clear, cos most of Stag's cronies have clambered into their hunting boats. I push open the door and throw myself flat as the hawks rush and squabble to flee the ship. In five heartbeats they're gone, and when I look up they're soaring, wild and free, across the moonlit clouds.

I watch as the hunting boats slice away through the water. My heart lifts, cos maybe the whales know to stay away from hunting boats – without Sparrow, Stag's got no way of summoning them.

But then Axe-Thrower lifts a long wooden stick into

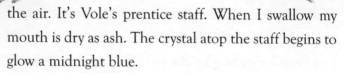

the air. It's Vole's prentice staff. When I swallow my mouth is dry as ash. The crystal atop the staff begins to glow a midnight blue.

Drifts of bright blue whale-song escape the crystal and twine into the air. The whales' voices boom in answer.

A humpback queen I often saw with Da and Sparrow, so many moons past, surfaces between the hunting boats and the ship. I recognise the whale's battle scars from skirmishes with orca and squid. 'Come about!' calls Stag. 'Ready your weapons!'

Thunderbolt wakes and starts to tremble inside my pocket. A puff of moondust tickles my nose, making me sneeze.

Heart stammering, I scuttle down the mast onto the deck and run to grip the rail.

As his boat turns, Stag spies me on deck. 'Glad you've seen sense,' he bellows. 'Join us!'

The whale's beast-chatter zips through the night air. *Where is little Tangle-Hair? Where has his song flown?*

In a rush I feel the force of her love for Sparrow. I remember all the times she was summoned by his whale-song, all the times she helped guide the *Huntress* through storms and sea-fogs.

I haul myself into the rigging and swing onto the rail, gripping it with my feet until I get my balance. The

184

whale's ancient, solemn eye reflects the frozen stars and her breath sprays into the air.

I meet her gaze. *Flee this place, dive deep, swim quick!* I call. In their hunting boats, Stag's crew lift harpoons onto their shoulders and aim. I stamp my foot on the rail and howl. My friends lift their heads and howl back from the boats.

'What are you doing, little fools!' barks Stag.

A spear grazes the tip of the whale's tail, before plunging into the sea. The whale-queen dives out of sight, white tail flukes melting into waves shaped like dorsal fins.

Stag stands and points at me. 'Don't you dare try to interfere with matters you do not understand!'

Hammer and Ermine inch towards the edge of their hunting boat, but a Fangtooth red-cloak yanks them back.

Axe-Thrower waves the prentice staff back and forth over the water and soon, between the ship and the Icy Marshes, whales breach the surface of the sea, singing with the staff.

Then the noise of weapons striking whales is constant and loud. The sea moans in pain and anguish. An iron stink of blood clogs my nostrils and catches at the back of my throat. My hands rush to cover my mouth. 'How could you do it to them?' I scream

through my fingers. 'How *could* you?'

Whales are tangled in the shallows of the Marshes. Tears gush down my cheeks, from a hurt that nudges and nips at my bones, stripping chunks off of who I am, half choking me. This is all wrong. I try to beast-chatter again but bile races up my throat and I gag.

The crew stand in the reedy water, wielding their blood-stained daggers. Stag's face is dark as a storm-cloud. 'Where is the *crown*?' he roars.

My skin startles, sweaty-sick. That's why he showed me the book. This whale hunt ent about earning a place in his Tribe, or being good enough to be a captain, or even providing for the crew. It's cos he wants the Storm-Opal Crown and he'll do anything to get it.

Stag bows his head, mouth twisting. I squint – looks like he's muttering under his breath.

'What're you doing?' I shout. His voice grows louder and I catch the wildness in his throat, recognise the beast-chatter.

Then I freeze as a distant wail makes all the hairs on the back of my neck prickle. I look around, scanning the sky.

Stag cocks his head. 'What is it, Mouse?' he calls. 'What do you hear?' He stares up at me, face streaked with blood.

Before I can answer it comes again, three times, from

different directions. A few Marsh-Folk milling around the harbour scurry for cover. The sound makes the dawn air tremble so much that I almost forget to breathe. Only one thing can do that.

'The terrodyls are coming!' I yell, waving my arms to warn the boats.

Stag's face cracks into a sharp-toothed grin. 'Excellent.'

27
True-Tribe

Sickness washes over me. He's summoned the terrodyls with his beast-chatter. I never knew a gruesome thing like that could be done.

Stag's own crew peer at the sky, quailing. 'Get the staff!' I yell to my friends. 'Use its whale-song to repel the beasts!' But when Ermine grabs the staff the crystal is clear – drained and useless.

I growl in frustration. 'Head for the Marshes!' I bellow at Erm. He nods and pulls at Hammer's arm. They jump into the water and swim away. The sea's got to be freezing, but at least it ent too far to shore.

The terrodyl calls throb closer, closer. A hunting pack bursts into sight, their shrieks shivering through the air like arrows.

I clamp my hands tightly over my ears. That stinking madman! I ent even got my longbow!

Terrodyls swoop down and rip into the whales' flesh. I cover my face, hands shaking. Stag's summoned them to do his bidding – did he send them terrodyls to us, right before he boarded our ship? Has he somehow kept them roaming, instead of making their winter journey to slumber? And *why*?

Find the crown! Stag roars. Then he ducks to avoid a wing, and stumbles. His boat almost overturns. A red-cloak jumps into the water and starts swimming frantically to get away – then there's a scream as a terrodyl plucks him from the sea.

Terrodyls drop whale hearts from the sky and they clunk into the bottom of the boats. Stag's hands are red and slick with blood. But he still ent found the Storm-Opal Crown. The rage boils off him like hot thunder. *Kill every last one. Bleed the sea to death if you have to. No one rests until I have the crown!*

The terrodyls snap their jaws at each other, squabbling over whale flesh.

Fight them! I scream. *Fight back!* In answer, a humpback's huge white fin rises from the sea and smashes into one of the boats, knocking a Fangtooth into the water. I whoop. Then a thought strikes me. *Raise your voices, like spears!* I chatter.

Stag curses at me, but a clumsy terrodyl wing sweeps him off his feet and sends him crashing into the bloody water. He stands, spitting, skin a furious purple.

Whales begin to sing. Throbbing blue notes rise

into the air. A terrodyl flinches and careens into a boat, overturning it.

I laugh at Stag. 'See? You can't control what beasts do!'

'Fire-arrows!' he barks, smashing the water with his fist. 'Strike the unruly ones only. No guns – they will send the beasts wild.'

As soon as the flat, dead word leaves Stag's lips, I know the thing he used to kill Grandma must have been a 'gun'.

Stag starts his beast-chatter again. For a heartbeat the creatures obey, but when the archers set light to their arrows, they sense danger and round on Stag. *The crown!* he grunts. *Bring me the crown!*

One terrodyl soars towards the horizon, jerking its head to try and rid itself of the whale-song. Another begins to slash at Stag with the edge of its wing. The last makes an eerie sound in its throat, like a cackle, and dives towards another boat, stabbing holes in its hull.

'Nock, draw, loose!' yells Stag, fear widening his eyes. His red-cloaks loose a score of flaming arrows. The terrodyls throw back their pointed heads and scream in fury. Stag crouches in the boat, clutching the sides with knuckles turned white. A terrodyl smashes into the water. 'Catch the child, she is sabotaging us!'

Axe-Thrower looks at me, lifts her axe high and bares

her fangs. She plunges over the side of the boat, water sloshing over her face, and swims towards the ship.

I crouch on the rail, not taking my eyes from hers. Then, as she gets closer to the rope ladders, I leap into the rigging. The bitter, woody stench of tar prickles the back of my throat.

A shout goes up from the crow's nest as a mass of red hair bobs away across the dockside – Squirrel.

'Run!' I scream. 'Faster!' I whoop a battle-howl of furious joy.

Axe-Thrower climbs over the rail and lands silently on the deck. She casts around and spies me in the rigging, then laughs. 'Poor little sea-slug. There's nowhere left for you to turn.'

Suddenly Frog springs down from the main-mast, his face ashen apart from the freckles. 'Axe-Thrower, my sister – she's the runaway.'

'Calm yourself, soldier,' she purrs, eyes cold. 'We'll catch her and deal with her. She is no longer your concern.' Why'd she call Frog a *soldier*?

'Please don't hurt her,' Frog begs.

'You speak out of turn.'

Frog backs away, helpless.

'She'll be all right, Frog!' I yell. 'She's True-Tribe, like us!'

Axe-Thrower lunges for my foot so I climb higher

kicking out behind me. My boot crunches against something hard – when I glance down, the Fangtooth holds her broken nose and blood runs into her furs. 'I'll roast you alive!' she rages.

I scuttle higher up the ropes and scan the horizon. The only choice I ever had stares me in the face. Since Dread's Eve it's been my only true home. The sea.

Stag climbs aboard while the Fangtooth fiddles with a bow, dripping blood all over the string. An arrow whistles towards me and I leap from the rigging, straight onto the wide seat of the privy that juts out from the ship's side. *Hope moonsprites can swim*, I murmur.

Thunderbolt makes unhappy belching noises from my pocket. *Ick, ick, uck.*

Tough blubber, I tell her. Below, the sea bubbles with a flurry of silver fish.

'Mouse!' brays Stag. 'Stop this foolishness! You belong to me.'

'After what you've done to my kin? Never!' I yell.

'Don't you want to learn to be a captain?' he clips, a vein bulging on his forehead. 'Growing up is about facing your duties, not running from them.'

I spit and he dodges. 'I learnt how to be a captain from the best, and we both know she was a hundred times the captain you'll *ever* be. I'm gonna find the kin I've got left and keep them safe.' I close my fingers around the smoothness of Ma's dragonfly brooch and feel my heart grow stronger. Then I touch Bear's amber amulet for protection, gulp a deep breath and dive down through the squatting seat, as the Fangtooth's arrow shears my thigh.

The moonsprite shrieks, her chatter brimming with fearful threats. *StopBlack-Hairnastystupidgrrrhatefulafraid notgoodideasnapteethroar!*

As I fall past the rowing benches, I glimpse rows of grubby faces, gleaming chains – and a deep, coppery pair of eyes. Bear!

Then he's gone. I tuck into the arrow of my dive.

The sea rushes closer and closer.

I'm sucked below the churning waves.

PART 3

Flight

28

Rattlebones

Seawater holds me tight. I can't hear a thing except my own heart, thumping against my ribs. Whale blood clouds my eyes.

Arrows plunge into the water. I kick off the side of the ship. Little floes of ice bump against me. If I can reach the Marshes, I'll lurk in the reeds until Stag gives me up for dead. Then I'll creep into a canoe. The Marsh-Folk are a Sea-Tribe who knew Grandma. Maybe they'll help me find Sparrow. And with heart-luck, Thaw will be waiting by his side, with the Opal.

A glimmering shoal of fish brushes my face with tails and fins. I bat them away, but then a pair of hands pushes through the shoal and I tread water, nerves jangling. *Mouse*, a voice calls. *You must come with me, or they will hook you.*

A merwraith appears, her hair a rust-red cloud, face moonlike in the dark water. Her filmy eyes search my face. She's the one who saved me from the gulper.

How did she find me again?

I trailed your ship, she answers, without moving her mouth. Her voice strikes deep into my mind. *Come.* She slips a webbed hand under my arm and with a flick of her tail we're coursing swiftly into deeper water.

Where are we going? The Icy Marshes are that way! I twist to look back at the reeds and house-stilts, lit by the moon.

You must trust me, she says.

I have to find my brother.

The little Tangle-Hair is far from this place. You must have the battle-spirit to find him. Only you can set things right. You are his guardian. You must bear the burden.

I've always known it. But the burden is too heavy. It's too hard.

It is not too hard. You saved the eye from the captain-killer. I will take you to a friend, someone who can set you on the right path.

Who are you? Why are you helping me?

I have watched over you all your life. I was there the first time your mother took you diving. Such heart-pride coursed through me! I am Rattlebones. Once I was a great captain. I was part of your Tribe.

Captain Rattlebones! A she-captain, like Grandma! Stag's wrong. Women were captains, even in days of old.

Rattlebones begins to chant. *Every . . . ship . . . has . . . a . . . soul . . . Every . . . ship . . . has . . . a . . . soul . . .*

It's part of the Captain's Oath; the words every captain must swear. But what will happen to the *Huntress*'s soul, if I can't save her?

A thrum fills my ears, deeper than my own pulse. Rattlebones chants in time with it. Is it a ghostly oarsman's drum, beating from within some ancient wreck? Then a huge whale looms through the murk and I realise the thrumming is the whale's call.

Before I even know I need to breathe, Rattlebones lets go of my arm. She rests her palm on the whale's skin. *You must surface*, she calls to me. *Rise, fill your pipes. Then your journey will continue.*

I burst through the surface and guzzle lungfuls of air. The Icy Marshes are a fog-shrouded speck in the distance. I'm getting ready to dive again when a mass of fish and bubbles fizzes at the surface. They're fleeing from a wide black hole, yawning beneath me.

I dive and try to swim out of the way but the whale glides after me. Rattlebones's voice drifts through the reeds. *Your path will bring you many dangers. But you must not fight your powers. Grow them. Use your fear.*

Darkness closes in. *Take her to the one who knows the way!* Rattlebones roars, as whale jaws snap out the starlight. I'm caught, falling fast down the whale's rubbery throat. The flesh is thick and dank, roughened with barnacles. I'm pushed fast and deep, headfirst into a pool of stinking slime.

The sea-god has eaten me alive.

At first I reckon this whale's gulped a throatful of stars. But then the lights at the top of his cavernous belly start skitter-chattering and I realise they're moonsprites. When the whale scoops up a shoal of fish – *circlecirclespinDART!spinspincirclecircle* – blobs of moonlight *plink* into his belly and bloom into moonsprites that bump against me, tittering. Soon I'm covered in silver footprints. Thunderbolt bristles with wishing she was the only one. *Grrr!* she snaps at them.

At least they're making it lighter in here, I tell her through a yawn. *And I reckon we must've been carried far from the* Hunter *by now, though I can't be sure.*

I sit cross-legged atop a rotting shark carcass. My eyelids are growing heavy and my head keeps nodding. Then suddenly I'm awake again. I can hear the whale weeping. *Sea-home red-churned.* The oarsman's drumbeat of his heart almost shakes my bones loose. *Love swum far. Death-sea?*

There's an ache in my chest and whenever I ent expecting them, tears for Grandma spring to my eyes. My spirit yearns to find her in the sea. *Make her a merwraith. Please, you great blubber-god, make her a merwraith!* I whisper.

Thunderbolt finishes one of her brawls with the other sprites and rushes down to stand on my knee. Most of her burns have healed. *It's all the stupid Black-Hair's fault.* Her moon-glow bursts with angry sparks. *Black-Hair turned her back on Tangle-Hair. Black-Hair said she hates him!*

I never meant it! My voice echoes off the slime-covered walls. Sparrow's look of hurt rushes into my head again. *Rather I'd left you in that bottle, would you? This whale's a friend of Rattlebones, so we should be on the path to find Sparrow. And at least we're far away from Stag.*

I pull Da's carving from my pocket and stare at the ragged strips of cloth. If Stag's read the message, he knows about my search for the Opals. The thought niggles away at the back of my brain. How could I have been stupid enough to leave the carving lying around?

But fight flickers through my veins. Stag won't know what the old song means, so maybe he won't be able to unlock the map. If he thinks he can stop *me*, he can think again, cos I've etched the message on my memory, together with the song.

The whale rises to the surface to breathe. My feet slip into the pool of watery blood and blackening fish brains; the bitter gunge begins to gnaw through my breeches. Reckon I've got to stay as dry as I can, so I dig my fingertips into the flesh of the shark and haul my legs out of the water.

Thunderbolt shrieks up onto the top of my head, her footsteps leaving cold, tingly traces on my neck. My teeth chatter and I'm shivering hard. Anemones, krill and silversides chime in panic, cos they're being digested alive. I can't stay still while the same fate seeks my bones. I've got to know when this whale's gonna spit me out again.

I leap onto a floating turtle shell. Planting my boots wide, I grab a broken barrel stave to use as an oar, but then dizziness washes over me and I stagger to my knees. I need fresh water.

Thunderbolt skates down my nose, lands on my wrist and chatters up at me in sharp bursts. *Black-Hair better not swim to the death-sea! Thunderbolt will tear out Black-Hair's eyeballs and feed them to the fishes!*

Just try it, you useless sprite. I ent dying! I scold. Then I double over and retch until my insides feel bruised and my throat stings.

Suddenly the whale stops weeping. Around me, strings of goo drip into the pool. *Two-legs?* the whale ponders. *Its kin churned sea-red. Brought death-sea to many.*

It gives a thunderous belch that makes my bones throb. When he opens his mouth to let the gas escape, ropes of saltwater stream in, drenching me. Then he pushes the water back through the filter of its baleen.

I weren't part of the hunt, and nor were my kin! I yell. I shudder at the memory. *Are we swimming closer to my brother?*

Why help any two-legs? Its kin flooded my home with ghost-gods, thunder-grumbles the mournful creature.

I tried to help the whales! My voice scratches. A tear trickles down my cheek, but I swipe it away roughly. The whale is silent. Did he hear me? I spit bile and snatch for breath, ready to beast-chatter again. But then a low groan shudders through the belly.

The whale's mouth is creaking open.

29
Thunder Heart

Seawater rushes in, but this time the whale don't push it back out. The gut-slime's gonna be up to my neck in a few heartbeats. I jump to my feet. Thunderbolt buzzes round in a panic, dazzling me with white spots of light. I reach up and grab her, stuffing her into my tunic pocket. *It's for your own good!* I rasp when she complains.

My head whirls but I try to focus. *I ent your enemy!* I call to the whale. But the water keeps rising, higher and higher.

Enemy? it mutters.

No! I'm not! Rattlebones brought me to you, she said you're a– Before I can say *friend*, I'm wracked by a vicious cough.

More water pours into the whale's belly. Moonsprites ping everywhere, squealing. The water's reached my chest and it still rises.

'Hell's bells!' I paddle closer to the wall. Limpets and barnacles are scattered across the flesh, rising up to the

whale's gullet.

I leap off my raft, using the sleeping creatures' shells as footholds. Quick as I dare I scuttle upwards like I'm in the rigging. At the top I clear my throat to try something that might work better than shouting.

Gods of the sea,

Ice-bright.

I'm not sure the song will fly high enough for the whale to hear but I keep going, even though my singing's naught like Sparrow's.

Moonlight, the lighthouse on the shore!

The whale starts to sing Sparrow's song with me. But the water keeps rushing in. My feet slip and I struggle to cling to the wall.

Its song is barnacle-coarse, but it bears the words of the little Tangle-Hair.

Aye, sea-god. You've got to let me out so I can save him!

The mouth begins to close, painful-slow, and finally the torrent stops. But there's scarcely two feet of air left to breathe, and I ent keen to put the luck of being born in the caul to the test again.

I try to swallow, though it's like gulping knives. *Have you heard the little too-soon's song?*

Song drew me, not long past, but stopped, sudden as thunder. Now I drift, alone. One voice I heard, from the old wraith. Asked me to carry two-legs to another it has need of.

My heart startles. *Who?*

The whale weeps again. *But why should it find kin, when I can't hear the song of my life-mate, the great queen of the deep?*

My stomach whooshes into my chest as the whale plummets into the darkest depths of the sea. *The battle-scarred queen?* My insides pang. *She must be alive somewhere, cos I saw her escape the hunt!*

Truth? he asks.

Yes! I bellow. *Please let me out so I can find my brother!*

The whale gives a groaning lurch and begins to glide upwards. I squeeze my eyes shut, trying not to retch again. Thunderbolt chatters and frets inside my tunic pocket. We're travelling faster and faster. I bite my lip to strangle my scream, cos I know I'm gonna fall if we don't stop – then the whale's mouth opens and there's a distant glimpse of blue sky, and the sweetest air I've ever tasted pours in and kisses my cheeks.

Blessings and thanks! My voice cracks. *Tell all the whales you meet that Stag wants to find the golden crown and claim it for his own head. Swim fast and deep, where he won't find you!*

The whale chuckles. *Glint-of-gold cannot adorn a man's head!*

Before I get a chance to ask what he's gassing about, the whale *thumps* against the shore and begins to turn back in the same movement, struggling not to beach. The impact knocks me off the flesh-wall and sends me soaring up and out through the whale's throat. He cranks his mouth wide, coarse baleen brushes against me, and I fly into daylight.

30

What the Sea Spat Out

I crash into the shallows, so hard that more bile is knocked from my sore stomach. When I can move again I twist around, in time to watch the whale's grey body disappear beneath the waves.

I've hardly got the strength to hold my head up. I'm drowsy to the marrow of my bones. A great flat plain of wet golden-brown land stretches away into the distance, crowned in the north by cliffs the colour of iron. There ent a soul in sight. The salty freshness of the sea is tainted by a sweet, rotten stench, like dead things have washed ashore here.

A high-pitched trill greets my ears. Rolling onto my back, I open my pocket and Thunderbolt runs out, straight up the bridge of my nose. She stands on my forehead and chatters insults down at me.

Now what's Black-Hair done? Retch-quaffling bilge-bones!

I got us out, didn't I?

But out to where? she babbles. *Where is Tangle-Hair? Find him!*

Gimme a flaming chance. I take some deep breaths and let my eyelids flutter closed. I wish I could just lie here and sleep, listening to the crash of the waves and the whip of the wind. But Thunderbolt's right. I've got to look for Sparrow. If – *when* – I find him, maybe I'll stop feeling so lost.

I splash to my feet and stare out across the water, thinking of home, though I ent got one now. Another memory of the hunt flashes behind my eyes, sending a shudder along my spine. I'm heart-glad that the sea's not blood-stained here. Maybe Stag can't really bleed the sea to death. Or maybe he won't need to, if he's already got the crown. Though what did that whale mean, about how it can't adorn a man's head?

With a shaky breath, I turn back to the land and begin to limp forwards. Thunderbolt buzzes around my head. On shore, the sky's just as big and the wind's just as fierce as at sea, but the dead-stillness under my boots is hateful. Imprints of little worms clutter the dark gold sand and when I step on them my boots sink.

The ground grows more solid for a few steps. Strange, bulbous seaweed gives a crackly *pop* beneath my feet. I bend down to touch the purple weed, wondering what new medsins Grandma could have boiled up with it. Bitterly I push the thought away. As I walk, the smooth cold sand turns to sticky brown gloop that sucks at my boots.

I sink with every step. There's a *squelch* behind me, like someone's following, but when I twist to look it's just the sound of my footsteps refilling with mud. The moonsprite grumbles, spitting glittery clouds of moondust. *Thunderbolt hates this place*, she moans.

Soon I'm up to my ankles and the ground's still softening. I flail my arms and climb out again, but when I take another step my boots sink deeper. My heart thuds. The land is swallowing me.

Mud stretches into forever. I try to turn back but my feet are stuck too deep. I struggle forward a few inches, but the gloop pulls me in deeper, until it's crept up to my belt.

'Help!' The scream rushes from me, but I'm a flaming fool – ent no help in this place.

Beneath me, the ground begins to wriggle like a bucket full of worms. When I try to run, I barely move. A low wail throbs into the air – it's rising from the earth. The mud moans and writhes, forming twisted shapes like human bodies that rise and fall under me.

I'm going to die. After everything, I'm going to die on *land*, in some gods-forsaken devil-mud.

I scream again as muddied, blood-smeared hands poke through the surface, grasping for my wrists, trying to drag me down. Frosty earth cloys its way up my chest, my neck, my chin. It locks tight around my thrashing limbs, until it holds me still.

I keep my neck straight and seal my lips tight. It's going to drown me – and the fire spirits never said a thing about whether I can drown in mud and sand . . . Thunderbolt's flitting to and fro, panicked.

Suddenly a shout goes up and a black shape dashes towards me across the sandy plain. 'Look what the sea spat out! Must be in one of her moods.'

'Hurry!' My hoarse voice splinters. Cold mud creeps up my chin, towards my mouth.

'What you doing out here?' shouts a boy's voice. 'You got a death wish or what?'

A figure in a tattered black cloak throws a plank of wood onto the mud in front of me. He steps onto it, muttering curses, and walks towards me, until all I can see of him is a pair of grimy, sun-bleached boots. He bends down and his warm breath touches my cheek, but I can't even move my head to see his face. He slips his hands into my armpits and pulls, hard.

The crazed wailing of the mud grows louder. I squirm and try to kick my legs but the coldness clutches me tight.

211

The boy's curses grow louder, right in my ear. 'Get outta my eyes, stupid doom-bug!' He shakes his head, trying to get rid of Thunderbolt.

Wetness trickles down my cheeks. Thunderbolt lands on the bridge of my nose, trying to smudge away my tears. Her tiny footsteps fizzle on my skin.

'Don't give up just yet, sea-slug!' the boy says.

'Just get me out of here!'

'I'm *trying*, but I don't want to use mag—' His words cut off as he pulls until it feels like my arms are gonna come off. 'Damn you, anyone would think you weren't centuries *dead*!' he shouts suddenly, startling me. He can't mean *me* – is he talking to the mud spirits? He straightens up and my skin pangs with fear that he'll leave me.

'Be still!' he yells.

'I ent moving a muscle!'

'Not you, shrimp-breath.' He stoops to pull a long black feather from his boot, then sighs heavily. 'Have it your way, ghouls.' The air ripples and time slows – even my heart settles. He throws the feather onto the mud and shouts a strange word, like an enchantment. A crackle splits the air and a hand shoots from the ground to snatch the feather.

For a heartbeat the earth around my body slackens. The boy grabs hold of me again and cries out with the strain of hauling and then I'm slipping through the mud, through the air, onto the plank of wood. I land sprawled across his boots and lie still, struggling for breath.

'You're welcome!' he says scornfully.

I look up. Two golden eyes stare down at me, set in a face wrapped in ragged black cloth, framed by shaggy red-brown hair.

'Heart-thanks,' I pant, trying to muster a smile.

The boy sticks out a hand to help me up. 'I'm Crow. And I reckon you're a long way from home, sea-slug.'

31
Crow

'Sea-slug?' I brush his hand aside, roll onto my knees and hurl myself off the plank of wood.

Crow pulls a face. 'Next time you can save yourself.' He leaps onto dry sand.

When I meet his eyes again I realise he can't have more than fourteen or fifteen suns. Then I frown. 'Ent I seen you somewhere before?'

He sticks out his lower lip and plucks at it with his fingers. 'Hm, don't reckon so.'

Thunderbolt blows raspberries in his ear, but when he tries to catch her in his fist she shrieks and darts into my tunic pocket.

I check myself over. I've still got the carving of the *Huntress*, the vials of medsin and a few merwraith scales in my pockets. Ma's dragonfly brooch is pinned firm to my tunic and Bear's amulet of amber is fastened round my neck. But my breeches are ripped and when I tug at my hair it's stuffed with clumps of slime from the whale's belly. I wrap my fingers around Bear's amber and squint hard at Crow. If it's bringing me protection, maybe this boy can be trusted. It couldn't be *him* that Rattlebones reckons I have need of, could it?

Crow strolls over to me, whistling. 'Someone don't look at all well, if you don't mind my saying. How'd you wash up here?' He steps closer and reaches out to grab at my hair before I can stop him.

I duck and swat him away. 'You don't look so pretty yourself, land-lurker.'

He holds up his fingers to show me the silver-grey fishtail he's plucked from my hair. 'Easy there, sea-slug. I ain't gonna hurt you. Unless you *want* me to chuck you back in that evil mud?'

Suddenly I remember where I've seen him before and I snap my fingers, startling him. 'Dread's Eve! You barged into me at the stone circle.'

'As I recall, it were you that barged into me,' he huffs. 'Then you pushed off without even saying sorry. Don't they teach manners out at sea?'

I laugh. '"Out at sea" there ent no time for *manners*. There's just life and death and naught in between.'

'Aye?' He cocks his head. 'Think that makes yer summat special? Life's no different on land, as it happens.'

I roll my eyes. 'On land you ent got the hardships,

you ent got the storms, you don't have to worry about running out of food or water or getting smashed to pieces. You wouldn't know real danger if it ran up and bit you!'

He stares down at me. 'Is that so?' he breathes. Then he shakes his head. 'All right, listen up. You can come with me to get yourself warm and fed, or you can take your chances out in the wilds. What'll it be?'

'*Gods.*' I glare up at him. 'Why should I trust you?'

'Maybe because I just saved yer life?' He flicks a lock of hair out of his iron-hard eyes. 'And you should know, there's folk in these parts that'd make me look like your best mate. You need me.'

Anger flashes along my nerves, but he's right – I need to get food and grow strong if I'm gonna find Sparrow and the Opals. And Crow did save my life – not that I'm about to admit it out loud. 'All right, all right,' I spit. 'Settle your flaming bones and let's get out of here. But if you can't help me I ent gonna hang around for long. And I'm *choosing* to go with you – I don't need you. I don't need no one.'

He walks away. 'Looks like it!' he yells over his shoulder.

I scramble to my feet and take one last glance out to sea before I follow him. Up ahead, the cliffs tower over the sand, with ragged chunks gone from the top, like giants have gnawed bites out of the rock. One of my legs drags and it feels like there's a drum booming inside my skull. The sky's almost as dark as the cliffs and the air's hot and damp – unless that's just my sickness.

'What *were* those things in the mud?' I call.

'Unrestful spirits,' Crow says grimly, tightening his jaw. Dark circles ring his eyes and his skin is slack and grey.

I lift my brows. 'Aye, and what did you give—'

'I gave 'em something to keep 'em quiet, is all you need to know, but it don't half take the wind out of me. They're trapped between sea and land, where they drowned. Not a pleasant thought for a little sea-slug.'

'Don't call me little,' I spit. 'If you don't wanna talk about it then I won't bother to listen.' I force one leg in front of the other. There ent a bit of me that don't hurt and every part of me yearns for my longbow.

The sand has deep ridges, like the scales of some slumbering beast. I remember the fireside tales again, of lurking land-beasts: bloodthirsty giants and scuttle-spiders as big as horses. My heart skitters and I walk faster.

We draw close to the cliffs. For a heartbeat I think the land-lurker means for us to climb them, but when we're near enough to see the moss and tiny purple wildflowers clinging to the stone, a sandy path appears.

Crow reaches a crack in the cliffs and slips through. He disappears fast and sudden as a bewitchment. When I follow, the rock closes around me and the path is straight as an arrow.

Suddenly Crow stops in front of a sharp overhang of moss-covered stone. Underneath it, the path vanishes, leaving just a deep pool of black water.

'Where's the path?' I call. I ent sure how much longer I can stay upright.

'I hate this bit,' Crow grumbles.

'What's going on?'

'We gotta swim the rest of the way, through Dead Man's Caves. There's a whole labyrinth of them, right under our feet. It's the only way.' He stares into my eyes, looking frighted.

'We've got to swim through there?' I ask sharply. 'Why?'

'To get you some food, water and safety. I ain't doing this for my health, you know. Wouldn't have thought a sea-slug would be scared of a scrap of water.'

I laugh. 'Scared? It's just a bit of diving! I'd bet my bootlaces it's *you* what's scared.' Without waiting for an answer I gulp a lungful of air and scoot headfirst into the dark pool.

32
Labyrinth

I bump my way along the cave-bed like a blind thing on the bottom of the sea. The water's thick and sluggish and when I kick my legs, bolts of pain shoot up my back. My strength's not even half what it should be, and it's not long before I realise I must've been tricked.

WrigglewrigglewriggleSLIMEwriggletothesea, gasps some desperate beast-chatter. Something rubbery brushes my wrist and I know what this water's stuffed with – hagfish; the foul snaking devils that turn the water near the seabed into slime.

Panic jolts through me. I stretch out my arms and kick as hard as I can but there ent no sign this tunnel's coming to an end. The stone scrapes my belly and the gunk creeps up my nose as I grope my way along tight bends. Stag's voice drifts into my head. *I could swim through underwater caves as deep and dark as the tomb.* Didn't he say that, once?

Suddenly something grabs my boot and drags

219

me backwards. My mind's turning to sleep-mush. *Spar-row*, my heart beats. *Spar-row, Spar-row, Spar-row. I'm sorry!*

I'm pulled faster, round a jagged corner. I feel a stab of pain as the skin's torn off my elbow. My head smacks against something hard and then the water falls from my face.

Someone roughly turns me onto my front and a hand slaps my back again and again and again. Then I'm gasping and wheezing and spitting out thick globs of filth.

Cave water runs out of my ears and hair and drips onto the ground. Hagfish and fat black leeches gorge on my blood.

I flail in Crow's arms until he lets me up. 'You never said the place was crawling with creatures!' I close my eyes and wait for the wave of sickness to pass but it just keeps getting stronger.

'You never gave me a stinking chance! I was just *messing* with you! *No one* uses the caves if they want to see another sunrise – you might have a death wish, but I don't!' His garb's stuck to his skin and his eyes blaze.

'What – there's another way?' I gasp, still half choked.

'Yes, you tawny frogmouth!'

Then a hot, metallic tide rises inside me and my belly clenches like a vice. Before Crow can jump out of the way I'm spewing my guts all over his leather boots.

'My best pair!' He groans, face in his hands. 'My *only* ruddy pair. This ain't my day.'

I'm doubled over, trying to breathe. 'Serves you right for your trickery.' I wipe my mouth with my wet sleeve and grin up at him.

'The trick only worked because of your pig-headed pride,' he spits. 'And you'd better stop giving me lip – I just saved your skin for the second time today.'

'Ack, shut your griping.'

Suddenly I get the feeling we ent alone. I glance up – while we've been squabbling, a ragged crowd of little 'uns have gathered in a half circle around us.

The cave has spat us into a cobbled town square, with ramshackle hovels packed round the edges. In the centre of the square is a fountain, set with a stone carving of a ship crashing into rocks. Water flows through holes in the ship's hull. The sight chills my bones.

The oldest of the group look to be about my age, but most of them can't be more than five or six. There's no full-growns in sight, which is strange enough, but I can't tear my eyes from their faces. They're staring at me like I'm some spekter.

'Where are we?' I ask. 'What're they all looking at?'

'This is the Orphan's Hearth,' replies Crow. 'They're just gobsmacked cos no one new ever comes in here, and no one ever—' He clams his pipes.

'No one ever what?'

He grabs my hands and tows me from the square. I'm too exhausted to stop him and I'm heart-glad to get away from the stares.

We hobble down a side street, me leaning heavily on Crow's arm. He stops at a peeling white door and knocks on it five times. It swings open.

He half drags me through the door. 'Will you help me find—' My voice is thin, weak. I swallow. 'Find out where my brother is?' My knees fold.

'Whoa!' I feel Crow's arms catch me.

The world spins. My ears and eyes fill with fog. Emptiness closes in.

When I open my eyes I'm in a whitewashed room, tucked in bed. Shouts drift up from the street and mingle with a breeze that stirs a thin curtain at the window.

Crow barges through the door with a tray. He sets it down on my lap and raises his eyebrows at me. 'All right, Rat?'

'Plug your pipes,' I hiss. 'It's Mouse.' I glare at him, but there's half a loaf of crusty bread on the tray, and a thick wedge of cheese and a gallon flagon. I tear off a chunk of bread and stuff it in my mouth, hardly stopping to chew.

Then Crow darts closer and slides his fingernail underneath a bloated leech on my wrist. He sticks out his tongue in concentration as he carefully plucks it from my skin. 'Thought I'd got 'em all,' he mutters. 'You've gotta make sure you get the teeth out. Y'know?'

I chew my cheek and shrug, already land-sick again.

'Look, I'm no good with names, so what? After that stunt you pulled at the caves, reckon I can call you whatever I bleeding well choose.' His eyes flash angrily.

'Well caught, boy. Very well caught,' slithers a different voice.

My head snaps towards the door. A man with dead blue eyes and a mop of dirty yellow hair has ducked into the room. It's the man from the red tent on Dread's Eve – reckon his name's Weasel. For one foolish heartbeat I'd thought he was Da. His face is still covered with seeping pustules and his mouth has widened in a brown-toothed grin. My skin prickles with disgust.

'What did he mean, well caught?' I demand, glaring at Crow.

Crow twists his mouth and looks away. Weasel shuffles further into the room and rests his hands on the foot of the oak bed. 'Welcome to our little hearth – the beating heart of Wrecker's Cove, jewel of the East.' He makes a sweeping bow, face full of mockery.

Wreckers. I feel my colour drain as I remember the

33

Wreckers

Weasel crosses to the window and hands a thick gold coin to Crow, who snatches it into his grubby paw quick as anything. The gold flashes as he pockets it swiftly and gifts Weasel a nod.

I think back to the square, when he stopped himself saying something. *No one ever comes in here. And no one ever . . .*

'No one ever leaves, was that it, you wretch?' I shout. 'I'll *kill* you!' My voice shatters and a painful cough bites my lungs.

Crow laughs. 'Not in that state you won't.'

'You sold me out!' Dread shivers through me. Why has Weasel paid Crow in gold? What does he want with me?

'You never asked me my motives.' Crow says, grinning. 'You don't ask, I don't tell.' What I wouldn't give to wipe that smirk off his stupid face.

'You lied about where we were. You lied about me being able to trust you.'

'Hmm.' He takes an apple from his pocket and tosses it from hand to hand, looking thoughtful. 'Did I ever *say* you could trust me? If I gave that impression, I am truly sorry.' He winks and loudly crunches the apple.

'I'll have to vouch for the lad on that one,' says Weasel, spreading his hands wide. 'A truth with a chunk missing still don't equal a lie. This little town *is* the Orphan's Hearth, hidden away in the middle of the cliffs. But it belongs to the territory of Wrecker's Cove. We've no more than the sand and the cliffs and a few huddled dwellings, where we scratch and scrape to eke our humble living.' He ducks his head slyly and rubs his hands together.

I gape up at him. 'You reckon I'm likely to feel bad for a bunch of ship wreckers? Bleeding shipworm! It's your gold-grabbery that dooms any ship unlucky enough to mistake your lights for safety.' I flood my voice with scorn. 'You ent *scraping*, judging by the look of that gold.'

Weasel blinks. 'That's a bitter speech for so sweet a face. It seems you've a grievance against me, Mouse, but I'd like to think you *have* been safe here. If you'd spent your time out *there*, your fate might have been very different.'

'Why? How long have I slept?' I ask, the fear

226

brimming in me worse than ever. I can't afford to lose time; I've got to find Sparrow.

'A whole day and a night. How are you feeling this morning?'

I ignore him cos I've twigged something else. 'What were you doing down there on the shore?' I ask Crow. 'You weren't just taking the air.'

Crow stops crunching his apple. A flush spreads up his neck and spills into his cheeks. 'Never you mind, sea-slug. I still rescued you, didn't I? Should've let the mud do its worst.'

'I've got your measure.' I struggle upright. 'It's your job to hang round the beach, scouting for ships to sink. Or do you watch for survivors to drown so they can't rat you out? Filthy scavenger!'

Crow won't meet my eye. His flush deepens as he reaches up to push a lock of hair out of his face. Then he turns on his heel and storms from the room. I don't know why I feel betrayed when I don't even know him. But I do, anyway, like a flaming fool.

I look at Weasel again. 'So why did you pay such a pretty penny for me? D'you think you can turn me into one of your murderous scroungers?' I turn my head and spit on the floor.

Weasel chuckles. 'A fella like me has to get by however he can, and that means forging links in high

227

places. Today is my lucky day, for there are folks on your trail that'll be ready to offer me a far greater reward than the single coin I just paid the boy.' His eyes gleam. 'Some of 'em ain't best pleased when little sea-slug girls destroy beasts that're rightfully theirs.'

I frown. 'What you belching on about?'

He makes a show of looking disappointed. 'Come now. Should a youngling have so short a memory? The Fangtooths won't have Trianukka quaking in her boots if little girls can skip around shooting their prized polar dogs.'

My breath freezes. The Fangtooths. 'Them frost-snots are leagues away in the Frozen Wastes. I ent scared.' Careless as I can, I lift the flagon and pour some liquid into a tankard. It tastes stronger than when Bear once let me sneak a thimbleful of rum, and it makes my head swim worse than ever.

'Oh, but you should be scared, girl. It's them and Stag that rule the seas of the north now. Together they'll rule all the waters of Trianukka, and the sky and the land as well. You could run to the end of time and you'd not escape them.'

Stag! Dread's Eve floods back to me again, when I heard Weasel in the tent. Them two blather-blubbers are linked. Despair snags me when I think of Stag filling the poor *Huntress* with guns; turning her into his warship for ruling the seas. Gods, I *won't* let him do it, I can't! I have to find those Opals before he does.

'I'd better get going then,' I say, but my face feels like a wax mask and my voice comes slow and muffled. My arms are so heavy they might as well be bound. 'What did you give me?' I wheeze, trying to force my eyes to stay open. *No.* This can't happen, by all the sea-gods, it can't. Panic bubbles in my chest.

'Just a little draught to help you sleep soundly. You ain't going anywhere,' says the ship wrecker. 'Who knows – perhaps by the time you wake up, the Fangtooth warship will have come for you.' He grins and slips from the room, eel-quick.

I open my mouth to scream, but no sound comes.

34
One Boss

Fingers claw at the window. *Scratch, scrape. Tap.* I startle awake. Thunderbolt trills from my pocket and I move to let her out – but I can't, cos my hands are bound. 'No!' I struggle, flail, twist, writhe, but the ropes tighten on my wrists. The room is dark except for two dried candlefish, skewered on a stick and lit as a lamp, fizzling and stinking. I sag sweatily onto the mattress.

Scratch, scrape. Tap. My nerves grow tense as bowstrings. 'Who's there?' I croak. But no one answers. Me and Sparrow need to get back to the sea as quick as we can. I wonder if he's as land-sick as me. All the times I moaned about being in our cabin with Grandma's snores and Sparrow's squirmings. What I wouldn't give to be back there, even for one heartbeat.

I've got to escape. I cast my eyes over the room. There's a fish hook on the back of the door that's being used to hang cloaks – I could wrench that off to use as a weapon. Or maybe I could use the iron chamber pot to bludgeon Weasel and Crow while they sleep. But how, if I can't even get out of this bed?

Thunderbolt, how long did that cursed potion make me sleep?

She squeals a reply but it's muffled by folds of cloth.

Maybe I could've dodged a knock to the head, but ent no dodging a potion, I whisper. I'm shocked by my own thought – but I *did* use a dream-dance to dodge Stag's fist and visit Grandma, I just ent certain how to bring one on at will. When I think how my dream-dances used to fright me I can hardly believe it, cos now I know they can help.

What if I could dream-dance to see Sparrow, like I saw Ma and Da and Grandma? I shut my eyes and try to get the feeling of the dream-dance, the questing and the push-pulling. My thoughts swirl and tell me that it ent gonna work; I ent falling asleep or getting knocked out, but I squish the thoughts and focus on Sparrow. Rattlebones's words drift back to me. *Use your fear.*

The thing outside scratches at the window. *Scratch, scrape. Tap.* Maybe a scuttle-spider has crept up to the window and wants to get in? I try to conjure Grandma's tough, crinkled face. *They're just fireside tales, girl. You ent frighted, are you?* My spirit tests the edges of my skin. I use my bowstring nerves to push it like an arrow, and

I'm *stepping out and getting ready to fly but then there's a heavy* thud and I flick my eyes open. My dream-dance dissolves.

The lamp by my bed has toppled to the floor – did I lash out by accident? – and little flames have started to lick at the bottom of the curtains. My heart gives a painful lurch. I realise the tapping on the window is just a tree branch striking the window, cos now I can see a spindly black branch in the firelight.

Thunderbolt! Thunderbolt! I hiss, eyes glued to the flames. I twist my hands in the ropes but they grow tighter. My heart lurches painfully.

The moonsprite struggles out of my pocket, spies the fire and scolds me in a rush of moon-sparks. Then she zooms across the room to my cloak, dives into the pocket and hauls out a merwraith scale. She lugs it over to me and presses it into my fingers. *No panic!*

Heart-thanks, Thunderbolt! I angle my wrist and slice the sharp scale through the rope of my opposite hand. The fire has gnawed most of the curtain and curls of smoke lap along the floor.

Finally, the ropes snap and I fling the blankets off, my seawater-stiffened clothes crackling. I pat my belt and my heart clamours even though I might've guessed it – the carving of the *Huntress* has gone. My half-rotten, stinking cloak is folded over the back of a chair and my dragonfly brooch is missing, too. Sweat springs out across my skin.

Go! chirrups Thunderbolt, diving into my pocket to shelter from the growing heat.

The tray of food's still on the table so I grab some of the bread and cheese for later. There's a flagon on a wash-stand, and it's full of water, so I take a quick mouthful, then hurl the rest over the flames. They're snuffed out with a damp, angry hiss.

Eyes streaming from the smoke, I snatch the fish hook from the back of the door and test the handle – the door ent locked, so I steal into the creaky hallway. The floors slope, like the house is sinking. I hurry softly down the worn wooden steps.

When I reach ground level dawn has broken through the shutters, staining the hallway with ghost-pale light. Murmuring voices drift from a door that stands ajar, so I huddle in the shadows to listen.

'– but I done what you said. I brought you the girl. I've not put a foot wrong!'

I clutch the doorframe. It's Crow's voice, and he's talking about *me*.

'Orphan's Hearth is for young 'uns. You're almost a man grown.'

'I'm only fifteen! Where d'you expect me to go?'

'Listen, I'm doing you a favour. There's every chance

Stag'll find you if you stay here, and I reckon you've caused him enough grief to warrant lying low for a while.'

I hold my breath. What has Crow done?

Crow laughs. 'I get it. You don't want Stag to think you're protecting me. You're saving your own hide.'

Weasel's voice grows steel-sharp. 'There ain't enough room here for the both of us. The Cove wants *one* boss, and that's me. You wouldn't be challenging my position here, would you, lad?'

'I never said that, did I?'

'Truth is, however much you try to prove yourself, you're soft in the heart as well as the head. You couldn't be the boss of a place like this if your stinking life depended on it. Couldn't even go back to Stag and finish the job proper.'

I suck in my lip. Finish *what* job?

There's a pause. 'Say that again, old man. I dare yer.'

Even as I crouch and listen, the shadows are turning tail and running from the day. My heart skips. I twist the fish hook in my fingers. I'll make Crow give me back what's mine, along with some bleeding answers.

'Get outta my house,' barks Weasel. 'And you better have the brains not to show your mug round the Hearth again.'

'You'll rue the day you met me,' says Crow in a voice grown danger-quiet. 'I never wanted to get tangled up in that business with the boy Stag needed rid of, but I still took him to market and sent him on his way to the Bony Isle, so the likes of you could keep your hands clean. Risked my neck on that particular errand, as I recall.'

Thunderbot shrieks bitterly inside my pocket. My blood freezes. All the hairs on my arms and my neck and down my spine start to tingle-fizz. It was *him* doing Stag's dirty work! My throat tries to growl but I clamp it quiet.

'Shut your griping and get out. Don't you speak of that business again, or might be you'll find yourself stuck in the devil-mud, with no one to pull you out.'

Crow gives a bitter chuckle. 'It's you that needs to watch your back, old hook-wriggler. One dark night you'll find a blade at your throat.'

The row fades in my ears. I don't know whether to laugh or wail. Sparrow's on the *Bony Isle*? I remember the night, moons ago, when we were tucked warm in our bunk and I told him the story of the Storm-Opal Crown 'til he slept. Castle Whalesbane is the only dwelling on the Bony Isle, but there's naught left now 'cept crumbled walls and terrodyl nests. *And* my brother, if Crow's speaking the truth. But Stag said he'd sold Sparrow to slavers at the Western Wharves.

My thoughts scatter when I hear boots striding

towards the door. There's a sudden smash as something is thrown against a wall.

Crow darts into the hallway, hands bunched into fists. Then he stumbles into me and his eyes widen in shock.

We stare at each other. I grip my fish hook so hard my hand shakes.

'You out of my house yet, boy?' yawps Weasel.

Crow springs forward. I leap up, grab a handful of his tunic and stretch onto my toes to press the fish hook against his neck – then he knocks it out of my hand with his elbow and lopes out of the house, his cloak scraping the stone wall.

35
Crew

'Bleeding blubber-brain!' I hiss, tearing after him. He weaves down the street, glances over his shoulder and picks up his pace.

His cloak flaps like salt-stained wings and his copper hair burns in the sunlight that's spilled across the rooftops of Orphan's Hearth. He turns a corner and I follow, down a street where two girls are hanging out sopping wet laundry.

Crow smashes past, overturning one of their baskets. 'Oi!' shouts the tallest. I hurtle after Crow, but the smaller girl's hanging out a sheet and I get tangled in the damp cloth as I try to pass. 'Get out of it!' she snaps. I burst through and stare down the street, but there's no sign of Crow. His footsteps lie before me in the mud, but they stop a few yards ahead. A slender black feather floats in the water that fills one of his footprints – must've fallen out of his pocket.

I tear past the feather, looking left and right down

237

twisted alleyways. There's no sign of him. '*Crow!*' I thunder, racing down a windy street. 'You've got nowhere to go, you stupid slackwit! No one wants you here!'

I search, heart loud in my ears, belly tied in knots. Then I turn a corner and he's sitting in the mouth of a covered alleyway with his back to a wall. He pulls a strip of dried meat out of his sock and starts chewing on it like he ent had a morsel in weeks.

He spies me, rolls his eyes and groans. 'Everyone thinks they can have a gripe at me,' he says, jerking his head to knock the hair from his eyes. 'But I ain't taking it no more.'

Thunderbolt shoots from my pocket and starts whizzing angrily around his head. He flaps his hands, grimacing.

I catch the moonsprite between my palms. 'Why'd you reckon that might be? Now give me back the stuff you stole.' I keep my eyes fixed on him.

His chewing gets slow and thoughtful. 'Don't know if they'd have sold, anyway.' He pulls a dirty rag from his pocket, then a bottle of sand, the gold coin Weasel gave him, a few small bones, a vial of dark liquid – blood? – and a tiny scroll of parchment.

'How much flaming clinker have you *got* in there?' I ask, goggling, as I drop Thunderbolt back into my pocket.

'Hang on.' He keeps digging. 'Here you go, mad girl.'
He hands over my dragonfly brooch and the battered
carving of the *Huntress*. I stoop to grab them.

'What's that on your arm?' he asks, eyes suddenly
curious.

I yank my sleeve down to cover Stag's *Hunter* mark.
'Ent none of your wretched business, bilge-breath. You
better start feeding me a half-decent plan for getting my
brother back.'

To my shock, tears fill his eyes. He scrubs at them
with his knuckles. 'I'm tired, Rat. I'm tired of this lot of
pilferers and I'm tired of flitting hither and thither to
do their bidding. I'm done with this place. All I wanted
was somewhere to call home. And this ain't it.'

I sink to my knees in the dirt. 'I understand how
that feels.'

He looks at me, eyes lighting up like the sun breaking
through storm-clouds. 'Not many do.'

I bite my cracked lips. 'But I've got you to thank for
that, ent I? I heard you with my own ears – you took my
brother to market!' Fury rekindles in my bones. 'You're
gonna help get him back, right now, or else.'

'You've got Stag to thank for it, most of all. But I'm
sorry, all the same.'

'Prove it.' I climb to my feet and dust down my
breeches. 'Get up. Let's go.'

239

He cocks an eyebrow. 'Hold your horses, little miss keen-as-peppercorns—'

'I told you, *don't* call me little! And I can't stand horses.'

He smirks. 'Don't blow your spout. I'm just saying the job would be tough for a man grown, let alone a girl-child of – what are you, ten? Eleven? – who don't even know the lay of the land. Look at you, all green around the gills, like a fish out of water.'

'It's being near *you* what's turned me green, slackwit!' I yell. 'And I'm thirteen, if you must know.' My cheeks are on fire, and Crow's chuckling, and my face keeps getting hotter. 'Ugh!' I turn and stride towards the corner of the square that leads to the underwater caves, wishing harder than ever that I had my longbow with me.

Crow follows and reaches out to grab my arm. 'Wait!'

I shake him off roughly.

He raises his palms in defence. 'Do you want my help, or not?

'Just tell me what you know.' I cross my arms. 'And I'll decide whether it adds up to more lies.'

Colour rises into Crow's cheeks. 'All I know is *where* the nipper got shipped to, I don't know who crewed the vessel. The Fangtooth ship Weasel was gonna trade with – your hide, to save his – docks here at noon. It's the only ship that won't get torn apart on the rocks –

240

owing to how her chieftain's got a deal with Weasel, if you catch my drift.'

I scratch my nose. 'Who does the ship-wrecking with Weasel?'

'Kids – that's why he keeps them here. If they won't do it, he drowns 'em in Dead Man's Caves.' Crow kicks up a cloud of dust and tugs his fingers through his hair. 'That's how I got roped into it, six years of age.' He flicks the hair out of his face, eyes grown stormy again.

A thing like pity settles in my bones but I keep my face iron-steady, which ent hard when I think of all the poor ships he must've helped sink. 'Didn't stop you doing the same thing to my brother, did it? Gods know what *he's* being roped into.'

Crow crosses his arms. 'Don't get me wrong, Rat. I weren't dancing a jig about it, but a man needs to eat. Weasel told me there was something the boss wanted taken care of. I went along and helped smuggle the boy off the ship. We took him west, then south past Haggle's Town to the old abandoned docks. A ship picked him up from there.'

I spit at his feet. 'Ent you got a shred of honour?'

He presses his mouth into a hard line. 'Stag would've had me help him out with more than just smuggling, I can tell yer. But I never went back, all right? That's why he's got it in for me. And you were right before. No one

241

wants me here. So I swear I'll help you get your brother back.'

'How?'

'We smuggle you aboard *Devil's Hag*.'

I lift my brows. 'Your cauldrons are bubbling, but no one's at home.' I wrack my brains, heart-certain I've heard that ship's name somewhere before, but I can't catch the memory.

'Smuggling's one of my specialities,' he says, puffed-proud, and I could hit him. 'You're desperate to find him, ain't you? There's no other way. If you can lie low for two nights and a day you'll make it to the Bony Isle.'

'How d'you know? They could raise sail for anywhere in Trianukka.'

'They'll be on course for the Bony Isle, all right. Stag's got them hauling prisoners there to sell to the mystiks. Word has it they get up to grim business – *I* fancy they feed 'em to the terrodyls.' He watches me to see if I'm shocked.

My temper lashes and I flood my voice with scorn. 'You can't faze me, stupid. I've seen stuff that'd turn your hair to ash.' I stare hard at his face – is he taking this seriously enough? Could the plan work? 'So once I'm aboard all I've got to do is flee another flaming ship captained by another flaming madman?'

'You saying you want me along for the ride?'

I open my mouth to shut him up, but something makes me pause.

Glee spreads across Crow's face. 'As I live and breathe – the girl admits she needs someone!' He pulls a ragged scrap of cloth out of his cloak pocket and winds it around his neck and face like a scarf, rubbing his hands briskly against the chill.

'I don't need *you*, slackwit,' I hiss through clenched teeth.

He laughs, golden eyes dancing. 'Whatever you say, Rat. But I'm your crew if you want me.'

Heat creeps up my neck. I flare my nostrils and look away. Guess Crow don't know that no land-lurker can ever be crew, or that my Tribe might cast me out for mixing with a ship wrecker.

'*What?*' His voice is spear-edged.

Why should I put a speck of trust in a boy who's troubled my life as many times as he's saved my skin? I grind the toe of my boot in the dust. But who else have I got?

I remember the dawn of Dread's Eve, when I stood on deck with Grandma. *Wear your armour close to your heart*, she told me. 'And your enemies closer,' I murmur.

'What did you say?' asks Crow. When I don't answer he turns away, shoulders stooped. 'Just forget it.'

More of Grandma's words float back to me, from

what feels like a thousand years ago. *A skilful captain learns to weather stormy seas, but only once she's learned to weather her crew.*

'Wait!' I call, and he turns back to me. 'My name's *Mouse*,' I tell him, forcing a grin. I take a breath. 'You'd better remember that, now we're crew.' I spit into my hand and Crow does the same, though he screws up his face in disgust. Then we shake to seal the deal, but behind my back I keep my fingers tightly crossed.

36
Bony Isle Bound

'Up for taking the dry land route today?' asks Crow, with a crooked grin that shows the gap between his front teeth.

I send him a withering look. 'You ever gonna let me live that down?'

He shrugs. 'I'll think about it.' He leads me back towards Dead Man's Caves, then turns and walks east, running his hand along the mossy town wall.

'What you up to?' I follow, frowning.

He searches the moss, eyes narrowed, then plucks that vial of dark liquid out of his pocket and unstoppers it. His lips are moving, and if I strain my ears I can almost make out the twang of garbled words from some other place. He daubs his fingertips in the liquid, then peels back a patch of moss and paints a blood-red smear across the stone underneath. Then my mouth falls open as he pushes the wall apart – but not just the wall – the whole base of the cliff it's nestled into, until a crooked path leads away from Orphan's Hearth. For a heartbeat he sways on the spot, drained of colour, a strange, dark power swarming around him like a cloud of flies.

That's the second time I've watched him weave his land-magyk and there's a sickly taint about it that unsettles my bones. 'What in the *gods*—'

'Fetch Weasel!' shrills a voice. I whip round to face the fountain. One of the laundry girls I pushed past is marching towards us, pointing. Another runs back through the square.

Crow grabs my arm with hot, shaky fingers. 'Let's go!' He darts into the doorway in the rock, drags me through after him and shoves the moss-covered door closed behind us.

We race down the sandy path between the cliffs. The sea tumbles in the distance, whale-skin grey. Icy rain stabs my skin. Crow skids to a stop where the sand starts to turn into sinking mud, and I crash into him, almost knocking him off his feet.

Knobbled mast-tops jut from the mud – the place must be a graveyard for wrecked ships. I touch my dragonfly brooch and think a prayer to the sea-gods. I remember when Crow saved me before, when he threw a plank of wood onto the mud . . . my chest tightens. It was a ship's plank.

I wipe my sweaty hands on my cloak. 'Blessings and

heart-sadnesses to you and your captain,' I whisper to the ship's dead.

A muddy hand rises from the depths and grasps for my leg, but I snatch it away. Barrels lie scattered across the ground. 'When the ship comes, how will we board?' I ask.

'You'll see,' Crow replies. 'Not scared, are yer?'

I pause, remembering when Grandma asked me if I was scared of Stag. Part of me wishes I'd swallowed my heart-pride and said *aye*.

'No,' I lie, digging my nails into my palms. In my heart I swear that when I'm full-grown I'll be stronger than iron without pretending.

Crow nods. 'Good, though maybe the pair of us should be.'

A ship prowls on the horizon, growing with every heartbeat. Her sails are dyed red and her oars are painted black. Suddenly I know her – she's the warship I saw on Dread's Eve when I stood on deck with Grandma. *Devil's Hag*. Ent no way she was a Fangtooth vessel back then – poor ship must've been thieved from her true captain, same as the *Huntress*.

I remember Vole's lessons about the Great Tribes. 'For more than a hundred years the Fangtooths have prayed to their frozen land-gods for our Tribe to perish,' I mutter to Crow.

'Maybe their prayers have been answered,' he replies.

'Not yet they ent.' The marrow of my bones shudders with rage. 'Not while there's wind in my sails.' It'll be down to me to claim our ship back. But first I've got to save Sparrow. Cos without him, there's no Tribe. I thought my dragonfly brooch was my last link to Ma. But it ent – Sparrow is.

'They're gonna see us any moment,' says Crow. 'Get in a barrel.'

'But they'll find us, slackwit.'

'No they won't. Look at the letters on the side.'

I crouch in front of a barrel and smear the wet sand away from the wood. Runes emerge, painted in white. 'Salted eels.' I wipe hair out of my eyes and look up at Crow.

Crow's face cracks into a grin. 'They'll think the barrels have been coughed up with the rest of the loot from the wreck. They'll throw them on board, with us hidden inside. They won't hang about to check – their dread of this place runs too deep.'

'You'd better be right.' I bite my lip. 'But what loot? There's naught else here.'

'Just get in, and keep *quiet*.'

'Oh, settle your bones, quiver-heart,' I tell him. 'I've done more dealings with Fangtooths than you've had widdles in your chamber pot.'

248

Crow erupts into a choked laugh but I turn my back on him and prise one of the barrels open with a merwraith scale from my pocket. I ease myself inside, sinking among the cold, slippery eels until my feet touch the bottom. Then I pull the lid over me. Thunderbolt gushes out a cloud of questioning moon-sparks. *Shhh!* I whisper.

As soon as the daylight's sealed out the air grows close and the stink from the eels clogs my pipes something fierce. A chink of light stabs through a gap in the wood, so I press my eye to it and watch Crow clamber into a barrel.

We wait. I keep one eye squeezed shut and the other pressed against the crack in my barrel. *Devil's Hag* creeps closer. I'm heart-sure she'll run aground; her tarred hull must be churning through the mud already. Then the drum stops beating and the crew drop anchor. A knot of Fangtooths leap overboard. They land in the shallows and wade towards the shore. I screw my hands into fists.

They draw close to the mud where I almost drowned, but then two of them cast a great criss-cross of wood onto the mud so they don't sink.

Where the Fangtooths tread, the mud begins to writhe, but instead of trying to drag them to their deaths, hands push things to the surface. The Fangtooths grab thick gold ingots, leather belt pouches, pocket watches, mud-crusted jewels, dull silver daggers. It must be some kind of foul land-magyk – to bewitch the mud and make the spirits thieve from the survivors of shipwrecks, and then drown them!

'Filthy snaffle-beasts,' I whisper.

Suddenly someone grabs my barrel and hoists it into the air. I wrap my arms around my knees and bite my tongue to keep from crying out. 'Heavy for salted eels,' a thick, fang-clumsy voice says.

'Mayhaps the dead've been double generous!' replies another voice, with a hearty belly-laugh. I catch his meaning, and it makes my blood seethe. Eels dwell in shipwrecks – that'd be why so many have been harvested here.

'Where's that sniveller, Weasel? He should have brought us the sea-slug girl by now,' says a shrill voice, after we've been carried aboard and set down on deck. My heart jangles when I realise she must be talking about *me*.

'He'd better drag his bones – and the girl – here soon,' gruffs another voice. A violent thud rattles through me and I press my hands over my mouth. Someone must've kicked the barrel. 'We won't linger, not even on Stag's orders.'

A shout goes up. 'The cretin has crawled from his eel-pit!'

The Fangtooths begin to laugh, jeering and stamping

their boots. I squint through the crack in the wood.

'Sorry to keep you!' puffs Weasel as he hurries up the plank towards the deck. 'I'm not sure how to tell you this, but—'

'But what, worm?' booms the Fangtooth chieftain, wearing a curve-toothed walrus skull for a helm.

'Well, it weren't *my* fault,' Weasel mumbles. 'I slip her a draught, tie her up proper, then come morning she's gone. Might've been some filthy sea-magyk—'

'He's been outwitted by a bed-wetting bairn!' declares the chieftain. 'Stag will hear of this.'

'Ah, come now, no need to tell the boss!' cries Weasel. 'Tell you what, I'll let you keep my share from that wrecking and we'll say no more to Stag.'

The chieftain steps closer to Weasel. 'Oh, you'll *let* me, will you?'

Weasel backs away, stammering. 'You can tell whoever you like, I really don't—' Then there's a short scream as he's hurled overboard, followed by a great splash.

I grin in the darkness of my barrel as the deck shudders with laughter. Then my heart flutters and soars into my mouth – I'm finally on my way to find Sparrow and the Opal!

37
Devil's Hag

My spirit squidges out of my body, through the barrel, and over the rail of the ship. I flick over the surface of the sea, dipping dream-fingers into the water. Sparrow, my spirit cries, are you there, are you safe? Up ahead looms an island, a ruined castle hulking on top of it. Waves lap against the shore and terrodyls swoop in and out of caves in the castle's crumbling walls.

I wake without knowing I've slept, a picture of a crumbling castle burned onto the backs of my eyes. Waves churn against the hull and the rigging groans. For a heartbeat or two I wonder what Pip's baked for breakfast, then I remember where I am with a start.

My throat's so dry and sore I can hardly swallow. The eels are slimy and their cold nibbles my bones. I've got to stretch my legs. I've got to find water. A chatter greets my ears. *Black-Hair finally wakes. Such a dreadful clutter-bones!*

Thunderbolt sits on the dead-eyed head of an eel.

Keep your moon-glow down, we don't want anyone to see light coming from this barrel. She puffs a cloud of jagged sparks but then does as I say. Her light dwindles to a pale beam that throbs with her mood.

My belly grumbles. Silently I pull out the bit of bread and cheese I took from Weasel's house. A thought strikes me as I wolf down the food. How will I know when we're passing the Bony Isle? Then I remember that I know what it looks like – I saw it in my dreamdance – and my tight breath loosens.

Fangtooth voices drift towards me. 'Chieftain says when they've set the boy to shaking, there'll be so many whales washed up on the Bony Isle that great cauldrons of blubber will be bubbling – think of the riches the oil will bring!'

'Never mind vats of blubber. It's them Opals and that crown my tusks are twitching for. You've heard the tales – gems like that hold untold power. They can turn the seasons upside down – our home will thicken and spread if the sea turns to ice. Might be the Frozen Wastes will cover all of Trianukka – then we can travel by sled instead of sail!'

My scalp tingles when I hear them talk of Sparrow and the Opals. Is that why Stag wanted my brother – cos he saw how his shakes drew the whales in that freakish storm?

I press my palms against the wooden lid and it lifts easily. Two Fangtooths in ankle-length walrus-skin coats are moving away from me along the deck, swigging from bottles. Only a Tribe what don't live at sea all the time would don garb that'd drown them as soon as they fell overboard.

A Fangtooth flag snaps and ripples atop the nearby main-mast: a leaping polar dog on a black background. The sky's bright with unshed snow, and when I put my hand to my face, my nose feels icy-cold. There's a *scrunch* as the ship sails ahead, and it takes me a few heartbeats to place the sound – the keel must be breaking through ice on the sea.

Da's message flashes in my brain. Could all of Trianukka really turn to ice? I send a quick prayer to the sea-gods that Thaw-Wielder's got the eye to Sparrow, cos that means at least I'll have one of the Opals when I get my brother back. If we can find the others and get them to the crown, we can stop this ice from spreading, keep the whales from getting trapped and stop Stag in his filthy tracks – gods know what else he might be plotting.

I'm among a cluster of about twelve wooden barrels, what must be full of loot. 'Crow?' I whisper.

After a pause, a barrel lid wobbles and lifts. Two angry eyes poke out. 'What do you think you're *doing?*'

he whispers, motioning for me to get down.

I chuckle softly. 'What? You ent *scared*, are you?' I reach across to offer him a bit of bread and cheese.

He shakes his head, face brightening. 'I'm all right, thanks. I've a belly-full of eels.'

I stare. 'They're meant for *bait*. You ent supposed to munch them, you great loon.'

'Nah, these are definitely for eating,' Crow replies, ducking out of sight to grab another eel from his barrel. He reappears, biting off a chunk of eel flesh. 'Prefer 'em in a pie, mind you, with cider vinegar and lovely hot potatoes.'

'Don't come blubbing to me when you're heaving up your guts,' I tell him. 'Eel blood makes for good poison. Your belly's gonna tie itself in knots trying to squeeze out raw flaming eels.'

'W – what?' stammers Crow. 'Why didn't you say something *sooner*?' He hurls his half-chewed eel away, quick as hot coals.

'Listen,' I whisper. 'We've got to find water. And how—'

Nearby, a door squeals open. I fall back into my barrel and pull the lid into place.

What trouble did stupid Black-Hair bring now? garbles Thunderbolt. I grit my teeth and drop her into my pocket.

Heavy footsteps thud across the deck. 'What's going on out here?' booms a voice.

'Don't spit icicles, Chieftain,' slurs another. 'Nothing prowls here but the dawn.'

'Rum softened your senses, has it?' The first voice comes suddenly closer. There's a heavy thud on the lid of my barrel. Then the world shakes as I'm rocked violently from side to side. I stuff a fist in my mouth and bite down to keep from crying out. 'Salted eels, my eye. Didn't any of you soft-fangs think to check the cargo before we sailed?'

Gods. I gulp a lungful of damp air.

There's a heartbeat of silence as the voice gets no answer. Then curses fly as the lid's lifted off my barrel. I stare up into the grinning face of the Fangtooth chieftain. His walrus-skull helm sits over his head, long teeth curving over his face and chest. 'Well, well. Looks like we've hooked ourselves a pretty young elver,' he purrs.

'Aye, might be I'm a prettier sight than *you*,' I spit.

His grin freezes. 'You!' he roars. 'You shot my polar dog, girl!'

38
Hooked

Did she really?' comes a mocking voice from my right. 'That was rude of her.' The Fangtooth looks around for Crow's voice and I take my chance, springing up out of the barrel, the chill damp of the eels clinging to my breeches.

I get behind the barrel so it's between me and the mountainous Fangtooth. His beard is dyed red to match the sails, so it looks like he's been drinking blood. Might be he has – Grandma once told me that if Fangtooths are shipwrecked most of them survive, cos they kill the weakest and drink their blood from a boot.

Crow bursts from his barrel but catches his foot on the edge, sending eels and lumps of salt skidding onto the deck.

The Fangtooth watches Crow with a slow grin, while his crew shout and stamp with laughter. 'Aye, she did. But no matter – I've a new hell-brute, now.' He puts his fingers to his lips and sends up a bone-piercing whistle.

A white blur rushes to its master's side. The beast stands as high as my heart and its lips are pulled back to show rows of dagger-sharp teeth set in black gums. A growl steams from its throat and its muzzle twitches as it sniffs our scent. Then it throws back its head and *howls*.

Swift as an arrow, I howl back, imagining I'm warning my Tribe of danger. The polar dog retreats a step, but it keeps growling and strings of spit fall from its gums.

Smell dead, no fresh blood, fish-scent, kill? Kill? Girl pup not pack master . . . KILL?

Its beast-chatter is thick with confusion – the salted eels must've covered our scent!

The chieftain's face furrows as he kicks at the polar dog. 'Useless beast!'

I grab a barrel, shake out the eels and heave it over the rail on the port side. It crashes into the water. Then I hurl myself into the rigging and use the ropes to swing myself onto the rail. The mood of the sea is heart-calm, but she's a long way down. The sky seeps snow.

I glance behind me. Crow's tensed in front of the polar dog and the jeering crew, wild fright smeared across his face. 'Come *on*!' I call.

'Enough merry-making!' shouts the chieftain. 'Fire-arrows!' Hatches fly open along the length of the deck.

Scores of Fangtooths pour out, hair and beards dyed blood-red, fangs long and curved.

Crow bursts into life, grabs a length of rigging and swings himself up to stand beside me. He almost tumbles overboard but I grab the front of his tunic.

The Fangtooth archers line up and there's a *clank* as they stand their war bows on the deck to string them. 'Nock!' yells the chieftain. A woman passes him a lit torch. The archers nock arrows to their bows and he walks the length of them, lighting the rope wrapped around their arrow shafts. The flames warm my face.

'Do *not* draw!' I shout. 'I'm the one Stag wants. Let the wrecker go.'

'The *wrecker*?' mutters Crow darkly.

'Cork your pipes!' rasps the chieftain. 'Or we'll kill you both. Don't bother trying to save him.'

I will my voice iron-strong. 'Then what'll you tell Stag? He wants me alive, not dead! And he'll want the wrecker to answer for the wrongs he's done.'

A murmur rushes across the deck. The chieftain curses. 'This Stag thinks he is *king*!' he roars. 'But Fangtooths don't take orders from men in brass buckles!'

I turn my head slightly, without taking my eyes from the chieftain. 'Can you swim?' I murmur under my breath, barely moving my lips.

Crow gives a stiff nod, eyeing the sea nervously.

'Them waves are the friendly ones,' I hiss, quiet enough not to be heard over the fizzle of the fire-arrows.

'Another move and arrows fly!' shrieks an old woman with polar sled tattoos stretching the length of her arms. 'You have three choices,' she keens, in an accent so thick I have to strain to understand it. 'You can jump, we can shoot you, or you can come by your own will and be taken to Stag in irons. Your scowling friend is dead flesh, whatever you choose.'

I spit onto the deck below. 'Not good enough!'

'Archers!' the chieftain shouts. '*Loose!*'

'Now!' I scream.

We jump as arrows streak past us, pushing bright balls of orange flame into the sky. One scrapes the top of my head and a singed smell fills my nose.

The freezing air rising from the sea hits us first. Our fall shatters a crust of ice and we crash through into a shock of icy water. The sea sucks me down. I push against the hull of *Devil's Hag*, fighting for the surface. When I break it, gasping, my breath steams and the Fangtooths shriek with laughter above us.

'Don't waste another arrow,' hoots the old woman gleefully. 'That water is grave-cold. The child must be ready to face her death-sea.'

Crow breaks the surface and swims a few strokes to

grab a barrel floating nearby. He pushes it over to where I'm treading water. Thunderbolt sits in his hair, shivering. When I look at her, she darkens like a raincloud and growls. *Black-Hair getting Thunderbolt almost drowned!*

Crow fishes a compass out of his pocket and stares at its wet face, but I grab the barrel and push it out in front of us. 'I know the way,' I tell him through numb lips. 'Hang on and kick, hard!'

He stays silent, mouth tinged blue. I grab his shoulders and shout into his face. 'We've got to swim for our lives, or we'll freeze to death!'

We kick, pushing the barrel through the sea's skin of ice. 'Why'd you have to show your stupid face round Wrecker's Cove?' Crow blurts, but then he inhales a lungful of seawater and spends half an age slumped over the barrel, spluttering. I'd kill the land-lurker for a single drop of wolf-fish blood to keep warm – as I think it, my belly leaps.

'Wait,' I mutter, reaching into the water to check my breeches pocket. My fingers curl around the two vials – one of wolf-fish blood, one of dragonfish eye drops. I whoop for joy.

Crow glares. 'Have your gills crusted over?'

I lift a dropper full of wolf-fish blood to my mouth and swallow, then lift it to his. 'Take a drop of this and you'll live to see another sunrise.'

261

He sticks out his tongue and when the blood touches it he pulls such a face that I press my fist under his chin to make him swallow. Then I gift a silent heart-thanks to Grandma and her medsin-making for saving our hides. A sunbeam pierces the clouds as though she's heard me.

We swim. I'm frighted witless that *Devil's Hag* is gonna follow and shoot us when our bones tire. But she don't – instead she veers south.

'She'll dock first at Riddler's Hollow,' says Crow, a spot of warmth in each cheek from Grandma's medsin. 'To find poor folk for the terrodyls to snack on, I'd bet.'

My spirit sags under the grimness of his words. I heave a sigh.

Snow falls, clouds thicken and thin, the sun climbs and falls through the sky. My muscles are screaming and my throat's cracked raw, so I take a turn at resting on the barrel, then force myself to kick again. As the sun touches the horizon, my chin dips lower in the water. I shake myself and look ahead – my heart lurches. 'Look!'

The rays of the setting sun have cast a towering, dark green island in a fiery glow. It looks like it's erupted from the seabed into a giant knot of mountain paths and trees, ringed by glittering white sand.

'The Bony Isle,' husks Crow. 'We were closer than I dared hope.' Now his lips are purple, his skin's tinged green and his eyes are bloodshot. I remember the raw eels he ate. Fear washes over me.

'Hang on,' I whisper, my own voice just as hoarse. 'We'll find fresh water soon.'

A castle crowns the island, high above us. The dark, spiny shapes of terrodyls flit in and out of roosts in its walls.

It must be Castle Whalesbane. Its golden walls have crumbled, forming caves like dark eyes, and in the crevices of the rock, huge black lumps sit in nests of bones – terrodyl eggs.

A fat black thundercloud hangs sorrowfully above the castle. Tendrils of purple light crackle through it, and every time the light flashes I can almost hear the cloud groan.

'Bleeding blood cockles!' Dread shudders through me.

'Didn't you know this place was evil?' asks Crow, glancing sideways at me. 'What's your plan now we're here, anyway?'

'I'm gonna find my brother and get him out of there.'

'I know that,' he says, like I'm some slackwit. 'But how d'yer plan to do it, exactly?'

I squint at him. 'What bit of "find my brother and get him out" can't you understand? I'll do whatever I have to.'

A smell of ash hangs in the air. When we can touch the sandy seabed with our toes, we let go of the barrel and wade. I know that light flickering above the castle – I've seen it before. It's the same colour and it gives the same smoky smell as Sparrow's lightning did in the storm. *Spar-row*, thuds my heart. *Spar-row.* I've got to get to him. I've got to make things right.

I struggle forward. My blood leaps with a brew of dread and joy mixed together. Cos what if my brother is . . ? *No.* I shutter the thought behind locks and bolts but it smashes through. *What if he dies before you can reach him?* whispers a treacherous voice behind my eyes. Thunderbolt *whirrs* through the air and settles on my shoulder, like somehow she knows how I feel. Suddenly I'm heart-glad she's with me.

But as I move closer, I realise Crow has lagged behind. I stop and turn to him. His face is worry-crumpled. A wave of gloom throbs from the Bony Isle, almost strong enough to make me want to throw myself into the depths of the sea.

'Rat, there's something worse than evil here,' says Crow, catching up to me.

'It's *Mouse.*' I look down. The water's so clear I can see my boots and the fine, chalk-white sand. Lengths of odd white seaweed bump against my feet. 'What's this seaweed? I ent seen nothing like it before.'

'That ain't seaweed, feathers-for-brains.' Crow's voice is flat and quiet. 'It's bones. The tales say that's what makes the sand so white.'

A sudden shriek pierces the stillness and something smashes into the water right in front of me. My eyes are filled with salt water, and the copper tang of blood touches my tongue.

I spit, then swipe the stinging water from my eyes.

At my feet lies a warped knot of bones, strips of flesh still hanging off it. The world slows. My mouth grows dry.

'*Run!*' I scream.

39
Blood-magyk

We run, seawater dragging at our clothes. Terrodyls screech loud enough to send Crow buckling into the shallows, hands over his ears.

I grab his arm and wrench him to his feet, shouting over the terro-wails. 'You've got to block them out! Keep heart-strong!' His eyes are wide and he struggles for breath, so I pull him along.

Crow grabs the back of my neck. 'Down!' he cries, and shoves me towards the water as a terrodyl dives for us. I scream without hearing my voice, then snatch a breath before the water covers my head.

The bone-sand scrapes the skin from my palms. I open my eyes underwater and see the giant claws of the terrodyl raking through the shallows. Elbowing Crow out of the way, I grab a merwraith scale from my pocket. The terrodyl stabs its beak into the water, and there's an explosion of pain near my eye. I slash at the flesh between two claws, and black blood seeps into the sea.

The terrodyl wheels away with a furious scream.

I drag myself upright. We've almost reached the shore and the cover of thick dark trees. Blood drips down my face and falls into the sea like rain.

Crow's grip on my arm is painful. 'Your *face!*' he says, but then the terrodyl dives again and this time it *snaps* to a stop right in front of us, like someone's caught it in an invisible net. It hovers in the air, breath reeking, great tawny wings edged with fire from the last rays of the sun.

Mouse, its voice creeps, making my toes curl. *Tainted, wicked Mouse! The evil comes from you! Turn away, turn away, Mouse!* slithers the beast-chatter. *Leave, or he will die!*

I can't tear my gaze from the terrodyl's. Its eyes are hot amber torches, glowing with rage. As I stare into them, something begins to stir in the back of my brain. The beast says my name again and now other terrodyls are saying it too.

Mouse! their voices swarm, except somehow it's like they're speaking someone else's words. *Run away, run far away, savage little monster!*

Suddenly I know who's speaking through the terrodyls. My skin crawls. It's like *his* voice has mixed with the beasts'. I gasp. I never knew beast-chatter could be twisted like that, and from such a distance.

267

Get away from us, Stag! I scream. Distantly I'm aware of Crow retching.

The terrodyl lurches forwards, as though it's shaken off the strange bond that held it in place. But before it strikes me the air ripples, like the edges of the world have grown thin and time has slowed. A smell like burnt mist clogs my nose. 'Run!' shouts Crow, in a croaky tone.

I twist to look at him and the edge of his cloak grazes my torn face, making me scream in pain. But then the cloak blurs and shifts, ripples and frays, becomes a pair of *wings*.

A gleaming black crow soars into the air, feathers smeared with my blood, bright gold eyes flashing. It flickers, one beat a ghost, the next solid and real. Then it barrels into the terrodyl with a piercing *thwawk* and plucks at the beast's eyes.

Crow's gone. I always thought Grandma's tales of shape-changers were just fireside stories . . .

'It was *you*,' I breathe, my vision painted fury-red. 'Stag's *flaming* carrion crow!' I stagger through the shallows, towards the shore, as Crow tumbles and circles in the sky, leading the terrodyls away from me.

Song of Sorrow

All that time aboard the *Huntress*, he was spying for Stag. That's why I couldn't hear the crow's beast-chatter – cos it weren't a beast at all. Crow must've been the one who told Stag I went diving, and about the carving. His was the voice I heard talking to Weasel at Dread's Eve. Weasel spoke of something in the water, like unguarded gold . . . flaming hell's teeth! What if he wasn't talking about an Opal at all, but our ship, cos they were in on Stag's mutiny?

I groan aloud as the vastness of all that's happened ripples through my mind. Crow heard and saw *everything*. I burst out of the water, across the crunchy bone-sand and through the treeline, cursing my throat to shreds.

Thunderbolt comes shrilling out of my tunic pocket, covering me in silver footprints. *Thunderbolt knew not to be trusting that dry-land boy!*

You and me both! So why *did* I trust him, even for a wretched heartbeat?

I'm in a clearing, surrounded by bare trees with branches jutting into the sky like antlers. My skin prickles in the chill. *Only thing that should block out the sun is a sail,* I tell Thunderbolt, in the old Tribe-Words. *Trees gift us ships and longbows, but I hate to think what creatures they might hide.*

Frost-melt from higher branches runs down the trunks. I run my swollen tongue over my thirst-cracked lips. Crossing to one of the trees, I crouch on the ground and press my mouth to the trunk to drink. Then I rip a strip of cloth from my breeches and make a bandage for my throbbing face.

Once my bandage is tied I stand and listen. The trees muffle the sound of the waves on the shore. Except for the needle-fine *whirr* of Thunderbolt's wings, there ent a sound in the wood. The quiet makes the hairs stand up on the back of my neck.

Suddenly the silence is shattered by a hoarse cry. '*Mouse!*'

I run towards the other side of the clearing. Ent no way I'm waiting for that gap-toothed sneak to catch up with me. Thunderbolt zips along by my side, sneezing clouds of moondust.

Stag's words from a lifetime ago come back to me. *She's just a trouble-making little girl, too small for her age. She'll never be captain.*

A painful lump lodges in my throat. Stag was right. I couldn't keep my own brother safe. How will I ever be captain? It's all I ever wanted. But why would I want it now, when a crew can turn on their captain like a pack of hungry wolves?

'Mouse! Wait!' Crow blunders through the trees behind me. I dart away from him, uphill along a narrow path. Between the tree branches I catch glimpses of the castle. Dark moss has swept up its side like a giant tentacle rising from the sea. The purple light flickers in the sky.

Glowing orbs peek from the trees – the eyes of unknown creatures, watching me. I'm heart-glad for Thunderbolt, showing me the path.

'Mouse?' calls Crow, voice thick with tears. 'I'm sorry! We're crew; you don't have to do this alone!'

Ice creeps along my spine, through my blood. I won't listen to Crow, not after everything he's done.

I push on, but my legs are clumsy-slow, and the cold stabs deeper into my bones. I breathe the clean air in ragged gasps, then trip over a knotted tree-root.

When I stand I try to run but it's like wading through mud. Tree-tendrils scrape against my face and the wood comes to life with hoots, caws, rustles, scratches. The trees whisper and the wind's breath seems to call, *stay away, stay away* . . . but then another sound pipes through the branches: a heart-sad beast-chatter, filled with regret.

Alone, afeared. Lostlostlostlostlost! Bad feather-flutter! Losteyelosteyelosteye.

Thaw-Wielder? I gasp, stopping in my tracks. Is it too much to hope for? I search the tree branches for her but it's too dark to see anything except blurred shapes. *Thaw!* I yell.

Then a flurry of rustling feathers and a little cloud of frosty breath shoots through the night towards me and lands on my shoulder. *Homehomehomehomehome!*

Oh, Thaw! It really is you, you made it!

My hawk toots, trills, peeps and hoots her heart-gladness to see me, right into my ear, until I'm weak with joy and laughter. Her bright yellow eyes stare up into mine. *Home!* Then she snuggles her head under my chin.

Yes, your home is with me, my brave hawk! But my joy fades as I realise what she was saying before – something about a lost eye. *Is Sparrow in the castle, Thaw? Did you find him?* She's still trembling under my chin so I stroke her head, waiting until she's ready to tell me.

Thunderbolt makes a low grumble-chatter that buzzes through the dark. *You keep going for Tangle-Hair, you promised Thunderbolt you bring him home!* She races in circles around my head.

Thaw untucks herself from me and stares daggers at

the moonsprite. *Bright-bug not there. Bug didn't see thing of many legs take eye!*

Thing of many legs? I ask her. *Was it a – spider?*

She turns to stare up the hill. *Creature from the sea, trapped under. I hear Tangle-Hair's song, fly closer to look, eye in beak – carry not easy, make hawk-heart flurry-skip! Then chased! By featherless beast–*

A terrodyl! My blood boils. I'd bet anything it was sent after her by Stag.

Thaw hoots in agreement. *Then, eye fall! Splash! Snatched by legs-beast. Heart-sorry feather-fear!* She hides her little head under my chin again and I stroke her back, full of pride in her.

Ent your fault, I soothe. *You brought the Opal here, just like I asked, clever girl. Let's go and get it and find Sparrow. Can you show me where the eye fell?*

Upupup! she squawks. *Up high!*

When we reach the hilltop, purple light crackles through the thundercloud onto the sprawling castle. Two towering iron gates face me. A full moon hangs in the sky, shrouded with a red veil. I shudder. Grandma always said a blood-stained moon draws bad things from their nests.

I crane back my neck and watch as terrodyls flit in and out of the caves in the castle walls.

Thunderbolt thuds into my pocket. *Want to go from*

here, Black-Hair! This is bad place, drifts her muffled voice.

You said I had to keep going! Ent no turning back now, quiver-heart. Somewhere behind us, down the hill, I hear Crow blundering closer so I step quickly towards the gates. I keep to the shadows, praying the terrodyls don't see me. The earth's all bumpy and lumpy with huge, buried tree-roots. *If my hawk says my brother's in there, and the Opal too, then we're going in after them.*

Thaw-Wielder gives a soft trill and leaps from my shoulder to glide along beside me. *Eye fell to bad-roost, in water below!*

When I press my palms against the gates they crack open easy as anything. I frown, cos I'd half reckoned on having to climb the walls. Skin prickling, I slip into a large courtyard, all the flagstones pierced by weeds.

I tiptoe towards a sweep of stone steps leading to a heavy wooden door. Fear steals across my skin. Why ent this place guarded? And where is the water below?

'Mouse!' calls Crow urgently. 'Wait!'

'Shut it, slackwit!' I hiss. I cast around, peering into the shadows of the courtyard, but the castle's blotted out the light, making it hard to see.

My breath steams in the cold. *Thunderbolt, can you show me the way?*

She answers with a half-sob, half-growl, but she flicks

from my pocket and zooms for the door, casting a trail of chalky moondust in her wake.

When I reach the door I shove against an iron door-knocker in the shape of a tentacle coiled around a whale's tail. The door creaks inwards.

Thaw lands on my shoulder and resettles her wings. *Feather-fear*, she trills. *Watchful-times for slither-arms!*

Why? Is this where the eye—

'Mouse, stop, you can't just walk right up to the door!' Crow rushes across the courtyard and grabs my arm.

'Get off me!'

Thaw nips his fingers. 'Yargh!' he cries, snatching back his hand. I step inside.

'Don't! What if it's a—' Crow starts.

Before I can draw another breath the stone slab beneath my feet falls away, dumping me into a slippery tunnel.

Thunderbolt sputters moon-sparks. *Black-Hair!* But me and Thaw-Wielder fall away from her, down into the belly of the earth below the castle.

41
Battle Scars

Thaw-Wielder, fly, quick! I scream, but the stone seals us in and shuts out even the faintest light. My hawk clings to my hair and my belly flies into my throat. I'm sliding so fast, down and down and down. The air smells of ash and salt, damp and rot.

I try to catch the walls, the floor, *anything* with my nails, but I'm just scrabbling at smooth stone. Here and there roots have broken into the tunnel and I grab at them but they snap cos I'm going so fast.

It dwells here! squeals Thaw, flapping herself into a frenzy.

That – ent – helping, Thaw-beast! I gasp, reaching up to try and get her claws out of my scalp.

How much further can this tunnel go? It twists and snakes left and right but always heads down, deep below the ground.

Finally, the tunnel widens. There's a bump in the stone and my belly drops away as I'm flung into the air.

Thaw tries to pluck at my cloak with her beak but I plunge away from her and crash down, down, down into stagnant water.

I break the surface, looking around me, but whatever place I've fallen into is blanketed in darkness. My blood leaps as I remember the dragonfish eye drops. Just one drop of liquid in each eye lights the cavern with fire as green as the fire spirits.

I'm in a wide chamber under the ground. Thaw zooms round and round in a panic. A voice, quiet at first, begins to sing from somewhere under the water. Something brushes against my leg as it gropes through the gloom, whispering some ancient battle song.

Surrender your kin, for the life of your king,
Let your blood stop and stutter, never utter a mutter.
Down in the depths they will drown.
Seek for the Storm-Opal Cro-o-own.

Your king's dead, I want to whisper, but my mouth's too dry. Something strong and rubbery twines around my leg. A yell rushes from my lips as it tugs me underwater. I reach down and my heart sickens when I feel the smooth, springy flesh of a tentacle. The suckers are clamped to my skin like limpets to the hull of a ship and I can't prise them off. This castle *is* guarded – by a giant squid.

I'll carve you into little pieces, comes a colder-than-death whisper.

The squid must be the slither-arms that Thaw-Wielder was talking about. It must have the Opal!

As I'm pulled deep underwater, black spots dance before my eyes. Below my thrashing legs, a green glint sparkles on the floor. My head grows light and woozy. I grab the merwraith scale from my pocket and jab downwards, slashing the suckers off me. The squid screams and snatches away its sticky tentacle.

I reach for the surface, burst through and gulp for air. Hateful whispers rise from the depths as tentacles reach for me again. I kick them away.

I swim towards one of the walls, but it's all slippery, with nothing to grip onto.

The squid tugs me again so I grab a breath before the water covers my head. Underwater I slash downwards with my scale, but the tentacle drags me faster until I'm on the bottom of the pool. I force my heart to slow and my muscles to relax, cos they're the rules for diving on one breath, and though Grandma always said it weren't my destiny to drown, now ent the time to put it to the test.

Deep in the depths they will drown, throbs the whisper

again, louder. My skin prickles. I stab into the tentacle around my leg and spring away from it.

When I look over my shoulder the squid spirals towards me, oozing swirls of black ink. Its skin's thin enough to show the huge black heart inside its body, quiver-pulsing. *Made the feathered one drop it once*, the squid rasps. *Not letting a two-legs steal it now!*

The squid shoots another cloud of ink straight into my face, but I slash forward. It dodges. As I squint through the murk I can still make out the flicker of the squid's heart.

Da's message flashes into my head. *There is grave danger – find the Storm-Opals of Sea, Sky and Land.* Thaw saved one of the Opals once. Now I've got to get it back.

I'll have to take another breath soon. The squid snickers hatefully. My mind grows foggy.

Creature, put down your sharp tooth. Sleep forever in my domain! the squid calls.

No! I throw myself onto the squid, putting all my weight on top of it, pushing it down. It flails and slams its tentacles against me. The suckers pinch and rip. Soon my skin is covered in sucker-shaped blisters, but I don't let go.

I raise my scale again and the squid hisses and tears at my face but I plunge the scale deep into its heart. Its blood threads into the water and its scream shakes the last breath from my lungs. I quickly cut away the tentacles that have suckered onto me and cast around for the Opal – there!

Rough stone scrapes my fingertips as I prise the green Opal from the cavern floor. I clench it in my hand and kick for the surface.

When I break through, sputtering and gasping, Thaw-Wielder thuds onto the top of my head with a relieved trill. I tread water and stare at the stone in my hand. It's Grandma's glass eye, all right. When I hold it to my own there are tumbled other worlds inside, just as there are beneath the sea. My blood rushes and thrills through my veins; I can feel the Opal's power.

Suddenly, there's a dredging, grating din, and more water slops into the chamber from a moss-covered spout on the wall. This cesspool ent just for keeping folk out of the castle – seems like it's for keeping things in too.

I drop the Opal into my pocket. The chamber is filling fast. Soon there won't be any air left to breathe. I cast around wildly. The water rises. I'm pushed higher, towards the ceiling. *Thaw-Wielder! Can you see a way out?* I call, but my hawk is a quaking ball of feathers, huddled on the spout.

'Mouse!' echoes a distant voice.

'Crow!' He's come looking for me – must've used his crow-shape to fly into the castle. Heart-gladness surges through my blood. 'I'm in here!' I splutter. 'The water's rising!' He don't reply and I smash the water with a fist in frustration. '*Crow?*'

There's a scuffling from beyond the wall to my left. 'I'm here!' he yells. 'There's a door but I can't get it open!'

'Is there anything that looks like it might drain the water?'

'I don't know!'

'Search! Quick!' I tread water, only a few feet of air left above my head.

'What do you *think* I'm doing?' he bellows.

The fire of the dragonfish drops casts light over the door he must be talking about. But I can barely make out its edges against the rest of the wall.

Thisthisthis, keens Thaw. She flits near the door, brushing her tail feathers against a rough, jutting piece of stone in the wall. Then she darts towards the ceiling as the water rises higher.

Clever hawk! I yell. 'I think there's a lever! Push it, quick!' I scream to Crow.

'I see it!' shouts Crow. There's a pause, and a groan. 'But it's stuck!'

Water floods the cavern in great gushes. Lumps of moss and old leaves splash in as well, and then a dead rat *plunks* sickeningly into the pool.

Deadthingdeadthingdeadthing! shrills my poor sea-hawk, almost out of her wits.

'Shove that flaming lever, unless you want us to drown!' My head bumps against the ceiling. Thaw-Wielder sits in the water next to me, eyes bright with fear.

When I tell you to, take the deepest breath you can, I whisper to her. *And you hold onto it.* But her beast-chatter's slipped out of reach, like she's too terrified to hear me. A great sob flees my lips and echoes through the chamber. *Thaw? Stay with me, brave hawk! You've done so much more than any sea-hawk should have to do for a girl. I love you so much.* It's my fault she's here; I put too much weight on her feathers. She should be flying free with her kin.

The water creeps up the back of my neck. 'Crow!' I shout. 'Help us!'

Thaw warbles low in her throat, feathers twitching. I reach into my pocket and wrap my fingers around the Opal that was Grandma's eye. So this is where the voyage ends.

Distant as a dream, Crow whoops. 'Hang on, I think I've got it!' There's a *crunch* of stone.

As suddenly as the flood started, water begins to gurgle and drain. I gather my shivering hawk to my cloak and kiss her head. Her feathers are freezing and beads of water roll off them. *We'll be all right now, Thaw.*

When the water drains below the door it bursts open. Crow stands there, hair on end where he's been pulling at it. Thunderbolt squeals and turns somersaults in the air.

'Heart-thanks,' I tell Crow. 'Let's go and find my brother and get out of here.' Thaw-Wielder nestles in my hair and my heart soars into my throat. I've got my brave hawk and the first of the Opals. I put my hand in my pocket and hold the Opal as we walk – it makes me feel close to Grandma for the first time since Stag shot her. Now to get my brother back, too. Together we creep along a slimy passageway, into the heart of the castle.

Castle Whalesbane

The moss-covered passage slopes upwards. Lamps hiss and sputter. We walk hunched, shoulder to shoulder, fists drawn up. The silence makes my breath too loud – it feels like creeping through a tomb. Thunderbolt skims along in front of us, shedding ripples of moonlight.

Every inch of me screams that I should run, cos what if Sparrow's waiting for me to save him?

Voices murmur in the distance. The walls are smudged with grease and stale air crawls into my nose. We step towards a spiral stairway and start to climb.

Sudden as thunder, footsteps ring against the stone. We crouch low in the gloom and peer over the top step into a dark passageway. Thaw trembles on top of my head and Thunderbolt dives into my pocket.

Stooped figures in rustling robes blur through the dark, then vanish from sight. I breathe out, listening to the echo of dripping water. *Plip, plip, plip.* It feels like even the warmth of my breath could betray us.

When the footsteps have dwindled, I make myself as small as I can, tiptoe up the last step into the passageway, and follow the robed figures. Crow scurries after me.

'Who were they?' whispers Crow.

'I don't know. But the legends say that when the last King of Sea, Sky and Land was alive he kept mystiks in a tower, who spun magyk to guard the Storm-Opals.'

'But why would anyone stay here?'

I glance around and catch his meaning – this is a place for the dead. Shreds of cloth hang in tatters at smashed windows, waving in the wind like the seaweed-hair of merwraiths. The walls have been devoured by damp and fungus, and sticky cobwebs hang from the ceiling. They grasp at my hair as I push through them. How could Stag send my brother to such a ghoulish place?

The deeper we pass into the castle the brighter Thunderbolt glows, and I'm heart-glad for her again. She *whirrs* free from my pocket and streaks ahead to light the way. Thaw flicks free from the crook of my arm to fly with her and I smile at Crow. My hawk's heart-strength is returning.

Suddenly there's movement to our right and I whip around to face it, fists bunched. Two boys stand there, one raising his fists back at me. He's got scrag-black hair, a blood-soaked scrap of cloth covering half his face, a sea-hawk and a bulb of moonlight hovering above his shoulder . . . I laugh, and quickly clamp my hand over my mouth to stifle the noise. My reflection in the looking-glass does the same thing.

I'm taller and thinner than I remember. My skin looks grey and my eyes shine wildly, but it must be me, cos Ma's dragonfly gleams on my cloak and Bear's amber necklace sits in the hollow of my throat.

Crow breathes out quickly. 'Ruddy place. Come on! I feel like getting this over with, don't you?'

'Wait, just a heartbeat.' I touch the dragonfly for heart-strength, step close to the looking-glass and snatch down the bandage on my face, wincing as it catches the ragged skin underneath.

The wound throbs sharply. It scrawls from the corner of my mouth to the outer edge of my right eye, slowly oozing blood. My chest squeezes as I pull the bandage up again and step away from the glass. Least I never was a preener like Squirrel.

'Vanity ain't becoming to yer. Let's go,' Crow whispers, tugging my cloak.

Soon we're on a balcony that looks out over a deserted long hall, with a great throne hunched on a raised dais. As I stare at three empty settings in the throne, each about the size of a Storm-Opal, a chain rattles in the passageway we came through.

Thunderbolt dulls her light and flies inside my cloak with a tiny growl. Thaw-Wielder zips onto the top of my head. I back away, pulling Crow with me until the balcony railing presses against us.

Two figures move across the balcony to another passage on the opposite side and pause before a door. One of them takes a key from a chain and turns it in the lock with a loud *thunk*. Then they slip inside and the door slams shut.

Thunderbolt rushes up my neck and into my hair, with cold soft feet. *Follow, Black-Hair!*

What did you think I was gonna do, dulse-brain? I whisper.

Dulse-brain, peeps my hawk. *Worms?*

I whisk to the door and press my ear against it. Faint voices ebb from inside, too quiet to hear the words. I step back. The mystiks – if that's what they are – might say something about Sparrow. I've got to get inside, but I can't let them see me.

You must not fight your powers. Grow them. Use your fear, whispers Rattlebones deep in my mind.

'What're you thinking?' Crow murmurs by my ear.

My heart thuds. I bend down to squint through the keyhole, and then it hits me – I know what to do.

'I need to go into a dream-dance.'

43
Dead Reckoning

'A *what?*' Crow asks.

I lean my forehead against the wood, listening hard for the voices inside, but they're too fleeting to catch. There ent time to fret too much about my dream-dance. I've just got to do it.

'It's a thing that – happens to me,' I tell him. Then I shake my head. 'No, it's different now. It's more like something I reckon I can do, travelling in the space between sleeping and waking.'

I turn away from the door and curl up behind a crumbling pillar. I shut my eyes and hook onto my fear for Sparrow, like Rattlebones said. A gouging sob rises through me, and I can't face the burden. But then I gather the power of my terror at losing Sparrow and try using it to pluck at my spirit. It drags, then pushes against the edges of my body, shoots towards the door and I fall through, dream-slow. The room smells of rotted kelp, oar-weed and barnacles. The blood-red walls are daubed with runes, lit by flickering lanterns. One of the cloaked, hunched figures paces up and down, whilst the other stands stiffly.

'A terrodyl brought Stag's news at dusk,' rasps the pacing man, face a shimmering blur. 'The sister has escaped. She is merely a girl-child, and no threat to us. But the crown is what concerns him – it eludes him still.'

'But what of the boy-witch in the high tower?' says the other. I gasp as he jabs at the air with a gnarled finger, and a picture of a skin-and-bones boy with yellow-gold hair throbs into being – Sparrow! He shivers against a wall, arms wrapped tightly around his knees. 'Stag may expect the Order of Mystiks to continue to aid him in his quest for the crown, but for how long must we let the boy shake? He may draw the whales to shore, where their bellies can be searched for the crown, but if he should die in the process, think of the waste!'

'The scattering of the Opals has unleashed the old magyk. It brought the terrible storm that increased the boy's powers – that is one benefit. But now we are at risk of an ice age, which would allow the Fangtooths to take over all the land! How could Stag let the navigator steal the Opals from under his nose?'

The second mystik clenches and unclenches his fist. 'The squid claimed the Sea-Opal when the bird brought it to our hearth. But Sky and Land are still unaccounted for.'

No, you rancid old molluscs. My spirit grins. I've got the Sea-Opal!

'The boy's powers could be great, yet daily he weakens. He must shake; we must draw the whales close. But before long, we may have blood on our hands.'

My dream-heart lurches in alarm. I've got to find the high tower and get Sparrow and my friends away from here! My spirit prickles and jolts, like tiny claws have hooked into it to pull me back to my body.

One of the mystiks looks up, quick as a snake.

My dream-dance breaks into jagged splinters, fracturing my sight and my hearing. The room fades as I blend through the wood of the door.

I lie quaking on the floor, Thunderbolt and Thaw-Wielder fizzing round like mad things. Crow leans over me. 'I've seen someone do a thing like that before,' he says, face pale and slack. 'Next time, you need a binding – elsewise how d'you know you'll be able to get back?'

'Get back?' I ask, fright nibbling at me. 'What's a bind–' Then the door clangs open and I lurch to my feet and run, quick as anything, through the cobwebs.

The mystiks rush out into the passageway. 'Halt, trespassers! How did you breach our walls?'

'Come on!' I yell to Crow, but one of the mystiks grabs his wrist and he staggers.

'Go, don't wait for me!' he yells. 'I'll find another way!'

290

'But—'

'Run!'

Thaw, Thunderbolt, with me!

'Stop!' one of the mystiks shouts.

I race towards a spiral stairway and plunge headfirst into darkness. Sparrow's in the tower, and that means *up*.

Thunderbolt? She answers with a spark of light that falls onto the grey stone of the stairway.

The mystik's footsteps slap closer and closer. As I turn each twist of the spiral, his shadow looms on the walls.

I slip and my outstretched hands slam against the stone, making me cry out in pain. But I get up quickly and run on. The stairway spirals higher and tighter, the steps narrowing.

A hand grabs my ankle. I kick out behind me, there's a groan and I run faster. A circular landing appears at the top of the spiral, lit by glimmering lanterns set in sconces above a door. I tear free of the stairwell, but my foot catches on the last step.

I land hard, the air knocked clean out of my lungs. My mouth opens and closes as I fight for air like a gutted fish. Thaw wheels around me, a brown and white blur of protection.

Run, stupid clutter-sculpin! chitters Thunderbolt.

291

I scuffle to my feet and wrangle with the nearest door. It's locked. I rattle the handle of the next one. The mystik wheezes to the top of the stairwell, a thin smile stretched across his gaunt face.

Orbs of purple lightning – just like Sparrow's in the storm – crackle at his fingertips.

44
Storm-brewing

'Where's my brother?' I shout, trying to wriggle the merwraith scale from my pocket. 'Sparrow!'

'You have no brother.' He throws a sizzle-bolt of lightning onto the floor, filling my eyes with smoke.

Grrrrrbrrrrrggg! growls Thunderbolt, flying into his face, but he flicks her away and she yelps when his lightning chars one of her wings. Thaw-Wielder scoops her up, breaking her fall, and she streaks the sea-hawk's striped wings with silver footprints.

'Talk sense,' I snap, as I blink and swipe the air to clear it. 'What you done to him?' Then a bruise-black tentacle unravels from the ceiling. I dart back and look up – rows of eyes stare at me from the rafters. They're squid, wallowing in damp, dripping foul slime. The tentacle sweeps towards me but I pull a scale from my pocket and drive its point deep into the flesh, gagging at the stench of its blood.

'There is a boy, but he has no family. We have given

him a home, and the power of knowledge. He was nothing before he came here.' The mystik's smile is like a knife-slash.

'*I'm* his family! His home is with *me*!' I yell, my tears blurring his face. That's when I know what Grandma meant about a cabin being naught but wooden walls – cos Sparrow and me will always have a home if we're together.

Another tentacle unravels in front of me, reaching for my neck. I curl my fingers around the scale but my hawk gets there first, sinking her talons into the tentacle. It slinks away.

'This is the ancient seat of power,' snaps the mystik. 'You have no right to maim the watchers!'

'Them beasts should be in the sea, not guarding some dead king's pile of stone!' I make my eyes danger-hard. 'I ent leaving 'til you tell me where my brother is!'

'Oh, you're not leaving at all,' he says, eyes glinting blackly within his cowl. 'You needn't fret about that.'

A tentacle thuds to the floor and creeps towards me. It grasps for my pocket. *Sea-foam gem!* oozes a fetid beast-chatter.

Ick, get away! I scold. As I tear another scale from my pocket, ready to jab the tentacle, the Opal bounces onto the floor. Eel-quick I snatch it up again but the mystik's face fills with hate. 'Foolish girl,' he crackles.

'You don't know what you're dealing with.'

Hot, sick fear spreads through my belly. I spin and wrench at another door and it flies open, almost knocking me out cold. '*Sparrow!*' I yell, tearing down the passageway. 'Sparrow! Where are you?'

The mystik zaps his lightning at my heels. I run faster. Thaw-Wielder glides by my side, urging me on with heart-bright yellow eyes, and from her back Thunderbolt sends up a tiny icicle-scream.

The floor blackens and slime squelches underfoot. Blue light flickers along the wall and there's a hot crackle in the damp, close air. I tear on, almost leaving my skin behind.

I fly along the passageway, heading straight for a door with purple light spilling from a crack underneath. Another lightning bolt strikes my heels and I shriek, shield my face with my arms and crash through the half-rotten door. I land in a crumpled bundle, surrounded by splinters of wood. Shaken, I lift my head.

I'm in a circular iron-grey room, full of that restless feeling before a storm. A gaggle of mystiks stand with their backs to me. Whale-song drifts through the narrow window, splintered now and then by terrodyl screams.

The mystiks chant eager, greed-laden words. 'Draw them, drown them, draw them to the land! Draw them, drown them, draw them to the land!'

They're loud enough not to notice me. 'Slackwitted old quahogs,' I mutter. But the mystik chasing me can't be far behind, so I scuttle onto my hands and knees. Something twitches and jerks on the floor beyond the mystiks. My gut flips as I drag myself to my feet. It's Sparrow. He really is here! My heart riots with gladness, and I run towards him—

'Drown them—'

I fall to my knees, then scramble up again—

'– draw them—'

And inch along the edge of the room to where he lies, an ache in my throat.

'– drown them on the land!'

The roof above Sparrow has crumbled away, leaving the room open to sky, where a thundercloud grumbles. I slip closer, with a quick glance back at the mystiks. They chant feverishly, eyes clamped shut.

Sparrow's eyes are open, but they're both veiled with white film. His yellow hair stands out at odd angles. I press my hand to my mouth as I draw closer, cos the sight of him after all this time and everything that's happened is too much spear-pain and soaring joy all mixed up. His arms are raised into the air, like they were that time when he shook in our cabin, moons and stars ago. Purple snakes of lightning thread their way from his fingertips to the thundercloud. Every few heartbeats, the room flashes the colour of a stormy sea.

Pain suddenly *whooshes* up my nose as the tears spring to my eyes. 'Sparrow!' I whisper. 'Wake up!'

'Draw them, drown them, draw them to the land!' drone the mystiks, drowning out my voice.

I move nearer to my brother, my throat choked. Black and purple bruises bloom across his skin.

'Drown them, draw them, drown them on the land!'

I'm almost close enough to touch him when raindrops slide from the thundercloud onto Sparrow's face, and his shaking settles. He starts singing a sad song, full of icebergs and ancient battles, but his voice ent the silver bell I remember. Now it's barbed with hate.

He's singing to the whales. But as the words of the mystiks strike deep into my brain, I realise they're setting a trap for the whales, to help Stag find the crown.

'Don't!' I drop to my knees beside Sparrow and press my wet face into the woollen robe he's wearing. 'Wake up, little too-soon!'

He stops singing and I rock back on my heels, watching his face. Slowly he turns his head towards me, blinking, but the membranes covering his eyes are thick. I choke back a sob. 'Who is that?' he demands.

One by one, the mystiks stop their droning and a

cold hush, like heavy black wings, settles over the room.

One speaks in a slither-scale voice. 'The one you hate most of all.'

I whirl around and glower at him. 'Shut it, triplewart! Why would he hate me?' But even as I spit the words, terror dives into my heart, cos Sparrow needed me and I wasn't there to keep him safe.

With a strained effort, Sparrow drags his lightning away from the thundercloud and gathers it between his hands. The light flickers across his skin, and his blind eyes never leave my face. It's like he's looking right into me, down to my bones. 'Mouse?' his voice quivers.

He goes blurry as tears fill my eyes. 'Yes.' My breath comes in ragged sobs. 'It's me. I've come to get you.'

'Stay away from me.' His voice is bitter, but fear dwells there too, and that's the worst thing of all.

I stare. 'But why – we've got to get out!' A sound echoes off the walls, like a trapped creature rattling around the room. The mystiks are laughing.

Sparrow's lightning sparks and gathers in a jagged knot between his fingertips. I can barely take a breath before he throws a crackling vine straight at me.

I flatten myself to the ground but the lightning shears my shoulder, sending a stab of pain down my arm.

The mystiks form a circle around us. 'You cannot alter fate,' says one. 'A greater destiny gathers here. You should never have come.'

'I'm his family. He needs me!'

'Is it not *you* who needs *him?*' asks one with a hunched back. Is he the one that went after Crow? My heart jangles. What's happened to the wrecker? The mystik's robes whisper against the floor as he creaks closer to me and stoops to hiss in my ear. 'You have *nothing*. He has power.'

'You addled loons.' My hand's so slip-slimy with stagnant squid blood I can barely keep hold of my merwraith scale. A skinny tentacle unravels from the rafters, slithers around my wrist and squeezes hard, until I drop it to the floor. 'You're killing him!'

'We have shown him his birth-right,' rasps another age-crackled voice. 'He has power that could be used to dominate and destroy, to bring the world to its knees. This is where he belongs.'

'He has power for good, 'n all.' I struggle against the tentacle bind. 'You don't know *nothing*. And he belongs with me!'

'His power for good is trifling. His power for darkness has only just begun to bloom.'

I fish around on the floor for my scale. There's a sizzle and I feel heat on my face. When I look across to him, Sparrow's raised another ball of lightning.

Before he can throw it at me, Thunderbolt flits

off Thaw's back and skitters towards him. *Tangle-Hair! Thunderbolt missed him so!*

Sparrow's eyes widen as he stares at the moonsprite. The lightning fades and seeps back inside his fingertips. His eyelids flutter. Are his eyes clearing? Can he see her shape? 'Thunderbolt?' he whispers, like he's dredging up a memory from a thousand years ago.

'I brought her with me, to find you,' I tell him. 'What I said was wrong, but now we've got to—'

My words are drowned out as the mystiks begin to chant again, pressing closer to us. A tentacle slithers to my chest and squeezes.

You keep away from him! chitters Thunderbolt. She stands on my brother's forehead, puffing furious clouds of moondust.

I thrash against the tentacle but it tightens, forcing out my breath. There's barely enough space for my lungs to fill again.

The hunchbacked mystik smiles, shark-sharp. 'We will make the boy shake enough to dredge the whales from wherever they've been hiding and bring them to our isle. And then, once we have found the crown, it will be for the gods to decide his fate.'

The whales have been hiding? Hope kindles in my belly. Maybe the whale that swallowed me spread my warning about Stag.

The hunchback turns to the other mystiks. 'When you have brewed a fresh storm, strong enough to make the boy shake again, throw the girl to the terrodyls.'

45

Tentacles

Thaw-Wielder sends up a mighty squawk and fixes the mystik with fury-bright eyes. She bolts towards him, powerful claws outstretched, and plunges them into his back. *Heart-care, Thaw!* I cry. The mystik drops to his knees with a yelp of pain and my hawk swarms around his head, screeching her fury.

I throw myself forward and bite deep into the flesh of the tentacle wrapped around me. My mouth fills with bitter slime. I spit. The tentacle uncoils like a spring, shooting back into the dark rafters. 'Get away from my brother, or else,' I rage at the mystiks, vaulting to my feet.

The hunchback turns back to me and grates a laugh, the others joining him. 'Or what?'

All around, tentacles thud to the floor from the rafters. *A mouse should have the sharpest senses of all*, says Bear in my memory. I grip his amber necklace and tune my hearing low. What if I can use my beast-chatter?

My ears sharpen to a dark muttering and a damp

breathing. I peer into the rafters, at the misery-laden squid. *Miss the sea, don't you?* I call.

The squid's wet, slithering breaths grow louder and they begin to shuffle their sore-ridden bodies like they're listening to me. But the tentacles creep closer, grasping for my ankles. I dart back.

'What is she doing?' hisses the hunchback. 'That sound, in her throat – it's not possible . . .'

I know that feeling, sucker-beasts. I miss her too. Inside I'm panicked, sickened. My voice shakes. A tentacle brushes the back of my leg. I whirl around and kick it away. *It's these blood-blisters that're keeping you here, just to make you do their bidding,* I cry desperately.

Around the room, a hiss rises into the air. *Sea,* pipes a damp voice. Thunderbolt clutches Sparrow's hair, eyes wide with fright.

The tentacles begin to writhe, clasping after the mystiks. Shouts ring through the gloom. Mystiks slam into walls, and screams echo as tentacles tighten around chests and over mouths. Lightning flashes as the mystiks battle the squid.

Sparrow is a wild thing crouched on the floor, cradling one of his hands like an injured animal. Hackles of lightning bristle along his back. I run to his side and bundle him up in my arms, yelping as the sparks burn me.

He wails, low in his throat, and bites and scratches at my face with nails like claws. I'm heart-glad for my bandage. 'Calm your grizzle-gruzzlings! We've got to go!'

He wriggles violently. 'Lemme be!'

'Wanna stay here with this lot of slackwits, do you?'

A frantic tapping comes from above. I look up and there's a crescent-moon window at the top of the wall. Crow's face is pressed against the smeared glass. He looks to his left and right, shrugs, and wraps his elbow in his cloak. Then he smashes the window. I cover Sparrow's face as shards of glass fall through the air. Crow drops a rope over the sill. 'C'mon!'

Thaw-Wielder and Thunderbolt flit up to join Crow.

I stoop to one knee. 'Get on my back!'

Sparrow scowls, but his blind eyes are fixed on the air next to my head. 'You lemme alone!'

'Don't be stupid—'

'I *ent* stupid! Why'd you always say that to me?' His fists are curled tight by his sides, and his charred fingertips look to be brewing up a tiny storm of purple light.

'All right, I take it back! But I came here to get you out, not to hang around bilge-belching. We have to go, now!'

Sparrow's scowl fades, leaving him skinny and pale

and frighted-looking. 'They told me over and over that you wouldn't come!'

'What do they know about us?' I ask fiercely. 'I promise, I'm gonna make you feel safe again. Come *on*!'

His face crumples. 'I'm always frighted! I'm frighted the shakes are gonna kill me!'

A lump swells in my throat. 'They won't,' I tell him, taking his hand. 'Not while I'm with you.'

I kneel and he climbs onto my back, hooking an arm round my neck to hold on.

'The *Opal*!' shouts the hunchbacked mystik, pointing up at us. 'Stop them!' Then he screams as a tentacle drags him off his feet and through a crack in the wall.

Crow casts worry-creased looks behind him and for a heartbeat I wonder if he'll shape-change and fly off without us. But even after everything he's done, I reckon me and Sparrow might've found a real-life land-lurker friend.

I move towards the rope and jump on, scuttling upwards as though I was in the rigging. When we reach the top Crow pulls us onto the window-ledge.

'Who's there?' asks Sparrow, looking around.

'Someone who can help us,' I say with a nervous glance at Crow. Guilt spills heat across my cheeks – not cos it's forbidden to crew with a land-lurker. I ent sure I care about that no more. It's cos I ent ready to tell Sparrow I've crewed up with the boy that smuggled him.

Crow's face is smeared with guilt, too. He jerks his thumb at the darkness outside. 'Shall we get going, sea-slugs?'

Outside, the spindly shapes of terrodyls clutter the night sky. Thaw-Wielder settles onto my shoulder. I squeeze through the window and the icy air helps clear my fuddle-head. Sparrow's clamped his arm too tight around my neck, so I pull at him until I can breathe easier and then start to climb down the wall. Crow scuttles out of the window after us.

Then Crow's boot slips, kicking me in the head. 'Argh! Watch it, pearl-brain!' My toe seeks for another foot-hold but there's naught to meet it but empty air. I fall through a black cave in the wall and land on a soft floor. I stand and prise Sparrow's arm off my neck as I blink against the darkness. Crow drops inside after us.

'Could you take a bit more care?' I snipe. 'We've got to get all the way to the ground and run!'

'I thought you could do with a rest,' fires Crow, eyes flaring. 'I'm that nice to yer, ain't I? Saving yer ruddy neck, *again* . . .'

'All right, I'm sorry!' I tell him, cos his face is thin and grey, showing the strain of the magyk he had to use to help us.

Sparrow tugs my cloak. 'Something's here.' Thunderbolt stands on his shoulder, and his blind white eyes shine in her light. 'I can hear scuffling and – *snuffling*,' he whispers.

As my eyes sharpen in the dark, the edges of the cave grow clearer. I put out a hand to touch the wall and snatch it away again when my fingers touch cold, smooth bone. 'Hell's bells,' I murmur.

46
Free Flight

'You, keep quiet,' I hiss at Crow. *Thunderbolt, to me.* The moonsprite leaves Sparrow's shoulder and flits to my side.

I stoop to whisper in Sparrow's ear. 'Don't move.'

Thunderbolt drifts deeper into the cave. I step silently after her, Thaw nervously nipping my earlobe. The moonsprite's glow touches a frosty cloud of – I stop dead – *breath.* We've landed inside a terrodyl nest.

Up ahead lies a great pile of bones, held together with clotted blood and torn scraps of cloth. A huge terrodyl sprawls there, her slumber-breath rattling through the cave, stinking and hot. A brood of youngsters sleep beneath her wings – but one of them is awake. It stares at me with amber eyes and cocks its head in curiosity.

There's another tug on my cloak – Sparrow's stumbled after me. Panic grips my throat. I put out a hand to keep him from getting any closer to the nest. 'What is it?' he whispers.

'Everyone freeze,' I mutter, not taking my eyes from the young creature. 'It's a terrodyl nest.'

Sparrow whimpers. Behind me, I hear the *whoosh* of Crow's breath. The terrodyl snaps its head towards them. Thunderbolt squeals and darts onto the top of Sparrow's head, hiding in a clump of tangled hair.

I put my arm across Sparrow and push him behind me. Then a thought leaps. If Stag's beast-chatter was controlling the beasts before, maybe mine can too, and maybe that'll be enough to save our hides . . .

Thaw, go to Sparrow. I crouch low, slowly stretch out a hand towards the watching terrodyl and clear my throat.

Fierce thing of the skies, I beast-whisper, bowing my head to appeal to the creature's bloated pride. The old beast-chatter wildness plucks at my blood.

The terrodyl blinks its lantern eyes. *Wingless crawler speaks to me? I chop the head off for my brothers.*

No, strong warrior. We worship your speed and grace as lords of the sky. I swallow but my pipes are dry and tight. *We ask you to fly with us, far from this place.*

The terrodyl spits strings of goo. *Big crawler, small crawler, flutter-feather and glow-bug are fit-for-foods, not fit-for-flyings.*

'What's it saying—' starts Sparrow, but I clamp my hand over his mouth.

309

But you are, great winged beast. You are made for flyings, even more than the sea-hawks. Come quick, come quiet. Only you are the best – do not wake the others.

I'm so starved and wounded that the beast-chatter takes the last of my strength. My head swims. But the terrodyl's eyes are agleam with pride, and it wriggles out from under its mother's wing. I think it's working! It totters clumsily down from the great nest and treads towards us, claws already as long as my forearm, even though it's still a bab.

It rasps its tongue across its lips and I bite my cheek to keep from gagging at the stench of rotten breath. *We will slurp crawler's challenge. But we will fit-for-food them later. We will drag them back to our nest*, it says.

Sparrow tears my hand from his mouth. 'It's not fair – you can hear it *and* see it. I can just see a shadowy lump. *Tell* me what it said.'

'It's going to help us,' I say, leaving out the part about gobbling us later. 'Climb onto my back again. We're going for a sky-ride.'

Suddenly there's a rustle and a snort from the nest. The mother's eyes are open, and they're full of fiery rage. She stands up. The spiny ridges along her back are tall enough to scrape the roof of the cave.

'Now!' I shout. Sparrow leaps onto my back.

The young terrodyl moves to the mouth of the

cave and spreads its wings wide, ignoring the clipped screams of its mother.

I run after it, loosening Sparrow's arm around my neck to keep him from throttling me. But he grabs onto me even tighter, tearing my cloak open in his panic.

There's a soft thud as something falls to the floor.

I whirl round. The mother is climbing down from the nest, and a whole row of curious eyes peer from their bed of bones.

On the ground, a few paces behind us, lies Ma's dragonfly brooch. My belly drops into my boots. '*Bleeding* viperfish!'

I race to the young terrodyl and heave Sparrow onto its back. 'Don't go!' he shrieks. Crow swings onto the terrodyl's back behind Sparrow, an awed grin raising the corner of his mouth.

'I ent losing that brooch now!' I sprint back into the cave.

'What are you *doing?*' yells Crow.

The mother terrodyl slinks closer and turns the brooch over with a huge, blood-caked claw.

That's mine, I tell her, rage and fear cutting my voice in two.

Mine, she replies, glancing towards her child at the mouth of the cave. Then all she says is one word.

KILL.

311

No. I plant my feet wide. The ancient wildness in my chest brims over and threads across the dark cave to the terrodyl. She snorts, steps forward and sniffs at me, but I scrunch my toes and think of Ma. Now I *know* I can control the beast. *Get away from my dragonfly.* I glare up at her, thinking *get away, get away, get away*, and she steps back. I walk forward and grab my brooch from the floor. Then I back off, without taking my eyes from hers.

At the opening of the cave I stretch up onto my toes and grab the spear-point of the young terrodyl's head, swinging into the hard space between its wings, in front of Sparrow and Crow. Thaw-Wielder thuds into my lap.

Thick, spiny nubs run down the terrodyl's back, fitting me in place. I grab onto the spine in front of me and Sparrow wraps an arm around my waist. When I look down and see his little hand, heart-gladness leaps along my nerves.

'What did you do?' he asks. 'Your beast-chatter went odd.'

'Your what—' Crow starts.

I answer Sparrow quickly. 'I don't know.' Somehow what I did sickens me. The night of the whale hunt flashes through my head again. Stag commanded the terrodyls with his beast-chatter, and he did it again when we reached the Bony Isle. Now I've done it, too.

You could know what it feels like to hold real power, he once said. Remembering his words brings the taste of bile to my mouth. I ent *nothing* like Stag.

The terrodyl's muscles tense as it steps to the edge of the cave. *That's it, Fearsome,* I croon, when it hesitates. *You're almost king of the skies!*

Then it takes off with a deafening hoot and swoops into the sky. Sparrow yells against my back, bunching my tunic up in his fist. Crow almost splits his sides with whooping and laughing. 'This is brilliant!' I hear him shout. 'Flying that don't sap half my strength!'

I tense, cos what if Sparrow guesses Crow's meaning? He might've seen Crow change his shape on the *Huntress*, when he smuggled him off. But Sparrow don't seem to notice.

Shards of sleet slice down from the clouds. My hawk bundles inside my cloak to keep dry. The wind pushes back my hair and makes tears stream from my eyes.

My frets disappear, cos all I can think about is holding on, especially when the beast wobbles under its fledgling wings, then zooms faster, trying to show off.

Suddenly we plummet too fast towards the earth. The ground rushes towards us. I gulp a lungful of air, my knuckles white where I'm clutching the terrodyl's spine. *Pull up!*

The terrodyl chuckles loudly. I screw up my eyes and

brace myself for the crash, but then the beast levels out and coasts along the top of the moss-covered flagstones, low enough that I could lean over and touch them. Then we arc away from the earth and swerve violently, almost slamming into the castle wall.

As we climb higher, I glance back down to the ground, my belly doing flips. The terrodyl flies towards the sea, over the path I took to the castle. I hold on, ducking my head low. Sparrow presses his face against my back.

I lean down, closer to where the terrodyl's ears might be. *Can you take us far from this isle, away across the sea?*

I can do anything I please! the terrodyl boasts. *Now I'm king of the nest!*

Soon the creature glides so high that wisps of moonlit cloud race past. When we reach the shoreline I look down, and there's a sweep of dark grey lumps across the bone-sand. Whales. Sparrow's shakings must've drawn them close, just like they did aboard the *Huntress*. At least he can't see them.

I stare ahead again and my gut gives a lurch as the ghostly outline of a ship looms on the horizon. What if Stag's come, to search the whales' bellies for the crown?

Terro-Beast, stay clear of all ships, understand?

Crawler utters stupids, it screeches. *I all-times stay clear of ships. They try to shoot us down!*

Suddenly, piercing screams wrench the night. I look over my shoulder – two full-grown terrodyls are careening after us. *Fear-Beast, fly away, as fast as your wings will carry you! See if you can be the quickest!*

Always am quickest! Fly faster than all! it gloats.

'Quick, go, go!' screams Crow. When I glance round at him, his eyes are wide as full moons, but when he sees me looking he sucks in his lip and tries to look calm.

We speed through the air, the wind whipping tears from my eyes. I look over my shoulder.

The terrodyls push closer. Ours gives a spurt of speed. *Fast beast, quick beast!*

Wisps of sorrowful blue whale-song drift up from the sea and soon the screams of the other terrodyls dwindle into the distance as they fall behind, shaking their heads and screeching.

Our terrodyl tosses its head and hisses when the song drifts past. *Dodge it!* I cry.

'Everyone, hang on tight!' We dart hither, thither, left, right, up, down.

Block out the whale-song, fierce creature! Stay heart-strong! I chatter. Even when we're almost turned upside down, and all the blood's rushed to my head, I still realise it's proper strange – how I've come to be telling a terrodyl to block out whale-song, like my Tribe always tried to block out terro-wails.

Thaw pops her head out of my cloak, then her pipes erupt with joy. *Worms!* She shoots into the air and slurps up wriggling strands of whale-song.

Soon the air is clear again and Thaw-Wielder nestles close. I stroke her head. *Well done, Thaw! And you, Fear-Beast!*

The spiny bumps underneath us ripple, making a clicking sound, and the terrodyl warbles a kind of *purr.* Then its wings settle into a steady beat.

Pools of moonlight cast a path across the ice-crusted sea. I've got my brother back, and even though so many whales are dead, at least Sparrow ent gonna be used to draw them no more. I smile into the wind, picturing Stag's face if he knew. He swore I'd never find Sparrow. But I proved him wrong.

I feel my muscles relax the tiniest bit, for the first time in gods know how long, cos the sea smells like home. I don't even mind the prickly terrodyl-hairs scratching through the cloth of my breeches, or its creaky bones shifting under me. Then doubt whips through my veins. *What am I, without my ship?*

I hunch over the spiny bump and grip Sparrow's hand. Shooting stars sizzle through the night sky. The sky-gods must be warring with fire and iron spears. As I watch, my eyelids grow heavy.

I jolt awake into a dazzle-bright dawn. Thaw stands atop the terrodyl's spear-point, burping up whale-song and spitting it away so it don't hurt the beast's ears. Below, a pod of lithe grey spinner dolphins leap in the swells, slivers of ice twinkling as they break through the thin crust. *Mischievous little shape-changers*, Grandma would say. Tears sting my eyes and nose. I sniff them away and call over my shoulder. 'Sparrow! The dolphins are dawn-dancing!'

He stays quiet. All I can hear from him is the tiny snoozing of Thunderbolt from his pocket. What if he ent really forgiven me? Or what if he's sick? And when will I tell him about Grandma? *How* will I? 'You all right?' I yell.

'Never been better, thanks for caring,' replies Crow, voice thick with a yawn.

'Not you, I'm talking to *Sparrow!*'

'*Sorry!*' snaps Crow, and then breaks off into a fit of coughing.

The wind buffets us and Sparrow cries out in pain. His hand feels clammy and cold. But he answers in his old voice. 'I'm sleepy, lemme be.'

I take a breath and lift my chin. We saved him and I won't let Stag win. I'll find the heart-strength to tell Sparrow about Grandma, just like the fearsome old captain would've done herself.

I think of Da, and my blood dances. I can't wait to find him and tell him about how we saved the first Storm-Opal! I reach into my pocket and hold it tightly in my hand, feeling how smooth and warm it is. As I grip it, I can almost feel a flicker of power lick into my palm. Da will be so heart-proud of me, I know it. I bring the Opal out of my pocket and watch gold flecks shimmer beneath its green surface.

Priiiiiip! trills Thaw-Wielder, swooping to land on my knee. *Eye makes heart flutter, deep in feathers.* Her eyes shine brightly as she watches the Opal. She taps it with her beak and the power I felt in my palm seems to fizz into her frost-sparkled feathers, making them spiky. That's when I notice how the waves beneath the terrodyl's huge black shadow are stirring as we pass.

Did the Opal help you find Sparrow? I whisper.

My hawk shuffles her wings excitedly. *Stone stirred sea-beasts above waves! Sea-beasts chitter-chattered to Thaw! Trilled of too-soon's song!*

The Opal brought you sea-helpers and they chattered to you about where he might be!

She squawks her agreement and nudges the top of her head under my chin, making me hoot with laughter.

Sparrow burrows his head deeper into my cloak. The old song laps round and round my mind like a spell. *We*

318

fly wild through the skies, fathoms deep and mountains high.

I glance back at Crow and he gifts me a wide, wild grin, eyes streaming. Then he punches the air and I can't stop laughing. As we fly further north the sea turns grey and wild, and ice slides from the sky to sting my cheeks. The terrodyl's skin grows tiny icicles and the white fog of its breath streaks past our faces. We're on our way.

This beast is soaring.

Thank you to my wonderful agent, Jodie Hodges, for awarding me the 2014 United Agents prize and kick-starting the epic adventure that followed. I've been pinching myself ever since.

To my incredible editor, Ali Dougal, for seeing potential and making my dreams come true – thank you for your patience, kindness and enthusiasm. Cally, Rebecca, Alice, Katy, Sarah, Ingrid, Laura, Lydia, Maggie, Tiff, Ben, Liz, Emily Finn, Amy, Emily Thomas and all the other lovely Egmontees I've been lucky enough to meet. Eleanor Rees for your awesome copy edit. Joe McClaren for your beautiful illustrations.

Giordano Aterini at Rizzoli and everyone at Carlsen publishing for bringing Mouse's story to Italy and Germany.

CJ Skuse for the priceless advice, encouraging my idea from the very start and for being the best manuscript tutor I could ever have wished for.

To my amazing workshop group – Alyssa, Annie, Becca, Lindsay and Emily – thank you for believing in me when I couldn't believe in myself. Thank you for the fan art, the s'mores and your endless positivity. Alyssa, thank you for sharing the tireless pursuit of research and driving us around the Icelandic ring road, not teasing me too badly for my sea-sickness and documenting my fermented Greenland shark experience . . .

To Irulan, Carlyn, Jess, Jas and the rest of the class of 2014. Lucy Christopher, Janine Amos, Julia Green, David Almond, Jo Nadin and Steve Voake, thank you for giving me the best opportunity I've ever had and the most magical MA year. Thank you to Lisa Heathfield for being such a lovely fellow Egmontee to learn from, and for understanding how surreal this is!

The ex-Naval Officer on the SS Great Britain who told me that 'every ship has a soul.' The amazing staff at the Mary Rose museum for answering all my questions about weaponry, arrowheads, light and conditions on board. Marina Rees, for compiling an anthology of Icelandic sea sayings.

Bryony – no words will ever be enough. Thank you for keeping me alive. For having always been proud of my writing and stoking my creativity with all of our nonsense.

Ruth – for illustrating my early efforts, writing the blurbs and for always being up for an adventure!

Reuben – thank you for pushing me closer to courage. For believing in me from the beginning, designing covers and writing blurbs.

Thank you to Mum and Dad, for your quiet strength and humility. For reading with me and listening to me read out my poems and stories. My grandparents – thank you for always being supportive and proud. Wish you had been here to celebrate this with me. Thank you to Nick, for being my brother and for bearing that particular burden with more patience than I deserved.

To all the NHS patients and staff I have had the privilege to work with.

To Mouse. Telling your story has been the greatest honour. Thank you for choosing 2013 to appear. And finally to all the authors whose books I've read and loved over the years, especially growing up. I believe that books can save lives. My life is no exception.

Fly with Mouse, Sparrow and Crow
as the adventure continues . . .

THE HUNTRESS

The trail of the Storm-Opals takes Mouse
further than she has ever been before –
and into an unknown world. This is a place
where the air crackles with danger
and secrets hide amongst the clouds.
Mouse's destiny burns fiercely inside her,
but evil is closing in . . .

SKY

COMING SOON

www.egmont.co.uk

EGMONT